BLOODSTAINS BY GASLIGHT

BLOODSTAINS BY GASLIGHT

Red Lagoe

BRIGIDS GATE™
PRESS

Edited by: Elle Turpitt
Formatted by: Stephanie Ellis
Cover illustration and design by: Red Lagoe

First Edition: March 2025

ISBN (paperback): 978-1-963355-22-2
ISBN (ebook): 978-1-963355-21-5
Library of Congress Control Number: 2024949552

BRIGIDS GATE PRESS
Overland Park, Kansas
www.brigidsgatepress.com
Printed in the United States of America

Brigids Gate
PRESS

To anyone who has been asked, "Why did you stay?"

The question should have been, "Why did they hurt you?"

Content Warnings & a Message from the Author

This is the story of one girl and her fight against intimate partner violence. Every person who has experienced domestic violence has a different story, a different reason for staying, a different path of escape (if they're lucky), and different thoughts, emotions, and reactions to their individual situations. Everyone has a unique story, and this is just one of them.

I escaped a six-year toxic and abusive relationship when I was 19 years old. The entirety of my teenage years was lived in the shadow of a threat. However, this book is fiction; it is not a detailed depiction of my experience (of course not, it's vampires!), but it *is* incredibly personal to me. I wrote this book with honest and raw emotions at its core. There is violence on the page, so those with abuse trauma (physical, sexual, and emotional) may want to proceed with caution.

www.loveisrespect.org

"Love Is Respect" is an organization that didn't exist in the late 90s when I needed help. There wasn't much of anything helpful online back then. This organization offers confidential support for teens, young adults, and their loved ones seeking help, resources, or information related to healthy relationships and dating abuse.

Please remember to clear your browser history.

Content warnings: intimate partner violence; physical, sexual, and emotional abuse; animal death

CHAPTER ONE

REESE

Who do you want to die first? You or me? The hypothetical question he'd posed was one of many reasons Reese Perkins knew it was time to break it off with her boyfriend. It had haunted her for months, but now she understood with excessive clarity that if she didn't gain the courage to end it with Michael soon, she'd slowly suffocate under his ever-tightening grip. She'd be sucked into a black hole, eternally trapped by his crushing gravity. She'd postponed her goals and aspirations for far too long, giving in to all of his wants and needs and ignoring her own. Teenagers are supposed to hang out with friends, drink in the woods around a bonfire, hit up Orange Julius at the mall, and go to prom. However, because of Michael, Reese had missed out on so much.

Despite wasting her high school years on a boy who had turned out to be a jealous, overbearing monster, her entire future was still ahead of her. Everything was going to be fine. It was only January, and she had five months until graduation. *Go Panthers, Class of 1997!* It wasn't too late to apply to colleges, and it would never be too late to break it off with her boyfriend.

Last week, he started talking about marriage, and it scared the hell out of her.

Breaking up with a boyfriend was hard, but breaking up with a best friend was The Worst. Make that break up with a guy who had danced with suicidal tendencies, and it was damn near impossible to walk away from the relationship she'd been in for the past three years.

She drove her 1984 Corolla past Michael's home. It was a single-wide trailer on a private lot of land, surrounded by pines along Halsey Road outside Byron. But she wasn't on her way to see him yet. He was still at work, manning the assembly line at the job he'd taken after he'd graduated last year.

The sun lowered in the west, scattering gold light across snowy fields. Salt and slush gathered at the edges of the winter-parched, winding road that cut through patches of forest and farmland. It was barren of traffic in the winter as many people chose to stick with the frequently-plowed main drag that went straight through town. Her old car was drafty, but she'd paid for it with her own money working at Fat Joe's. She wore a brand-new pair of button-fly jeans and a black T-shirt with racing stripes down the sides. Two sections of her ash blonde hair were pulled back with butterfly clips, and she'd spritzed herself with sun-ripened raspberry body spray before leaving her house. Fortunately, she didn't have to work after school today, which meant she wouldn't be reeking of fry grease.

Most Friday nights, Reese would get off school and wait for Michael to come over, but tonight she made other plans. Sebastian Belinski was her partner for a school project, and he'd invited her over to perfect it before their presentation on Monday. It wasn't some scandalous affair, but knowing how Michael would react made it feel that way.

Michael's jealousy and violent outbursts were becoming so predictable Reese knew he would totally and completely lose his shit over this. And when he did inevitably lose his shit, she would have an undeniably justified reason to finally dump his ass for good.

In her cassette player, Alanis Morrisette's latest album played on side two for the two-thousandth time, but she couldn't focus on the songs. All she could hear was the pounding of her own heart as she neared the fork where Halsey split to Centerville Road.

After the slight turn onto Centerville, she spotted a dark patch on the pavement ahead. Reese eased off the gas and slowed to a roll as she neared what appeared to be a patch of black ice, but the roads were bone dry. The massive splotch in the road caught a glint of sideways sun and reflected its red color. Blood. There was no sign of a carcass, no chunks of rotting flesh scattered across the pavement, and no vultures circling above that she could spot from her position. Bright crimson was painted across the road from the center to the shoulder, indicating something big like a deer had likely been struck by a vehicle. Reese pulled as far off to the side as she could and came to a stop with the bloody scene in front of her. If something had been hit, it could have dragged itself off the road where it appeared the snow was compacted down. The embankment was too steep to see to the bottom from inside the car, but she imagined some poor creature twitching and bleeding out, gasping for its last breath, terrified and alone. She should've continued down the road, but she couldn't allow the poor thing to suffer.

She checked for oncoming traffic, unbuckled, and stepped out of the Corolla. The sun skimmed the tree line across the field beyond an old dilapidated barn standing like a scar among the pristine white landscape. She edged toward the shoulder, where the trail of blood went through tangled, thorned brush, down the embankment, and across the field. No animal lay suffering below, but within the bloody trail was a single set of boot prints through the foot-deep snow.

From her elevated position, she lost track of the prints as they faded into the field, but it appeared that whoever created them may have headed toward the barn in the distance. Perhaps it wasn't a deer, but a *person* who had been struck by a vehicle, or attacked by a black bear. Maybe the person was in shock, or escaping some traumatic abusive relationship, and they sought refuge in the distant barn. What if they were out there now, dying from blood loss and hypothermia?

Reese grabbed the branch of a flimsy young sapling and descended to follow the injured person's tracks. Her Nikes and wide-leg jeans were hardly the attire for trekking through the snow, but someone had to help them. All the reasons why she shouldn't follow the trail of blood rocketed through her mind: it would be dark soon; the person could already be dead; the person could be a murderer; it might be a trap.

Fear could not keep her from doing what was right. Someone had to help. As she took another step down the embankment, a sound crept across the landscape. It began as a low hum in the distance, then gained intensity and volume. A man's scream echoed across the field, and even though the sound scattered and bounced off of the walls of distant tree lines, she was certain the primal call came from the old barn in the middle of the field. The guttural, desperate cry crescendoed into a shriek like she'd never heard before. She halted her descent and reconsidered the risk, but if someone was hurt out there, nobody was around to answer their cry for help other than Reese.

Chapter Two

Trevor

Despite the ravenous need to sink his teeth into a pulsing human vessel, Trevor kept to his promise of never harming another person. It had only been a couple of days since he'd left Syracuse on foot, but it'd been over a week since he fed. He wouldn't make the rest of the trip if he hadn't acquired sustenance of some sort.

Trevor drew his teeth from the jugular of the deer carcass, and the sour taste of roadkill dripped from his fangs onto his tongue.

His darkened vision began to clear and he fell back onto his ass, leaning against a rotting beam in an abandoned barn in central New York. He wasn't too far from the hunting grounds pa used to take him when he was young.

Trevor was not fully sated, but the animal blood subdued the rising beast within.

It had been excruciating earlier in the day when his insatiable need for human blood became more than he could handle. He'd stripped the shirt from his skin and tried to plunge a wooden stake through his own chest, without success. The wood had splintered into pieces, leaving nothing but a scratch that had since healed. He tried again and again, but he wasn't allowed to get off so easily. *You're not allowed to do that,* Jensen had said.

The setting sun's slanted light crept between decaying barn planks, highlighting the precise point of one of the wooden stakes he'd carved.

He'd used the spindle leg of an old chair and a small utility knife to whittle it down. Bits of shaved pine had fallen to the barn floor, forming a pile between his steel-toed boots. Boots that would never stand on another construction site again. No more long days working under the summer sun. No refreshing iced tea on the back porch when he came home to his family at the end of the day.

He'd carved the apex of the stake into a point that was sharper than any spear he'd ever seen.

It reminded him of the candy canes his boys used to work to a point using nothing but spit and determination. They'd twist the cane in their mouths, wearing down the red stripes until it all turned white. His youngest, Devon, had a dark-skinned cherub face that lit up brighter than the Christmas tree when he held the candy cane spear for his dad's approval.

A lifetime of memories haunted every waking moment.

What he'd give now to sink into the couch on a Friday night with his too-tired-to-go-out wife, trying to decide what Blockbuster rental to watch. Trevor preferred thrillers and action movies. He'd pick out a movie, like *Seven*, but Rebecca didn't care for the dark stuff. She'd rather watch that newer Sandra Bullock film about the internet. The movie didn't matter because their youngest, Devon, would be knocking on the door ten minutes into the film, interrupting Trevor's futile attempt to have sex with his wife.

His life hadn't gone the way he'd imagined, but he'd take it back in a heartbeat. A few weeks earlier, when he'd stormed out of the house after an argument with Rebecca saying he'd be back later, he'd meant it. He just needed some space.

Then someone jumped him in a parking lot and his life changed forever.

Trevor had awoken a day later on a twin mattress in an upscale apartment. His attacker sat beside his bed and introduced himself as Jensen. Jensen apologized, of all things, claiming he couldn't control the instinct to feed.

Bullshit. Everyone has a choice. At least that's what Trevor believed at the time.

Weeks passed since his attack, and things had gotten out of control. All Trevor knew with complete certainty was that he had to leave everything behind. His things, his vehicle, and what was left of his family. It stayed in Syracuse as Trevor walked out of the city wearing a black, hooded windbreaker, the scarf his wife had knit him, which obscured his face from the light, and a pair of polarized, wrap-around sunglasses.

He hiked west, keeping to the back roads that weaved in all directions, but he planned to head to the forest north of Byron. His pa had an old cabin there, used for hunting weekends. The secluded, off-grid location would be perfect for Trevor to learn control.

But last night as he walked alone, his thirst grew. His eyes blackened along with the increasing need to sink his teeth into somebody's—*anybody's*—veins. A barking dog behind a fence enticed him to take a little, just enough to hold him over, but Trevor refused the desire. He walked all night down pitch-black country roads until the sun rose, searing his flesh on the back of his neck. He covered himself with Rebecca's black and white houndstooth scarf, then found shelter in the old barn.

The dilapidated structure sat a football field's length from the road and could easily be overlooked by passersby. It blended into the backdrop of dormant trees and a snow-covered field. There were no homes within a quarter mile. No way for him to hurt anyone, at least for today.

After failing to kill himself, he'd nearly accepted his fate of losing himself to the beast swelling within. His former sepia-toned skin became dull with pale blue undertones. His body needed blood, and salvation came with the sound of a jacked-up truck driving too fast on this old country road. Tires squealed and the meaty *thunk* of the doe smacking into the grill echoed across the field. After the driver left the scene, Trevor ventured out to retrieve it. The minor burns inflicted by the sun as it lowered in the afternoon sky were worth the temporary pain.

After feeding, he sat on his heels and admired the dance of dying sunlight upon the snowdrift along the inside wall of the barn. Though he had difficulty sensing cold, he shivered as the animal blood pumped through his body, and those burns and blisters from the sun already began to heal.

The sun sank below the horizon as he dragged the drained deer outside. He had another few hours of walking ahead of him before reaching the hunting cabin. As Trevor rounded the corner of the barn to head to the road, he spotted another vehicle parked where the doe had been struck. He kept close to the wall, narrowing his gaze on movement as a person seemed to be heading down the hill.

His blackened gaze returned, eyes flooding with darkness that made it difficult to see anything beyond a few feet. He hurried to the backside of the barn as his gums swelled, teeth retracting in preparation to feast on what his body truly desired. He should've known animal blood wouldn't be enough.

"No!" He clenched his fists, jaw, and every muscle in his body, fighting the instinct within as a scream climbed his throat. His hunger and frustration, his fury and desperation roared, released across the snowy twilight field. Whoever crossed his path tonight would not survive.

CHAPTER THREE

REESE

The scream stopped and the open field fell silent. A braver person might have charged across that field to help, but her mom had trained her well when it came to self-preservation. She wasn't about to get herself killed. Reese waited a moment, wondering if someone might come running from the other side of the barn, but with each ticking second on the hand of her watch, she began to doubt whether what she'd heard was a person at all.

Reese hurried to her car, locked herself in, and started the engine.

Sebastian's house was only a few minutes down the road. Earlier today, when he'd invited her over to work on their project translating Hamlet's soliloquy into modern-day speech, Sebastian handed Reese a scrap sheet of paper with his address. Out of fear of sounding like a stalker, she didn't tell him that she already knew where he lived. Michael had hated the Belinskis ever since he spent a summer mowing their yard in sophomore year, so he drove by one day with Reese and pointed out their place.

It was a warm and inviting two-story home that sat secluded in a clearing among towering pines. Michael made it seem like the Belinskis were loaded with Ferraris and ten swimming pools, but it was simply picturesque.

Sebastian greeted her at the door and invited her in. Upon stepping into the foyer, she told him about the blood in the road and the scream she'd heard.

"Oh, my goodness," Sebastian's mom said from a sitting room adjacent to the foyer.

"I bet it was a buck." His dad's eyes peered up from a newspaper.

The mother eyed him suspiciously.

"Remember when we went to Yosemite and heard those elk? They sound like demons!" His dad smiled. "Maybe buck sound like that, too."

"I've never heard that around here," his mom said.

"Tell you what," Sebastian's dad said. "I'll call animal control and let them know about it. How's that sound?"

Reese nodded. "Thank you."

"Bastian," he said. "Grab me the portable phone from the library?"

"You have a library?" Reese asked.

"It's just an office," Sebastian said. He headed into the opposite room with two walls of bookshelves. He grabbed the phone and the yellow pages from the desk and carried them across the foyer to his dad. "My parents like to think they're fancy by calling it *the library*."

"We are fancy, darling, aren't we?" Mr. Belinski turned his chin up and held his hand out to his wife, who smirked. They got along the way Reese imagined married couples should get along. Like a classic TV show. Her life had never been anything like a classic TV show, but she would've liked that for her mom.

Sebastian led Reese upstairs to his room, and his mother shouted out after them, "Nice to meet you!"

His room was a dark and geeky space with a bookshelf built into the wall. A *Mystery Science Theatre* poster hung over a twin bed. Fox Mulder's *I want to believe* poster was taped above the beige box of a computer. Star Trek toys and stacks of science and philosophy books—some written by Stephen Hawking—covered every surface. There was no doubt Sebastian had read them all. He was one of the biggest geeks in school and he owned it with pride. Reese wished she could carry herself with the same level of confidence.

The red glow of a lava lamp offered a comfortable yet sexy ambiance.

"Do you always keep it this dark in here?" she asked, opening the fat brick of a book that was the *Heath Introduction to Literature*.

"Yes." He flashed a devilish grin and flipped through the book. "I'm hoping if I stay in the dark long enough, maybe my genes will mutate. I'll evolve a bioluminescence." Sebastian chuckled maniacally and thick dark curls fell over his eyes.

Reese cracked a smile.

"If I can *glow*," he said, "then it'll help my parents keep the electric bills down."

"If you could glow, maybe we would have enough light to find the right page," Reese said.

Sebastian turned on a second lamp and the room lit up.

"Page 683," she said, trying to stay focused on the work, instead of how much she suddenly wanted him to draw closer.

They only had a few lines to work on to wrap up the project, and before long, they were both belly-down on the bed, shoes off. Sebastian's feet extended several inches beyond the tips of her toes. Books sprawled open. Scribbles of all the failed Hamlet jokes about "aye, there's the rub" and "bearing fardles" that wouldn't make their final modern translation. It was the most fun she'd had with anyone in a long time, maybe even years. She and Michael used to have fun back when they first met, but it wasn't anything like this.

"I'll be heading to New York this summer," Sebastian said. "I got into Columbia."

The mention of him moving away deflated the balloon growing in her heart, but she feigned a smile. "I heard. What are you going for?"

"Computer Science."

"I should've known."

"What about you?" Sebastian asked.

Reese sat up and swung her feet over the edge of the bed, setting them on the floor. "I don't know yet. Originally, the plan was to stay here, keep working—"

"You mean at Fat Joe's?"

"Yeah. They're opening two more stores and need assistant managers. I'm one of the people they're considering for the Cortland location."

His eyebrows knit together so tight she thought they might battle each other.

"You're not going to college?"

"It's complicated."

Sebastian grimaced. "I'm a smart guy. Try me."

"I help my mom pay the bills, so there's that. And college seems too expensive." Reese had started paying rent last month when she turned eighteen. Her mom didn't need the help, but she wanted to teach her a lesson about responsibility.

Sebastian's face couldn't hide his disappointment. "I thought you would've been off to study astrophysics or something. You're brilliant with that stuff."

It was the first time anyone had expressed concern when Reese said she wasn't going to college. Mom said that the college kids at the diner were all idiots, and she often pointed out how useless a degree was. Even the school counselor, after a one-on-one meeting with every senior, nodded at Reese's decision to stay in the fast-food industry and simply said, "Good luck."

"I'd love to go to Berkeley," she admitted. "They have a new Astrobiology class, so I've read."

"Astrobiology?"

"I read about the class in a magazine. They study life here on Earth, like extremophiles and bacteria living on the vents at the bottom of ocean floors. Then they look at places in the solar system, like Mars or Europa or Titan, and figure out whether life could thrive in those extreme conditions." Passion spilled from her whenever she talked about space. "But I'm definitely not smart enough to do something like that."

Sebastian shook his head. "You're smart enough. You're everything enough."

She wished she could express to Sebastian how serious she was without getting into the whole conversation about her overbearing boyfriend. "You know, maybe I'll apply."

"We're halfway through senior year," he said. "You better get moving on that."

"I know, but I've had a lot going on."

"Do you want to talk about it?"

"No." She began packing her books into her bag. "Not yet."

"Well, you know where I live if you ever want to talk."

The project was complete and aside from wrapping her arms around him, she couldn't think of a reason to stay any longer. Reese shoved her feet into her sneakers. "I should head home. I have an early shift at Joe's."

"How early?"

"5:30."

"Ouch. On a Saturday?"

"I'm off at two, so it's not so bad."

She headed downstairs with him trailing behind. At the bottom of the steps, Sebastian's mother, Marissa, shrugged into a winter coat.

"I have to go in, sweetie," she said.

"I didn't know you were on call."

"I'm covering Doctor Sato's on-call hours this week." She opened the door and smiled. "So lovely to meet you, Reese. Drive safely going home, okay?"

Reese agreed to be safe and Marissa Belinski closed the door behind her.

Reese stood inside, physically ready to leave, but she couldn't propel herself away from Sebastian. The silence between them became so thick, she thought she might choke on it. She needed to say something, anything. Maybe something about how she was going to break up with her boyfriend, or how she was starting to like Sebastian, or how she was serious about taking control of her future, or about anything other than a simple, *"Bye, See you on Monday"*.

"Your parents seem cool," she said.

"They're okay."

"Your mom's a doctor? What's your dad do?"

"Artist. What about yours?"

"My mom's a shift manager at Ray's Diner, and I never met my dad."

"Oh, I'm sorry."

"It's okay. I'm actually going to get to meet him next week."

"Seriously?"

"Yeah! He lives in Florida near Cape Canaveral, and he's taking me to the Kennedy Space Center."

"Score!" Sebastian held up a hand for a high five, beaming with excitement as if he really had evolved the ability to bio-illuminate.

She gently tapped his palm.

"Are you flying down with your mom?" he asked.

"Going solo."

"Your mom is letting you fly to another state alone?" His luminescence faded.

She shrugged. "She knows I can handle it."

"And you never met the guy?"

"I was a baby when he left." She waved airily. "Anyway, I'll have to remember to send you a postcard."

"Cool." Sebastian bobbed his head as he opened the front door for her.

Reese stood at the threshold between the dream she'd been living for the past two hours and the reality into which she had to return. Sebastian's room invited her back. To sit in the glow of a lava lamp, laughing about nerdy things and casually elbow-nudging each other until those nudges became something more.

Reese zipped up her coat and flipped her hood over her head. "Okay."

Sebastian braced an arm in the doorway. He stood several inches taller than her five-foot-six frame.

Reese stalled, fiddling with her keys, looking to her feet, looking for something else to say that would keep her there longer.

"I should probably close the door," Sebastian said, "or my dad might yell about heating a barn or something."

"Those heating bills, right?" Reese laughed. "Maybe instead of bioluminescence, you should be working on evolving radiant body heat."

Sebastian let out a laugh. His eyes creased at the corners with his smile.

Reese's feet remained cemented to the floor, thinking of how radiantly warm his regular, unevolved human heat might be, and whether she should slide in for a casual hug to find out.

Sebastian leaned in and whispered. "Seriously, though. If you're still standing here in five seconds, I'm gonna have to kiss you."

Reese froze. Arm hairs rose to attention. Her eyes drew from her feet to his mouth. His full lips invited her to touch them.

Not yet. At least break up with Michael first.

"Five." Sebastian stepped forward, the tip of his socked-foot grazing her sneaker. "Four."

Oh crap, he's actually counting. Her heart raced. Or maybe it wasn't so much racing, as it was swelling larger than she could handle. So big it pressed against her lungs and she couldn't breathe.

She should've turned away before it was too late.

"Three." Sebastian placed a hand on her hip.

His fingers touched her coat so gently, she couldn't feel his hand through the downy fabric. Maybe the sensation she'd felt was the charged particles between them, sparking with excitement at their newfound connection.

"Two." He used his other hand to draw her chin up.

Their eyes locked.

He looked panicked. Not as confident as he normally was. His big, sad eyes showed fear this time. As if he couldn't believe this kiss was about to happen. Like he expected her to run away, but there she was standing before him, waiting to be kissed.

"One," his trembling voice whispered. He paused, giving her another chance to leave.

Reese held steady.

"Okay." Sebastian moved his hand from her chin to the space behind her ear, like he'd learned it from some romantic movie. His lips landed softly. She'd kissed before, lots of times, but this one was different. It was a nervous kiss, attentive, like he was unsure if the world as they knew it would come to an end, so he made it the best possible kiss in the history of the universe. In that moment, nothing mattered but existing, and it was possible their kiss would open up a black hole and it would be an end to all life on earth and everything in existence.

It was worth the risk.

Before she could raise her hands to pull him closer, he withdrew.

"Wow," he said. "I didn't think you were gonna let me do that."

No massive black hole formed, and there Reese stood with the universe intact and nothing but fireworks in her brain. The kiss sent feelings downstairs and she imagined, for a brief moment, pushing him up to his dark, weird bedroom to make out until they couldn't keep their clothes on any longer.

Instead, they exchanged shy smiles and Reese backed away. "I guess I'll see you?"

"I hope so." Sebastian stood in the doorway while she walked across the gravel driveway to her car. As she pulled away, his silhouette was framed in the light of his happy home, inviting her back. But she couldn't see him again.

Not yet. Not until she officially broke up with Michael Braxton.

CHAPTER FOUR

MICHAEL

Standing outside of Tessa Plastics, Michael Braxton shifted his weight from one foot to the other with the payphone receiver pressed against his ear. He'd used the last of his change to call Reese, but she wasn't picking up.

Tonight, he'd gone to work, got his paycheck, and after only three hours on the production floor, he told his piece of shit foreman that he quit. Reese had tried to convince him to keep working until spring when he could pick up a roofing gig, but he couldn't take it any longer. Harry, the second shift foreman, had done nothing but ride Michael's ass over every little thing since he started working last summer. His hours had been cut just before the holidays, so most Fridays, he was out of work by 8:00 PM, and Reese was always at home waiting for him.

"Pick up," he whispered into the receiver, scuffing his worn boot on the edge of the curb.

"Hello?" Reese's mother, Tammy, answered.

"Hi. Is Reese there?"

"Sorry, hon. Her car isn't here right now."

"Where is she? At work?" Michael asked, but he didn't expect Tammy to know. She wasn't the most observant of parents.

"Probably."

"She doesn't normally work Friday nights," he informed her.

"Well, I don't know then. But you know her. She's probably out with her telescope again, or—who knows—at the library or something."

Michael's frustration grew and he tried to keep his cool while on the phone with Tammy. The woman meant well, but she was clueless half the fucking time. In addition, Reese had been distant lately. He felt her pulling away again and it scared the hell out of him.

"I'll tell her you called," Tammy said.

"Thanks." He hung up the phone and crossed the salt-crusted, dry parking lot under the glow of flickering sodium bulbs. Plowed snowbanks as tall as him were pushed to the edges of the lot. He dug for his keys in the pockets of his knock-off Carhart coat as he neared his '83 Ford Ranger.

He pulled out of the parking lot, pealing his tires out and holding up a middle finger in case anyone happened to be watching. Mom would be pissed with him, embarrassed her son was such a pathetic loser. Hell, he was certain Reese wouldn't be too impressed with him either.

How would he support a family if he couldn't even keep a job? He gritted his teeth together, jaw locked, nostrils flared. His anger boiled within, but he'd been trying harder to keep it under control lately.

He was so close to the life he wanted. Reese would graduate in June, and he could officially ask her to marry him. She was the best thing that ever happened to him. His parents, his coach… everyone… they could all disappear forever and he'd be fine. But Reese kept him whole. She inspired him to be a better man.

Why the hell isn't she home? Michael navigated the sea of possibilities, including work, the library, and her telescope, as Tammy had suggested. Reese had spoken about an asteroid or meteor or something cosmic like that being visible, but she said it was in the morning, not at night.

Michael drove the back roads in the dark, keeping a watchful eye for deer and potential patches of black ice as the temperature dropped, even though the dry roads weren't likely to have patches of ice. Reese might have taken advantage of the nice weather and headed out to some random field for stargazing, but she was usually smart enough to tell someone when she was going. As reckless as she could be sometimes with safety, she at least knew better not to go setting up alone at night.

What the fuck is she keeping from me?

She'd been pulling away for weeks. Making excuses as to why they couldn't hang out. She tried breaking it off with him before, but he couldn't allow that to happen. He won over her heart time and time again, because they were meant to be together forever. *Soul mates.* The thought of her leaving him stirred up his insides and made him feel like pulling over to puke. He turned onto Halsey Road and would be home soon, where he'd try calling again.

What reason would she have for not being home, unless …

Unless there was someone else.

Michael grumbled under his breath, and felt the stir of disgust churn up something hateful. The simple thought of her being with anyone else made him want to kill whoever fucking dared to get near her. These were the thoughts he wasn't supposed to give power to, but the more they crept into his mind, the more power they had over him.

"Fuuuuuck!" Michael screamed, punching the steering wheel repeatedly until he had no more breath in his lungs to yell. When he stopped punching, the hairpin turn of Halsey Road was already upon him. He slammed his breaks, but a man stood in the path of his truck, raising a hand in a worthless attempt to shield himself. Michael swerved, but not fast enough to avoid clipping the Black man in the hooded windbreaker.

Chapter Five

Trevor

After the barn, Trevor staggered down a dark road with deer blood trudging through his veins. Feeding on an animal curbed the intense desire, but now his body wanted it out. His gut twisted and wretched with the sudden need to purge. Scarlet vomit spewed forth and tainted the moonlit snow on the edge of the country road.

The stake he'd crudely carved was tucked away under his black coat. Jensen had told him last week that killing himself wasn't an option.

You can't do that, he'd said. People like them weren't allowed to harm themselves, but Trevor hadn't believed him at the time. It wasn't until he'd tried driving the stake through his own chest that it all became real.

The whisper of tires on salty pavement and the hum of an engine carried on the wind behind him. Trevor stepped off the shoulderless road onto a packed snowbank. Wind shear from the passing car lashed against his face, along with bits of gravel and salt.

Dancing in the blast of wind was the subtle hint of an aroma. Iron-rich, warm, pulsing blood. The kind of blood that wouldn't make his gut tighten in unbearable knots. *Human* blood. Trevor's eyes darkened at the thought of it, obscuring his vision, but he pushed onward down the road.

He'd walked for only a few minutes before the hiss of vehicle tires could be heard again. Headlights glowed at his back, casting a long, monstrous shadow of himself onto the road. The rev of the engine grew near, but Trevor sensed something dangerous. An instinct to watch his back. He twisted around. Headlight glare pierced his dark eyes, blinding him. Tires screeched. A horn blared. Trevor shut his eyes and raised his head to the heavens, refusing to speed out of the way. Maybe *this* could put an end to his pathetic existence.

The Ford pickup truck veered, its grill crashing into his shoulder. The front end of the old vehicle crunched, and Trevor's shoulder snapped.

He was thrown across the pavement as the grinding halt of metal against trees screamed into the night.

Trevor lay flat out in the middle of the road. Weakened due to insufficient energy, it took him a moment to climb to his feet and snap his busted shoulder back into position. The truck had veered off the side of the road over a high snow bank and wrapped itself around a sturdy pine. The truck bed was planted in the mountain of packed snow. The cab suspended above the ditch several feet off the ground.

Trevor's shoulder throbbed and his face was scraped up from the pavement. The wounds would have typically stitched shut within moments, but as he was athirst for sustenance, the cuts itched, struggling to heal, and his cells were slow to regenerate. He leaped to the driver-side door, at least five feet from the bottom of the snow-filled ditch. Music bled from inside the cabin, an angst-ridden song from a band his oldest son Ryan liked. They sang something about being a *creep* and a *weirdo*.

He'd heard Ryan listen to it before, and he remembered calling it garbage. If only he could have that time back, he'd let him listen to any song he wanted just to spend another day with him.

A body lay inside the cabin, flopped to one side. The jammed door wouldn't budge on his first try, so he gripped the handle and yanked as hard as he could. Metal groaned and warped under pressure.

"Come on!" He dug deep, grunting at the stubborn door until he finally mustered enough strength to rip it free from the chassis. The cab lights blinked on, and he shielded his sensitive eyes from the glare.

For a brief moment, he entertained the idea of using this strength to do *good*. He could've joined a rescue team as a walking Jaws-of-Life, capable of ripping car doors off and leaping impossible heights to save those in need. But that ephemeral moment of virtuousness bled into darkness as the scent of blood hit his nose.

The pockets in his upper gums stretched. Wretched teeth slid down from swollen conjunctiva, and the long, needle-like structures scraped his bottom lip.

A thirst rose from his core, clawing through empty veins. Rapid breaths, like that of a panting dog, took over. He steadied the animal within and tried to remind himself of his humanity. A glance in the rearview mirror revealed a filtered view of himself through ink-black eyes. Every time he lost control, his vision blurred as if a cheap welder's mask had been pulled over his face. He turned away from the image and annihilated the intense urge to take what his body desired, what it needed for survival.

Trevor tugged on the man's Carhart sleeve, but there was no response. He shook his arm, but it was dead weight.

It would have probably been best to continue on down the road. Leave this guy to his fate. Trevor hovered over him and his fogged vision began to clear.

"Hey." Trevor's teeth retracted into the pockets over his canines.

He yanked the man by the shoulders and pulled him upright. The smell of blood slid across Trevor's olfactory sensors. The man's thick, muscular body moved with ease, ribs cracking as he held him upright.

Trevor cringed at the sound. "Sorry."

His pasty white face was badly cut from the shattered windshield, but despite the swelling and severe wounds, he could tell it was just a kid. Buff as hell, but a teenager nonetheless. He lifted a wallet from the floor. Inside, a school photograph of an ashy blonde girl was tucked into a plastic sheath. Behind it, a driver's license. Michael S. Braxton. Date of birth: May 12, 1978. The young man would be nineteen years old soon. About the same age as Ryan, who'd started at SUNY last year. What he'd give to see his boy again. To see them all. To look into Devon's eyes, Ryan's eyes. Watch them grow.

The ache inside pressed against his bones. It burst at its seams. His body wanted to detonate into a million pieces of blood and pink bits, splattering across the snowy woods, but this was his burden to bear.

He couldn't leave this kid to die alone on the side of the road.

Though, if the kid was already dead, Trevor could've taken a little blood while his body was still fresh. No need to let it go to waste.

Trevor questioned what the hell he was going to do while the radio continued to play, *"I'm a creep ..."*

The longer he sat with the body, the seeping blood called to him, and gloom fogged his vision once again.

This time, he let it stay. The lure of the jugular enticed Trevor's mouth closer. There was a pulse. Faint.

He let the black clouds swim into his eyes, placed teeth over the vein and aligned them perfectly with the vessel. A skill he wasn't taught, but instinctively knew the moment he woke in Syracuse after being attacked. The weak pulse teased him to take what he could.

He gave in, piercing the stubbled flesh of the boy's neck. Blood geysered through hollowed teeth and into Trevor's body, filling his veins with the life-giving fluid needed to survive another week.

Trevor reluctantly pulled away, easing his spindly teeth from the vein. He pressed his hand over the puncture wounds and leaned back. Blood dripped from the tip of his extended teeth. It dribbled down his lip and into his goatee.

"He's gonna die," Trevor whispered between trembling lips. "He's gonna die, he's gonna die."

Surely, the kid had a family. Maybe that ashy blonde girl from the photo was a sister or girlfriend waiting for him to pick her up tonight. A mom and a dad were worrying why their boy was late getting home. If Trevor walked away now, the kid would die from his wounds.

But if he *turned* him, then Michael S. Braxton could live, not in the way anyone enjoyed living, but he'd at least *survive*.

It'd be one less life Trevor would be responsible for taking. All he had to do was …

Drain and replenish, Jensen had said.

Blood seeped from between Trevor's fingers as he pressed against the puncture wounds in Michael's neck. The kid's pulse weakened further.

Fuck it. His teeth sank into the vein again. He pulled hard, drawing in as much as he could, then easing so as not to collapse the vessel. He worked at it, mindlessly, body acting on impulse. With darkened vision, nothing existed in this moment other than the blood. Life surged through his veins.

When there was nothing left to pull from his neck, Trevor sat back, satiated, but the job wasn't complete. Michael's injuries and pre-existing faint pulse had caused blood to pool into his legs. His pulse was not strong enough to defy gravity, and Trevor needed to take more if this was going to work.

He unbuttoned Michael's Wranglers and pulled them over bulky thighs, down to his knees.

"I'm sorry, man." He pulled a knee toward him, pushed up the fabric of his plaid boxers, and hovered his teeth over the main artery of the inner thigh. No pulse was discernable, but he could smell the blood in his extremities.

Trevor pierced the pale and hairy flesh, found the femoral artery, and drew from it until Michael had nothing left.

Trevor bolted upright, alive with a surge of energy, like a breaker was flipped and all the electricity zapped through his wires too fast. He pulled in deep breaths to gain control of the power moving through his body.

Michael lay lifeless. Pale, blue lips hung open on a slack jaw.

Trevor tapped his fingers against the kid's face. "Come on. Wake up, man."

From what he understood, all Michael had to do now was wake up and eat. Get new blood in him. They could hunt down a rabbit or a deer, it didn't matter, so long as he fed. But Michael wasn't opening his eyes. And if Trevor had taken even a moment to think this through, he would've realized he didn't have any idea how long it could take Michael to wake up. It took a couple of days for Trevor to come out of it after being attacked.

"Shit!"

Rebecca had always said he was too impulsive. He could hear her voice screaming in his head: *What are you doing?*

A set of headlights approached, but this time the vehicle did not pass by without notice. It slowed to a stop about twenty yards away.

Blue and red emergency lights flashed with no siren.

Trevor fumbled the jeans back up around Michael's waist. "Wake up, kid."

The police vehicle's door shut and a flashlight beam aimed toward the wreck.

The cop couldn't discover him here, and if Trevor could subdue him, Michael would have someone to feed upon when he woke. Then there'd be more bodies to clean up. More people exposed to their truth.

What are you doing? Rebecca screamed in his head.

He jumped from the truck and landed a swimming pool's length away from the crash, farther than he'd ever imagined possible. He ducked into the shadows and sprinted through the woods away from the cop.

Branches lashed his face as he tore through the woods, losing the moonlight under a dense canopy of pines. Twigs snapped and crunched around him as woodland creatures scattered. Weeks ago, he'd feared the noises in the pitch black of the surrounding forest.

Now, the things in the darkness feared him. The power was overwhelming. His muscles were stronger than ever before. His mind clear and decisive.

He slowed to a stop, not because he was tired, but because he realized he was holding something. Michael Braxton's wallet. Distant flashing lights pierced the woods. He had to go back and find out where they were taking him. It was wrong to claim this much power and leave the kid behind. He'd failed enough kids for a lifetime. If he couldn't take care of his own boys, he could at least take responsibility for this one

Chapter Six

Reese

Reese pulled her Corolla into the driveway at home. All the lights were on inside her single-story house. The front walkway was covered in a few inches of snow because nobody ever used the entrance. The small window to her basement room was covered in snowdrift. She'd have to clear it away soon. Mom worried it would melt and leak into the house, which had never happened. Reese was more concerned with frozen squirrels than she was with snowmelt. Two winters ago, she'd seen a squirrel's fur pressed against the window of her room. The poor thing had likely burrowed in to soak up whatever heat it could from her bedroom. But it wasn't enough. It nestled into a tight ball, slipped into sleep, and froze solid overnight.

Mom stood framed in the kitchen window and disappeared as soon as she noticed Reese had pulled in. Before Reese could get out of the car, Mom opened the pedestrian door in the garage and trudged outside through the compacted snow, wearing a bathrobe and winter boots.

"Where have you been?" Mom's curlers were rolled up against her head, and she had a full face of makeup, getting ready for a night out.

"I was doing homework." She sat in the driver's seat with the door open.

Mom waved her hand "There's been an accident. Michael's mom called and said they're at the hospital now." She tightened her robe over her chest.

"What?"

"Michael called earlier but you weren't here, then just a little while ago, his mom called and said he was in a car crash. Seriously, where have you been?"

Reese's lungs tightened, her breath catching in the back of her throat—a brick of a breath withholding oxygen.

"Anyway, he's in Auburn."

Reese restarted the ignition and her little Corolla roared back to life.

Mom held the door and kept her from closing it. "Maybe you should take a minute. I don't want you driving in hysterics."

She gripped the wheel at ten and two o'clock and looked at her mother with the calmest, collected manner she could manage. "Is he okay?"

"She didn't say. She just wanted you to come. I'm sure he's fine, though. It would've been a different kind of phone call if he wasn't okay, you know?"

This wasn't enough to ease Reese's worries. Eleanor Braxton always spoke in a soft, passive voice. She was a devotee of the church. The kind of person who could take any negative thing and pray about it until she felt that all was healed.

Mom let Reese close her door. She rolled down the window so they could talk.

"I was going to meet Barb tonight for a post-work pow-wow. Do you want me to stay home? In case you need to call me?"

Mom loved her Friday nights out and Reese didn't see any reason to have her mother waiting around for news.

"No, go out. I'm sure everything's fine."

***

Everything is fine. Reese had said this to herself every day for years.

Her mother was more interested in partying than parenting: *Everything is fine.*

Her estranged father was suddenly interested in meeting her after years of neglect: *Everything is fine.*

Her boyfriend would kill himself if she left him: *Everything is fine.*

She wondered, driving to Auburn, what kind of accident Michael had been in. A couple of months ago, she'd answered the phone at one o'clock in the morning while Mom was still out at the bar with friends. The voice on the other end was difficult to discern, but it was no doubt Michael crying. He threatened to step into traffic on the highway. This just so happened to be the day before she'd planned to break it off with him, and subsequently his cry for help postponed her actions.

Halfway to Auburn on a long stretch through farmland, tears blurred the blacktop and yellow lines, but she wiped them away and forced herself to drive on. If she pulled over now, she might not have kept going. She might've folded in half, crying on the side of the road. She might have never gotten to the hospital, walked through the doors, and have had to look Michael Braxton in his eyes and tell him she didn't want to be with him anymore. She *couldn't* be with him anymore. No, Reese Perkins sucked it up like the cruel world taught her to and powered forward.

At the hospital, she entered a waiting area outside the emergency room where Mrs. Eleanor Braxton sat with her hands in the lap of acid-washed denim. Her head was bowed, tears soaking into the ruffled collar of her button-up magenta blouse. Her poofy, eighties-style hair lacked the height today. Eleanor typically spent at least thirty minutes in front of the mirror teasing her hair into a perfect symmetrical puff. Tonight, it was clear her hair didn't matter. Only her boy.

Eleanor looked to the man beside her. Pastor Dan from their church said, "Amen." Reese had met him before. The same comb-over and Burt Reynoldesque mustache stood at a podium the day Michael asked Reese to attend church with them. She'd zoned out that day, watching the pastor's impossibly thick mustache wriggle like a fat caterpillar over his lip while he preached about self-sacrifice and the Golden Rule. Church wasn't really her thing, but it made Michael and his mother happy.

"Reese!" Eleanor rushed to her. She stood several inches shorter than Reese and wrapped her arms around her, squeezing like she'd never let go. Eleanor's body convulsed with her sobs.

Reese pulled back and tried to get information, but Eleanor was too distraught. She waved her hand and collapsed into a chair.

The pastor approached and placed his hand on Reese's back, guiding her a few feet away from Eleanor. "Hi, Reese. Thank you for coming."

"Is he okay?"

"His truck was found in a ditch on Halsey Road, not far from the house. He was almost home. Right at that bad bend, you know the one?" He placed his hands on his hips and sighed deeply. "It was wrapped around a tree." Another sigh. "He was unconscious, and the police used the registration in the glove box to find Eleanor, so she came in to ID him. He's very pale and banged up, lost a lot of blood."

Reese waited for more. The question hung in her head, but nobody would answer. *Is he okay?*

"Let's just say the doctor isn't optimistic."

Something hit her. It felt like a sheet of heavy plastic dropping over her head; the kind her mom used to cover the floor when she painted the kitchen orange. The weight of the news shrouded her vision and her airway. It blurred her reality, muffled the words telling her that Michael wasn't going to make it. Her best friend in the world was dying and the only emotion that could come through was guilt. *Guilt* for being in a make-out session with another guy while Michael lay dying in the hospital. The room pulsed with her heartbeat and bile tried to force its way up her esophagus. Reese locked her jaw and controlled her emotions.

"Let's say a prayer." Two hands stole her cold palms. Pastor Dan, Eleanor, and Reese stood in a circle. He prayed aloud, asking God to save this boy. Asking God to show mercy on him. He prayed for Michael as if Michael were some innocent kid with no faults.

The prayer was over, and Reese's lips parted to say *Amen*, but nothing came out.

Eleanor retreated back to the comfort of the stiff waiting room chair, her hand never leaving the palm of her pastor's. His thumb caressed her skin, and his other hand rubbed her back.

Reese wandered outside in the cold winter air, bundling her coat tighter, and sat on the bench by the cigarette disposal. Two nurses in scrubs snuffed out their butts and left her alone outside while the moon shed light on the shadowy places of the parking lot. The moon always did that for Reese. When things got dark, like when she'd first learned as a child that her father was an alcoholic who wanted nothing to do with her. When Mom wasn't home because she was out on a date with the new beau of the week. When Michael grabbed her wrist so hard he'd left a mark. And, worst of all, when she had to decide to either let him kill himself or continue to hurt her.

The moon and the stars were always there for her. Little lighthouses calling her home when she was lost. They grounded her, allowed her a moment to catch her breath. And now, with the passing of Comet Hale-Bopp, she had another hopeful light to keep an eye out for. Currently visible during pre-dawn hours, she'd been trying to catch a glimpse of it since she'd read about it. But every morning it was either too cloudy, or she had to work, or she couldn't seem to get her telescope to focus on the spot where it was supposed to be. It was an ancient sign from the heavens that signified a new beginning, or perhaps an end of an era.

"Everything will be okay," she whispered.

They were two broken kids who fell in love. Michael would have been perfect if he hadn't let his anger take over. If he didn't drive away her friends, if he hadn't undergone this tragic transformation from high school sweetheart to controlling asshole, maybe she'd feel differently about his depression. Maybe she'd have more compassion. He was no longer a nice person, even if he wanted to be. It was that *desire* to do good Reese knew was there, deep down inside of him. But no matter how many chances she gave him to do better, he continued to resort to jealousy and violence.

The automatic doors to the ER entrance opened and out of the corner of her eye, a person in a hospital gown staggered out.

Michael stopped in the moonlight, pale skin reflecting a ghostly luminescence. IV tubes dangled from his arms, dripping blood onto the salted walkway.

Reese jumped to her feet, relieved to see him standing.

Michael staggered toward her, arms open, IV lines dragging behind him. His face was battered and swollen with lacerations so deep they'd surely leave scars. Crusted blood coated his lip, and sticky black clung to his matted hair.

"Reese." Her name was spoken in a single exhale, like he'd been holding it in his mouth, waiting for her to come. As if she were the only one who could help him. Even with all the doctors, nurses, his mom, and his pastor there, Michael needed Reese more than anyone. She was the only treatment, the only medicine that could save him, as always.

Eleanor argued with a nurse as the doors opened and closed. The nurse urged that he remain inside or he might not survive. "He needs more blood."

"Please don't make me stay," Michael whispered to Reese. "Please." His eyes were swollen, puffy like he'd been crying. Bloody vessels bulged against his sclera.

"He says he's fine," Eleanor said. "He's in God's hands now."

"Eleanor," Dan interjected. "Perhaps we should let Michael stay a little longer. Make sure he's not in shock or something."

The hospital staff, Dan, and Eleanor argued. Their raised voices became muffled as Michael drew in closer to Reese. All she saw and heard was his desperation and vulnerability.

"Take me home," Michael said. His lips and the skin around his jaw had swollen, like wads of cotton had been stuffed in his mouth.

"They're saying you should stay here."

He shook his head. "I can't be in there. My eyes hurt. Everything hurts." Michael leaned into her, trembling in her arms. "I don't want to stay."

Reese allowed him to remain tucked in the comfort of her embrace. Michael was almost half a foot taller than her, and at least fifty pounds heavier, but she adjusted her stance to hold his weight.

The nurse approached. "Sir, I need you to come back inside now, okay?"

"He's coming home with me," Eleanor said.

"Ma'am, I understand this is your son, but he's an adult—"

A woman in a white coat rushed through the doors and Reese recognized her immediately as Sebastian's mom, Marissa Belinski. She tried to turn her head so as not to be noticed, but it was too late.

"Michael," she said. "You need to stay. Let us monitor you overnight and—"

Michael backed away, hands up. Bloody tubes hung from his arm. "I can't."

Dr. Belinski dropped her head. "Then you'll need to sign an AMA form." She turned her attention to Eleanor. "Just so you know, if he leaves against medical advice, his insurance won't cover it if anything happens to him."

"I don't care." Michael staggered into the parking lot. His open hospital gown exposed his strong, muscular back and acne-ridden behind, then he took off running.

"Great." One of the nurses threw her head back, then reached into her pocket for a pack of cigarettes.

Eleanor collapsed into Pastor Dan and she looked to Reese, silently pleading that she help. Her panicked eyes pierced through a wall of tears. "Will you bring him home, Reese? Please. I'll take care of it here and meet you at home."

Reese promised she would. She didn't know what kind of arguing and paperwork had to be done in the hospital with Michael running off, and she didn't care. She had a single task: find and help Michael.

As she darted toward her car, footsteps rushed up behind her. Dr. Belinski caught up, worry in her eyes.

"Talk him into coming back," Dr. Belinski said.

"What will happen to him if he doesn't?"

"He didn't receive enough blood. He's anemic, cyanotic. He won't do well … No. Let me clarify: he probably *won't survive* without further treatment."

***

Within seconds of pulling her car out of the parking lot, she spotted his gown. Bare feet trudged through the sidewalk's deep snow. His arms hung limp.

As she neared, he stopped and leaned against a telephone pole, dropping to his knees.

Reese pulled over, putting the car in park.

The moment was all too familiar to the position he'd put her in not long ago. She opened the car door and hesitantly went to his side. She couldn't stomach seeing him so broken and helpless. It was akin to leaving an abused puppy on the side of the road. She climbed over the solid snow bank and knelt before him.

"This feels nice," he said. "Just leave me to die." His face contorted, clenching his teeth through sobs. Cracked lips stretched, breaking scabs and bleeding down his chin.

"Don't say that," she said.

"I'm sorry." Michael rested his head against the pole. "I'm sorry for the person I've become."

Reese sat in the snow beside him, wrapping her arms around her knees.

"I said I would never be like him, and I turned into him anyway." His swollen lips quivered at the mention of his father. "Fuck! Fuck! Fuck!" Michael smacked himself in the head with each word.

She grabbed his arm. "Stop." Then she set her palm softly against his heart. "You don't have to be like him. You get to choose."

His eyelids were inflamed, distorting his appearance into some horrific version of himself. It was hard to see Michael beneath the wounds. After enough injuries marred a person, it's hard to see anything but the scars left behind.

Under the blood stains and swelling, something else came through. Something she'd never seen in him. Lifelessness. A depletion of hope, bleeding out into the snow around him.

Reese took his forearm into both of her hands, twisting to examine the IV. "You can't leave these tubes hanging from your arms, you're dripping blood everywhere. What'd you do, cut the tubes?"

Michael extended his arm. "I think I chewed through them." He let out a brief huff of a laugh. "I had to get out of that room."

The bulging veins that once webbed across his muscular arms were flatter due to the loss of blood. She peeled the medical tape and gauze from his skin, pressed a finger over the IV catheter, and slid it out of his vein. She covered the puncture hole with the used gauze and told him to hold pressure while she removed the second IV.

"Thank you," Michael said.

"You should get in the car and warm up."

"I'm not cold."

"You've gotta be in shock or something."

"I'm okay. I just want to go to bed."

Reese sighed and got to her feet, brushing compacted snow off her bottom. "Your mom told me to take you home, but I think it's best if we get you back to the hospital."

"No."

"We can ask if they can dim the lights. Make it—"

"I said, no!" Michael burst to his feet with a threatening lunge.

"Okay," she said. "But Dr. Belinski is worried you might not make it."

"I feel fine. Just need to sleep."

Michael allowed her to guide him over the snowbank. She opened the door, and he collapsed into the passenger seat.

The walk around her vehicle to the driver's side was sickening. Every sensible thought in her head told her to behave in the exact opposite way: *Don't take him home! Go back to the hospital. Don't be nice to him. Don't help him. Don't give into his attempt to garner sympathy.* Instead, she followed her heart and did what was kind, and she opened the driver side door, slid into the seat beside her best friend, and drove him home.

CHAPTER SEVEN

MICHAEL

One moment, he was pressing his palm against the needle holes in his arm, waiting for Reese to get into the vehicle, and the next he was in his driveway, buckled safely in the passenger seat with her winter coat covering him like a blanket. Reese was small but strong, helping him out of the car and keeping him from collapsing as she guided him to the trailer steps. He'd never felt so lucky to have her in his life.

Her bare hands plucked the spare key out of the snow-filled flower pot by the front door, and she wiped the snow onto her pants. His trailer home sat on a square lot of land tucked into the woods on Halsey Road several miles outside of town. Buster, the old yellow lab, barked at the end of his chain. Mom didn't like having a dog in the house, but she wanted to keep him around for security. Who the hell was going to rob a shabby 1970s-era trailer home in the middle of nowhere? Reese had tried on numerous occasions to convince his mother to let Buster stay indoors, especially on bitter cold winter nights. It wasn't all that uncommon for people out in the country to have outside dogs, and Michael figured Buster was fine with plenty of hay in his dog house to keep him warm. But Reese was naïve, innocent, too big of a heart for this cruel world.

Reese had told him that no living thing should have to live their life on a short chain, but he sided with his mother. He always sided with her. How could he not, after everything his father had put her through? Taking his mother's side came as naturally as breathing. But if he wanted things to work with Reese, that would have to change soon. Maybe it was time to start taking *her* feelings into consideration. Time for him to grow up and be a man.

"Did he eat tonight?" Reese asked, nodding to the barking dog.

"I don't know."

"Temps are dropping this weekend—"

"I'll bring him inside tomorrow before it gets too cold."

She didn't say anything else as she slid the key into the door and looked up. Michael followed her gaze to the clouds moving in. "No stargazing tonight, huh?"

She stepped inside and flipped the switch. The overhead ceiling fan lights cast a yellow glow on the living room. Michael braced himself on the arm of the brown, plaid recliner and lowered himself into the seat, wincing. Every joint and muscle in his body ached.

"I'll get you some clothes." Reese cut through the kitchen to the hallway bedrooms, while he remained seated in the recliner, staring into the massive projection TV that stood as tall as Reese. The screen was black, casting a distorted dark reflection of his face.

Reese returned holding a pair of Dallas Cowboys sweatpants and an old gray sweatshirt.

"Is my face all fucked up?" he asked, squinting into the screen.

"You're swollen, but it's fine." She held out the clothes. "Sit up."

Michael obeyed and leaned forward, while she untied the strings of his hospital gown at his neck and let it fall over his shoulders to his lap. Dried blood mottled his arms. A long strip of bruising stretched across his chest from his shoulder to his opposite hip.

He ran his fingers along the purple marks. "I should sue the seatbelt company."

"It saved your life."

Michael closed his eyes, unsteady sitting upright, his torso swaying like a dead branch in a breeze.

"Maybe you should shower, get some of this blood off you before you sleep," Reese said.

"It hurts too much to shower."

"Then a warm bath?" She touched his arm.

The sensation of her fingers against his flesh sparked new life into him. Warm flesh against his sent heat through his veins and touched his heart. If he weren't covered in blood and agony, he'd pull her into his lap and use her as a bodywarmer.

"You're freezing," she said.

He leaned back in the chair, letting the cushions swallow him. "I just need to sleep."

"Don't sleep yet." Reese hurried to the kitchen and grabbed a hand towel. She dampened it with water from the faucet, filled a small bowl, and rushed back. She made room on the end table for the bowl of water and placed his mom's TV Guide and Redbook magazine onto the floor. The crusted blood from his arms broke loose under the wet cloth. He pictured them together fifty years from now. Gray hair, wrinkles, and she was nursing him to health after some hip surgery or flag football game with the guys. Then his imagination brought him to the near future, five or six years from now—maybe with his child—cleaning the blood off a scraped knee with tender care.

Reese reached for his face with the damp cloth, hesitating for approval.

He nodded, and she worked from the top of his forehead, down to his eyebrows, scrubbing away dried blood on the parts of his face that were unmarred. The sutured lacerations across his cheeks must've been hard to avoid, but she did her best to clean around them.

"Do you think you'll go back to the hospital?" she asked.

"No."

"You're very pale," she said, but he could tell she was withholding something from him.

"Let me see," Michael said. "Get the mirror from Mom's vanity?"

"You have a lot of bruising on your neck." She gently ran her fingers at the site. "It looks like little holes." She leaned closer, the scent of that raspberry body spray she loved so much turning his stomach.

"Let me see."

Reese fetched the portable makeup mirror from Eleanor's vanity in the master bedroom adjacent to the living room and returned to Michael.

He gathered the strength to stand, legs unsteady beneath him.

"The swelling will go away and the cuts will heal." She handed him the mirror. "Don't freak out."

Half his lower lip was as swollen as a concord grape, split open and exposing grey-pink flesh beneath. The stubbly skin above his lip was puffy, like bread rising in the oven. Thin, broken skin stretched over bulging eyelids, inflamed and near-shut. Cuts, nicks, and bruising spackled his neck. At the center of the dark bruising on the left side of his neck were two small puncture wounds. A haphazardly stitched gash dissected his cheek, as if the doctors didn't expect him to wake up needing a presentable face.

His shoulders dropped and his fingers lost grip on the mirror. Michael's legs gave out and all one-hundred-and-eighty pounds collapsed into Reese, but she was strong enough to support him and guide him back into the chair.

"It'll heal." Reese placed her hand on his shoulder and hovered over him, checking for wounds on his back.

He leaned forward, closing the gap between them, lips nuzzling into the nape of her neck. His body shook as he fought to hold his emotions. "I'm not good enough for you."

Without a word, she pulled away and readied his gray sweatshirt before him. She stretched the fabric as far as she could to avoid brushing it against his wounds and slipped it over his head.

Everything she did, she did for him.

Michael worked his arms into the shirt and leaned back into the recliner. She knelt before him, opening the sweatpants and feeding his feet through the holes one by one, while Michael cried. He broke, tears spilling into open wounds and his body retching with each sob. She gave him a moment, sat back with her hands in her lap, his pants around his knees.

Get it together, man!

Michael huffed out a few short breaths like he was preparing for a fight. "Sorry." He clenched his fists and tried to pull it together. "I'm good."

Before pulling his pants up the rest of the way, she tilted her head, inspecting his leg. "What happened here?"

Michael put his hand over his crotch and examined his legs. Blood smears on his inner thigh surrounded a circular blue and purple bruise similar to the one on his neck. Reese leaned in with the washcloth and wiped away the mess, exposing two small pinpricks.

"Are those needle holes?" she asked.

"Maybe the doctors needed to get to a vein down there."

Reese pulled his pants up to his thighs. There was something about her kneeling before him and cleaning his wounds that got him going. He'd never wanted her more, but he lacked the energy to grab her and take her to his bedroom. There was no way she'd want to kiss him now anyway, with his face all jacked up.

Michael wriggled the pants up the rest of the way and forced himself to stand again. He hooked a few strands of Reese's hair with his finger and brushed it back from her face. "I like your hair."

Her brow wrinkled slightly and she looked away.

"What?"

She whispered. "You didn't like it last week."

"What do you mean?"

"The Sun-In spray? The highlights?"

"It looks good," he said, trying to force a painful smile.

Reese's jaw clenched. "You yelled at me for 'trying to look hot for other guys'."

"I didn't yell at you." Her accusation was disheartening. Here he was picturing their lives together, and she was pissed about some non-issue that happened a week ago.

Reese backed away from him, disdain replacing any sign of concern in her expression. Maybe she *was* hiding something from him after all. Where was she this evening? Why was she wearing body spray? Why was she highlighting her hair? Some interest in another guy?

The trauma of the accident must have temporarily blinded him from the facts in front of his eyes.

Reese's expression shifted back to concern as she leaned closer, fishing into his eyes with suspicion. "Did they give you painkillers or something?"

"I don't know, why?"

"Your eyes are dilating."

Michael squinted against the overhead lights and Reese's face faded with his blurred vision.

CHAPTER EIGHT

REESE

Michael shielded his eyes from the overhead lights. He closed the gap between them and grabbed her arms. She couldn't tell if he was being affectionate or if he was angry, but she knew exactly how to calm him down.

She placed her palm on his chest and took a deep breath. "Let me turn off the light."

His pupils had taken over his irises. She wasn't an expert in biology, but she knew that light was supposed to make pupils constrict, not dilate. Michael let her slip out of his grip, and she flipped the switch on the wall, sending the room into darkness. Her eyes adjusted to the darkened room, lit only by the dim stove light from the kitchen and outdoor light seeping through the sheer curtains.

"Your pupils are dilating a lot," she said.

"Weird."

"Maybe it's a concussion? Or some medication they gave you?"

"I was pretty out of it. I don't remember what they gave me."

"Do you remember anything about the accident? What happened?"

"I was coming home from work. I left early. I don't remember crashing. Just waking up in the hospital."

Reese tried to find some missing piece of information deep in his eyes. In the low light, his pupils constricted a little, but they were far from normal. The vast empty black pools in his eyes told her nothing.

Buster's barking pierced through the aluminum walls.

"I think your mom's finally home," Reese said, moving to the curtains to look outside. The only vehicle in the driveway was her Corolla. "Maybe not." She stood with her back to Michael, careening her neck to get a glimpse of what Buster might've been barking at.

"I don't deserve you," Michael said.

"That's not true." The words spilled out of her. The sound of her lying voice sickened her, but what would happen if she said, *You're right, Michael. I deserve better.* If she broke it to him right now, dumped him in this moment? Michael, bloodied and broken, might stagger into the woods and let the frigid New York winter take him. Or maybe he'd slip into that warm bath after she left, slice open his wrists to match the gash in his face and the gaping wound in his heart. His death and his blood would be on her hands. People would say things like, *She dumped him after he got in an accident and turned ugly.* Reese would be the monster, and no matter how much she'd try to explain he was no good to her before the accident, they'd say she was lying.

They'd ask why she was bringing up his abusive tendencies now. Just like they'd asked when that volleyball player from Weeds accused the high school coach of sexual assault after she'd gone off to college.

Why didn't she say something back then when it was happening? they'd asked. Reese had asked the same question, not realizing how damn hard it was to simply say something. Not realizing the power of fear and humiliation, the power of being under someone else's control.

As fed up as Reese was with having no control of her own life, she couldn't break up with him tonight. The trauma of the car accident was too fresh. She didn't know when. Maybe tomorrow. Maybe next week. But she had to do it soon.

Reese took a deep breath, took his face into her hands, and placed her lips upon his broken, swollen mouth. His scabbed lip trembled against her, and the taste of blood lingered after she pulled away. She still loved him, for some stupid reason she couldn't explain. But she couldn't be with him anymore.

"You're going to be okay." It was the most honest thing she could think to say in that screwed-up moment.

***

Michael fell asleep in the recliner before Eleanor and Dan returned. They stood over him, hand in hand, keeping watch so Reese could finally go home.

Buster's barking persisted as she left the trailer. Her car was parked to her left in front of the detached garage with an obnoxiously bright floodlight. A Ford Camry was parked behind her, blocking her in. A brisk wind caught the storm door, tearing it from her grip, and it crashed into the side of the trailer. As she reached for the handle, she caught a glimpse of movement in her periphery. A shadowy thing vanished around the righthand corner of the trailer. Buster's attention was on the line of trees along the property. Reese hesitated on the steps, staring into the blackness of the yard, beyond the floodlight's reach. She would have chalked it up to a shadow cast by the swinging door, were it not for Buster's incessant barking into the woods. Reese stepped into the worn, snow-packed path leading to Buster's dog house. He yanked on his lead, fixated on the woods.

Michael's place was no stranger to deer and the occasional black bear, and Reese was no stranger to pushing beyond fear when she needed to. She stifled the paranoia in her mind, and headed toward Buster. His filth-crusted food dish broke free from the icy ground, and she carried it to the forty-gallon bin of dog food against the side of the house.

Exhaustion began to kick in and Reese yawned, sucking in bitterly cold air, ice crystals freezing in her throat. The temperature was dropping quickly.

Reese set down the dish and pet Buster, who'd given up on barking to scarf down month-old, dry dog food. The tips of his ears were cold to the touch.

"I'm sorry," she said, tears forming in her eyes. She couldn't imagine how hard it was for him, confined to an eight-foot radius, never experiencing a cuddle or a warm couch. Never tasting scraps from dinner. Never doing anything or seeing anything beyond this yard, not unless Reese walked him. At least once a week, she tried to make it to Michael's house to take Buster for a walk down Halsey Road, simply so he'd have something to look at other than the rusting trailer and overgrown lot. He pulled hard on his leash during those walks, sniffing everything and pissing all over without control. For thirty minutes, one day a week, he had some semblance of freedom. She often wondered how awkward it would be if she broke up with Michael, but continued to visit Buster.

Reese returned to the side of the house and brushed snow off the tarp covering a stack of hay bales. Snow slid into her sleeve, chilling her wrists. While bent to get a grip on the twine securing the hay bale, she spotted tracks in the snow beside her. There were a lot of footprints along the snowy path leading from the front door to the hay, but a single set of large boot prints extended in the other direction, beyond the worn path, along the house where she'd thought she'd seen the shadowy thing.

Reese sprung upright and stared into the woods where the boot prints vanished.

She filtered and processed the barrage of possibilities of who could've made those fresh prints through the snow, but it didn't matter right now. Whoever created that path *ran away*. And that was enough for Reese to break from her petrified state and carry the hay bale over to Buster. She tore off a few sections, fluffed the flakes, and crawled half-way into the dog house to line the inside walls. Then she hauled a couple more bales closer to the dog house and placed them a few feet from the opening as a windbreaker.

As she stood up, her eyes stole back to the woods. Deep in the shadows, where the boot prints ended between dense trees, a face stared back at her. His features were dark in the shadows, but she could make out facial hair and a dark jacket. Her body tensed, waiting for the figure to move, to lunge out of the woods and attack. A moment of fight or flight was upon her, but Reese wasn't good at either. She froze, staring at the man, wondering if he was really there. Buster no longer barked in that direction, so maybe it was a trick of the shadows.

Reese walked backward, carefully placing each foot, afraid to lose sight of the shadow man in the trees, but the shriek of the rusty front door breaking free and smacking against the side of the trailer startled her from her gaze.

Dan stepped outside and fixed his comb-over as it blew in the opposite direction. "Reese! You're still here."

She glanced at him then back to the forest, but the shadow man—or whatever she thought she'd seen—had vanished. She squinted, leaning in, trying to get sight of it, but there was nothing.

"I was feeding Buster." She hurried away from the dog house, feeling as if the shadow man was right on her shoulder the entire way.

"I just wanted to tell you that you are a blessing to this family," Dan said, burying his hands deep in his tweed coat pockets.

"Oh, I don't know about that." Reese brushed by him and opened her car door. Dan's vehicle was parked behind, blocking her in.

He followed and stood with the Corolla's door open between them. "If you need anything or just want to talk, let me know." He extended a business card. "This is my personal number. I know you are close with Eleanor and Michael. If they need *anything …*"

"Okay." She took the simple white business card. A gold cross in the upper left corner and dark blue lettering: *Daniel Delgado, Pastor at Grace Cross Church*. She slipped it into her coat pocket.

"Thanks, Mr. Delgado."

"Just Dan. I've been spending a lot of time with Eleanor, as you must have noticed." He sighed. "I care a lot about Michael's mother. And I know you care a lot about Michael."

Reese shrugged, eyes drifting back to the woods.

"Look. Between you and me, I think Michael should go back to the hospital."

This drew her attention back to him.

Dan looked over his shoulder to the trailer and lowered his voice. "I wish I could stay the night and make sure Michael was okay, but I don't think that would be appropriate. I prayed with Eleanor, and Michael is in God's hands now. Will you pray for him tonight, too?"

Reese nodded to make him feel better.

Dan smiled. "All right, let me move my car out of the way so you can get home. Your mother must be worried sick."

Doubtful. Reese started the engine and pulled the buckle across her chest. As she backed out of the driveway, she didn't dare glance to the woods where the shadow face had been. She didn't have to. She could feel his eyes on her every second of the way home

CHAPTER NINE

TREVOR

The instinct to feed was hardwired. Like a lion needing to hunt or a mosquito siphoning blood from sweaty flesh on a summer day. There existed now within him a mindless call to land upon some unsuspecting soul and claim that to which he had no right. Trevor had tried to deny it for weeks, at a cost too great. Jensen's spewed rhetoric about surviving as a species was appalling to him before, but now it was beginning to make sense. They were a community species, like ants, apes, or even humans. If they didn't look out for each other, they'd fail.

With new power surging through his veins, Trevor felt stronger than ever. He'd drained the kid in the car, and now an electric current coursed through his body. Palpable immortality tickled his veins. A new sense of brotherhood took over his mind, like he was part of a pack or pride, and he couldn't let the others down. It was the only way to survive.

Finish the job. Turn the kid.

The crash scene was overrun with emergency vehicles, and instead of following him to the hospital, Trevor trusted his instincts, and waited for Michael Braxton to turn up at home.

He tucked the wooden stake deep within the inside pocket of his coat and read the address of the kid's license. *Halsey Road*—the same stretch of desolate, narrow road he was already on.

***

He waited for hours in the woods. So long he began to wonder if the kid had woken up in the hospital and devoured a nurse. He pictured bloodshed and screaming and needing to call Jensen to help him out of the mess he'd created. The dog outside Michael's house caught a whiff of Trevor on the breeze, barking and lunging at the threat standing just beyond the tree line. If it didn't shut up soon, he'd have to silence it. Trevor imagined its pulsing, hot jugular in his mouth; however, having bled Michael dry, Trevor wouldn't need any more blood for at least a week. Only the greedy must've felt the need to feed constantly.

A vehicle pulled into the driveway in the middle of the night, and a teenage girl stepped out. The ashy blonde from Michael's wallet. She helped Michael inside. Seemed like a sweet kid. Too bad she was as good as dead. He tried to reject the thought as it cropped up in his head, but it was the truth. If left alone for too long, Michael would turn on everyone he loved. It was their nature, and it was Trevor's responsibility to make sure it didn't happen, to do better than Jensen had done with him.

Trevor spied on the kids through the window as she cleaned his cuts and kissed him goodbye. Michael's wounds should have been healing, but without the replenishment of blood, the process would be slow.

Another vehicle turned in, and Trevor waited in the woods nearby for things to settle down. He was certain the girl had seen him, but he held as still as possible. Her eyes were locked on his and, for a moment, he darkened. The threat of discovery aroused his senses, and his instinct urged him to bleed her and the dog until they were no longer in the way of his mission. Fortunately, she turned away, and he was able to subdue the beast within.

The girl and the older man left, and the dog barked on and off, eventually losing interest and retreating to its shelter.

Once all the lights were off in the trailer home, Trevor spied through the boy's bedroom window and tapped on the glass. A few seconds passed without a stir, and he tapped again. This time, the curtains parted. Michael stood with pinched eyebrows and a scrunched face.

He opened the window. "Who the hell are you?"

Trevor held out Michael's wallet. "You dropped this during your accident." He leaped headfirst into the window before Michael had a chance to shut him out. His jump was as calculated as a cat's as he dove through, landing softly with a summersault onto the carpeted floor. His newfound skills surprised him, and he fought to hold back a smirk.

"What the—" Michael staggered backward, body unsteady and swaying with dizziness.

"They gave you blood at the hospital?" Trevor guided Michael toward the bed where his knees buckled, and he dropped onto the bare mattress. His pulse was weak. "You need more blood, or you won't survive more than a couple days."

Michael's eyes shut before Trevor could explain anymore.

Rest first. Then replenish, kid. I got you.

Trevor waited in the corner of Michael Braxton's room all night, watching over him. Posters on the walls, a bed with no sheets, dingy green carpeting threadbare and worn down in the middle of the room. A photograph of his mother and one of his girlfriend flanked a Jesus candle on the dresser. His high school diploma was taped above a full-length mirror leaning against the wall by the window.

The kid was face down, sweatpants leg bunched up around his knee. This kid, though far more fair-skinned and muscular, reminded Trevor of his oldest boy, Ryan. It's a father's instinct to watch after his boys. To raise them to be the right kind of men. Trevor needed to be here for Michael, to teach him how to navigate this curse with as much humanity as possible.

As dawn's light threatened to creep through the windows, and when Michael's mother was up and moving about the trailer, Trevor closed the blinds and hid in the closet. The mother, Eleanor, tiptoed into the room and pressed the back of her hand against her son's forehead. She pulled a blanket over his shoulders. "You're cold," she said.

He groaned and rolled away.

"I need to work a double today, but there's soup in the cabinet." She whispered a prayer over his sleeping body, begging God to take care of her boy.

Trevor's heart ached at the beauty of the sight—a mother caring for her child.

What are you doing? His wife, Rebecca, had screamed, breaking his trance in the predawn hours weeks ago. She'd stood in the doorway of Devon's bedroom while Trevor woke from a nightmare. Her shriek was etched into his brain matter like grooves of a record, skipping, repeating, forever screaming. If she hadn't screamed, Trevor might not have pulled away so violently, tearing his baby's jugular. The little boy's futile struggle ended. Blood gushed from his neck. The weight of Devon's bleeding body was still nestled in the crook of Trevor's arm like a palpable ghost.

He fought the urge to cry, but failed, wiping the drops of blood that leaked from his ducts. The iron-rich blood on his finger reeked of Michael, whose blood still coursed through his veins.

The mother, Eleanor, brushed a few stray hairs off the kid's brow, kissed him on the forehead, and left in a beat-up old Chevette that looked like it could've shattered into pieces if it hit a bump.

After Eleanor left for work, Trevor covered the windows in the trailer with blankets and towels to cut down on the amount of sunlight pouring through. He unplugged the phone from the wall so nobody would disturb them, then he waited for Michael to wake.

Within a few hours, the kid woke strong, thrashing out of his bed, fists swinging, eyes dark as oil, but he was too anemic and disoriented to keep up the fight. "What the hell are you doing in my house?"

"I returned your wallet. Remember?"

Michael furrowed his brow, gears turning in the kid's head.

Trevor gestured for him to have a seat on the bed. "We have to talk."

Chapter Ten

Reese

After dropping off Michael the night before, she'd crept into the house to avoid waking her mom, but instead of silence, Reese was met with the rhythmic squeaking of her mother's bed. She cringed at the thought of Mom having sex and wondered who was in there this time. A few months earlier, it was *Handsy Hank*, who had "accidentally" brushed Reese's ass with his palm. Mom sent the guy packing but never bothered reporting his actions to anyone. Mom had said, "There ain't enough proof to do anything about it." The entire incident was swept under the rug and never spoken of again. Mom didn't care much for uncomfortable conversations, so it made it easy to keep the secret from Michael. If he'd ever found that out, Handsy Hank would've ended up bludgeoned to near-death.

Reese had tiptoed to her basement bedroom out of earshot of the squeaking bed, plucked her Fat Joe's uniform from the dirty laundry, and gave it a sniff check. The clothes reeked of sweat and grease from the day before, but she didn't care enough to do a load of laundry. She collapsed into bed, and by dawn, Reese had only gotten a couple of hours' worth of broken sleep.

She put on her filthy fast-food uniform and drove to work in the dark. She tried to catch a glimpse of the comet which was supposed to be low in the eastern sky, but there was far too much atmospheric haze to see anything. She should have gotten out and seen it months ago, as it was turning out to be the next Haley's Comet, or so it seemed, but she was so busy doing everything Michael wanted to do, she'd stopped tracking what was happening in the sky. According to the articles she'd read recently, Comet Hale-Bopp would brighten as it made its approach over the next few months, so she'd have her chance to see it soon enough.

Much of the day was spent on auto-pilot, as the memory of Sebastian's soft lips against hers was haunted by the ghost of Michael's swollen, bloodied mouth. She dreamed about what was next. *The breakup.* Dating other people. Applying to Berkeley and driving her car cross-country to get there. She dreamed of independence. A horizon of hopes and dreams was, for the first time in years, visible and attainable. All she had to do was walk away from him.

At the end of the work day, Reese finished mopping the lobby, left her apron hanging on the rack, and punched her card into the time clock.

Outside, parked next to her old Corolla, was a dark blue Pontiac Grand Am. Sebastian Belinski leaned against the door with his arms crossed like Jake at the end of *Sixteen Candles.* She'd always identified a little with Molly Ringwald in that film. Not because of the pathetic crush on a popular boy, but because of how her family overlooked her.

Being the only child, she should've had all the attention a kid could get. However, Mom had always stressed the importance of women being independent. *It's the nineties!* She'd been training Reese to take care of herself since she was young enough to carry a latchkey. *We are women, hear us roar*, she'd say. Reese had a hard time letting out that roar. Her kitten mews were always silenced before she could figure out what she needed to say.

As she approached Sebastian, he tilted his head with a smile. A knit beanie covered his curls, and he'd never looked cuter.

"You here for lunch?" she asked.

He grinned. "No. I couldn't wait until Monday to see you again."

She tried to avoid his gaze and focused on the trash bins, the curb, the other cars in the lot, anything but staring directly in those devastatingly kind and enticing eyes.

"Is this your car?" she asked.

"I bought it with all the money I make doing absolutely nothing." He laughed. "No. It's my dad's."

"I like the color." She regretted it the second she said it. *I like the color*—like something a toddler would say. *Say something smart.*

"Do you want to …" He scratched his head through the beanie. "I don't know, hang out again? My dad built a stone oven outside. He's christening it tonight by making pizzas."

Reese was eager to blurt out a *yes*, but she already promised herself that she'd end it with Michael before seeing Sebastian again.

"I mean, who doesn't like pizza? Aaand …" He shrugged. "My mom told me to invite you."

"Okay." She didn't know how the hell she was going to pull it off, but she couldn't resist the temptation of spending time with him again.

"Come over around six?"

"Sounds good." A ridiculous checklist appeared in her head:

2:00 PM, Go home and change

3:00 PM, Break up with Michael

6:00 PM, date with Sebastian

Sebastian took a step closer, and if she was reading the look on his face correctly, it meant he wanted to kiss her again.

"I hope your dad is making enough pizza." Reese turned away, pretending she didn't notice his advance and rubbing her belly theatrically. "He hasn't met my appetite yet!"

Sebastian laughed. "I'll tell him to be prepared to serve an army."

"He'd better be."

"But what will I tell him when no army shows up, and it's just some little blonde?"

Reese's jaw dropped. "Some little blonde?"

"That came out wrong."

She shot him a smirk. "I'll let you make it up to me." She slid her key into the car door and realized her comment and the flirtatious look she'd given him may have come across as sexual. "I mean, you can make it up to me by ensuring there's enough pizza."

It was official, Reese was the most tragically awkward girl in existence.

She started her car and pulled away without looking back. Her galloping heart failed to slow down after her narrow escape from another adulterous kiss. She drove home, gathering her courage to proceed with what she was certain was going to be the most difficult moment of her life.

Chapter Eleven

Michael

Were it not for the disorienting feeling of being on a rocking ship, and the weakness in his muscles, Michael could've ripped Trevor's head clean off his body. Instead, he gave into his rage by flinging his forty-pound plates. Trevor was too quick and strong, deflecting them easily.

How the hell was he supposed to react to someone telling him they'd robbed him of the only life he'd ever known? That they took away his soul in a fit of animalistic passion? He'd never felt more defiled, more confused, more insane. Michael undulated between careful contemplation and wrathful denial. It was all too surreal, like he'd fallen into some nightmare and couldn't wake up. Nothing made sense.

In a fit of frustration, Michael tore down a blanket from his window, and sunlight flooded the living room. White, hot incandescence struck his face, rendering him blind. He twisted away, arm blocking the burning glare. "Shit!"

Trevor shielded them with a blanket and lifted it to the window. He secured it on the rod and crossed his arms. "Best to avoid the sun. Burns like a bitch. Cover your body with something. Definitely wear sunglasses. Overcast isn't as bad, but I still recommend coverage, especially for the eyes."

Michael panted and paced, hands on his head. "This can't be real." He looked to his mother's crucifix on the wall.

"Those don't work," Trevor said. "It feels like a curse, but not that kind of curse."

Michael crossed the room, lifted it from the nail, and cradled it carefully. "What if it's not a curse?"

"Doesn't really matter what we call it," Trevor said. "We're predators. And *people* are our prey."

"No. That won't be me."

Trevor laughed. "That's what I said."

Michael hung the wooden crucifix back onto its nail. "Well, I'm not like you." He squared up to Trevor, but he was too fragile to be a real threat. Michael sat down and rested his hands on his knees. "God doesn't let us carry more than we can bear, right?"

"What the hell are you talking about, kid?"

"I don't know yet, but I don't feel cursed. I feel *good*." Michael flexed his biceps and rubbed his hands on his chest, examining his body and noting the bruises had faded. His fingers moved to his face, exploring his features. The ridge of sutures ran under his fingers. "My cuts."

"They've healed," Trevor said. "Mostly."

Michael dashed to his dresser mirror to examine his face in the dim light. He poked at his skin, laughing. "Vampires? You gotta be shittin' me."

Trevor shrugged. "Not really. There are a lot of stories out there. A lot of myths. I think those who were here before us agreed to use the word *vampire* simply because it fit and everyone kept using it. Whether we say *vampire* or *evolved species* or *monster* doesn't matter. What matters is what we do with it."

"Like a purpose?"

"Right. We should be purposeful with our actions. Beat the instinct to the punch by getting blood in other ways."

"And you're certain it has to be blood?" As he thought about it, biting into someone's flesh, drawing hot blood into his body, an urge came over him. One that might come over a predator in the wild. He wanted it, craved it. Michael quickly rejected the desire. "That's gross."

"Eat anything else and you'll cramp up. Nothing goes down. Our bodies cannot digest anything anymore."

"But it can digest blood?" Michael threw his arms in the air. "Do you hear how insane this sounds?"

"We don't really *bite* people. The teeth are more like siphons or something that draws blood into our bodies. And if you don't get blood in you soon, you won't survive."

"I'm not siphoning blood into anything."

"I need to get you to Syracuse. They'll have blood bags to help you transition."

"Transition? How?"

"There are people in Syracuse like us who look after each other. They're organized. There are blood donors. There's *help*. If we make a mistake, they have these clean-up crews and folks on the inside to help cover our tracks. Cops and doctors and stuff. Now that you've rested and began the healing process, I'll call Jensen and someone will come get us."

"To go to Syracuse?"

"Yes."

"I can't go."

"You have other plans?"

"Yeah, asshole. I do. I have a job and a girlfriend and—"

"I know this is hard to hear, but your life as you know it is going to be very different now."

"No shit, Sherlock." Michael scowled at him. "I can't just drop my life and leave everything behind."

"Sadly, that's what we all have to do."

Michael's shoulders tensed and he clenched his fists through his frustration. "I wouldn't have to leave if you didn't do this to me."

Trevor's face dropped and something like regret painted his expression.

Michael headed toward the kitchen. "I gotta call Reese."

Trevor stopped him with an outstretched arm. "You can't tell anyone."

Michael tried to shove him away, but Trevor was far too strong to move.

"That's the price we pay to keep our loved ones safe. You can't see them anymore."

That would never be an acceptable option for Michael. "My mom needs me here. You don't know what she's been through."

"More than anything, she needs you to stay away. You can't trust yourself anymore."

"But I can trust you?" Michael puffed out his chest and got Trevor's face. He used all the strength he could to shove him, but Trevor didn't budge.

Trevor was a brick wall. "Of all people on this planet, you can trust me, and me alone."

"Yeah, right." He rolled his eyes.

Trevor shrugged. "I'll meet you in the middle. You stay here. Don't go anywhere. Don't call your little girlfriend. You *will* hurt anyone who comes near you. Hell, I wouldn't be surprised if you slaughter your own dog while I'm out getting you the help you need."

"What the fuck is wrong with y—"

"I will be back with blood so you can replenish. Your mother said she was working a double."

"You talked to my mom?" Michael lunged, but Trevor held him back with a single outstretched arm.

"Calm down. I overheard her this morning. She's working a double. Where's your girlfriend?"

"Why?"

"Where is she?"

"At work."

"Good. Leave her alone. Stay here. I'll be back before your mother gets back. *Don't do anything.*"

Trevor shrugged into a black windbreaker, wrapped himself in a black and white scarf, and pulled a pair of polarized sunglasses over his eyes. He sprinted out the door faster than Michael had ever seen anyone run in his life.

Thick scattered clouds blocked the sun, but Michael had to use an arm to shield his eyes from the light. He slipped into his silver and blue Cowboys jacket, now faded to a gray and grease-stained navy, and pulled the hood over his head. A blanket from the couch thrown over his head like a cape offered extra protection from the light outside. He slipped his feet into a pair of muck boots by the door and stepped outside. His eyes had trouble adjusting, and he kept his lids near shut as he navigated down the steps toward Buster, whose incessant barking hadn't stopped for more than a few seconds at a time.

He could smell the blood pumping through the Labrador's veins. Hot pulsing sustenance lured him to feed. He longed to draw closer, to nuzzle up against Buster's jugular. To part his lips to a mouthful of fur and be rewarded with what his body needed.

Michael staggered backward, rejecting the desire. He rushed inside, locked the door behind him, and knelt before the crucifix on the wall. "Please help me. Don't let me hurt anyone." The longer he sat before the wooden cross on the wall, chanting a prayer, the longer he wondered if God was even listening anymore. If he'd ever listened. Not once had a prayer ever been answered. Not when he begged for help in catching the attention of college scouts. Not even when it really mattered, like when he stepped between his cowering mother and his father's fists. Not once in his life had God ever helped him, and he feared it would be no different now. If he didn't get what his body needed soon, he'd die. He felt himself withering. Like an old dog that knows it's their time. His vision darkened while the dog barked outside, and Michael closed his eyes to fight the urge.

You better fucking hurry, Trevor.

CHAPTER TWELVE

REESE

Mom wasn't home, so Reese paced the kitchen, waiting to make the dreaded phone call. The walls had been painted orange a few months ago. The cabinets were beige and the counters yellow, and the clashing of tones always made her feel uneasy. The stove and sink were sectioned off by a peninsula counter, and on the opposite side was a small breakfast nook with a wooden table and chairs. She paced the area in front of the table and whispered to herself, practicing the words she'd use to tell him it was over. They say to never break up with a person over the phone, that you owe it to the other person to say goodbye to their face.

She owed him nothing, but society had a way of deciding what girls owed to the men in their lives.

Michael was a grown man now—an angry man—and she had every right to leave. It was time to stop feeling as if she were in debt to him simply because of the years they'd spent together. Simply because they'd been best friends.

Previous attempts to break up always led to Michael at her doorstep with a bucketful of wildflowers he'd picked on the walk over. A tear-filled apology and promises of being a better boyfriend followed.

Not this time. Today, she'd call him, tell him it was over, and head straight to Sebastian's house where Michael would never find her.

The answering machine blinked as she paced, signaling she'd received three new messages while she was at work. She pressed play. All of the messages were from Eleanor, asking if Reese could drive over and check on Michael, who hadn't been answering the phone all day. Each message sounded more desperate than the last.

"Damn it." Reese dialed his number, hoping he'd answer so she wouldn't have to drive over there, but nobody picked up. She slammed the handset down, banging it into the hook repeatedly. "Answer the phone!"

Next to the phone, her plane ticket poked out from Mom's address book. She slid it out from between the papers. On Tuesday, she could get away for a week. She could get out of this town. Get away from Michael so he couldn't show up and beg for her to take him back. Away from her mom's skeevy boyfriends. Reese had been looking forward to meeting her dad since they started talking a year ago. Even though Reese was reluctant at first, she eventually eased into the idea of having a father figure. She didn't know how to feel about George, or *Dad, Father, patriarchal failure, Bio-dad*, whatever she was supposed to call him. They'd exchanged postcards and letters and it wasn't until he'd talked about watching a launch at Cape Canaveral that Reese was finally interested. At least if ol' Bio-dad was a major disappointment, she'd get to see a rocket launch. So, Reese agreed, and George sprung for her round-trip ticket. Her suitcase had been partially packed for the past week, but she wished she could hop on that flight right now, go to Florida and never return. She wasn't much of a beach person, but she could get used to it. Maybe she'd apply to a college there, watch rockets launch, get a job at Kennedy. She spiraled into a daydream that had Sebastian meeting her in Florida for spring break. They'd hang out, and get coffee or pizza.

The hall toilet flushed, startling her out of her daydream and into a frozen panic. Mom was at work today, she was certain of it. Reese checked out the kitchen window to see that her Corolla was the only vehicle in the driveway.

"Hello?" a man's voice said from down the hall.

Reese dashed for the block of knives on the island counter. It was set of Ginsu knives that Handsy Hank had bought for Mom as a birthday present. Mom never used them much, but Hank could be found on numerous occasions slicing open watermelons and beer cans. They never seemed to cut with the force and precision as portrayed in the popular commercials, so she assumed either the knives were dull or Hank was inept. She believed the latter.

Reese grabbed the largest of the knives as a stocky man in athletic shorts and a T-shirt emerged from the hallway. "Reese? Is that you?"

She held the knife by her side and stepped out of the corner of the breakfast nook into the open space of the kitchen. The door to the garage was only a dash away behind her on the opposite side of the kitchen.

"Whoa." His hands went up at the sight of the knife. "I'm sorry." He grabbed a fleece jacket from the back of the kitchen chair by the telephone. "I'm a guest of your mother's. She said you'd be at work today."

"She didn't tell me anyone would be here." Reese put space between them, backing toward the other half of the kitchen and the exit to the garage.

"I should have left already, but I used your internet to check my emails." He pointed to the Gateway computer in the living room. "Then I used the bathroom and lost track of time. I apologize."

"Where's your car?"

"I rode with your mother last night." His eyes flicked to the knife and back to Reese.

The knife's metal handle warmed in her grip. She imagined the mechanics of defending herself with the knife as she held it to her side. She'd have to arc upward and out. It would be much more effective to hold it close to her shoulder, like she'd seen in the movies, prepared to stab down, but she didn't want to be dramatic and raise it.

"I'm Quentin. I apologize if I gave you a fright. I'll just be on my way now." He thumbed over his shoulder, shrugged into his fleece jacket, and backed toward the front door. "I look forward to meeting you properly in the future." He disappeared around the corner into the foyer. The click of the deadbolt followed, and cold air rushed into the house.

Quivering Quentin.

Perhaps it was a little ridiculous holding him at knife-point, but if Mom wasn't going to leave a note saying some random guy would be in the house, what was she supposed to do?

Quentin walked through the snow out front and stopped in the driveway. He pulled his foot to his buttocks in a stretch for a few seconds, then took off in a jog down the street, along the long row of trees on the opposite side of the road.

Reese locked all the doors and showered the stench of Fat Joe's from her body. As hot water fell in curtains over her face, she couldn't help but worry about Michael. Eleanor said he was sleeping peacefully this morning when she'd left the house. His pallid, sunken skin the night before was an indicator he was not doing well at all. But if Michael's mom was willing to pray the anemia away, who was Reese to argue?

After her shower, she got dressed and tried calling Michael again. For a brief moment, she entertained the idea of mailing him a break-up letter, but she pushed through her fear of facing what needed to be done and picked up the phone for another attempt. Still no answer.

An image crept into her head. Michael was dead, slumped over the plaid recliner where she'd left him. Flies buzzing around his rotting corpse. Piss and crap crusting in his Dallas Cowboys sweatpants. His poor mother would leap from a building if she found him that way, and it was Eleanor's fragile mental state that enticed Reese to keep trying.

After countless phone calls, her nerves sparked, stoking her anger. A rageful thing that said, "Screw him. He's not my problem."

Maybe Michael succumbing to his injuries would be good for her.

Maybe this was her way out.

With that thought, darkness swept over her, like that feeling of the thick plastic shroud over her head. It clouded her mind and seeped into her heart, blackening it with heinous thoughts. Reese covered her mouth, gasping that she had, even for a second, wanted Michael to die so she wouldn't have to suffer through the fallout of a messy breakup.

You have to do this.

She'd been kidding herself to think she could break up over the phone anyway. She grabbed her keys and headed toward Michael's house, either to find his dead body or to deliver the emotional blow that might kill him.

CHAPTER THIRTEEN

REESE

Reese stepped out of her car, heart so heavy with dread she didn't know if she'd make it to the trailer door or if the weight of the universe would buckle her knees. She'd rather collapse, bury herself under the packed snow, and let the buzzards find her thawing corpse in the spring rather than tell Michael they were over. No vehicles were in the driveway. Michael's Ford had been totaled and his mom's Chevette was still at work. Hopefully, Reese could say what she needed to say and be out of there before Eleanor got home.

Buster pulled at his chain, whimpering to see her. Saturday was the day she normally walked him after work. Before going inside, she headed toward Buster, grabbed his leash from the mound of junk against the side of the trailer, and asked him if he wanted to take a walk.

He jumped, spinning and dashing side to side while she struggled to connect his leash to his collar. The dense tree line beyond lured her eyes, seeking the man she'd seen the night before, but there was nothing.

She could load Buster in her vehicle now, head home with him, and never look back. But it wasn't that simple.

"Come on, handsome," she said. "Let's take one more walk."

Nobody in that house would take the time to walk him ever again. It was a brief walk on the shoulder down Halsey Road, not more than half a mile total, and tears burned her eyes as she thought about Buster being trapped in these living conditions.

Her wide-leg jeans soaked up snow and salt, saturating the denim as she headed back to do the inevitable. Her breath froze in the falling temperature. It was supposed to drop into the single digits later that night. Maybe taking Buster with her when she left wasn't such a bad idea.

She connected the grimy old dog to his chain, gave him some food, and made it toward the front door.

Please don't be dead.

Her stomach went sour with the thought of finding a corpse. She opened the front door and stepped inside to hear music coming from Michael's room at the other end of the trailer.

The living room was darker than normal. A thick, fleece Cowboys blanket hung over the front window where typically sheer, dingy white curtains allowed in daylight.

The window over the kitchen sink was obscured with a bath towel. Reese flicked the light switch, but it didn't work. She gave it another try, then spotted the missing bulbs from the ceiling fan fixture.

Music seeped through the kitchen from the room down the hall. A Red Hot Chili Peppers song mixed with the rhythmic clinking of metal from the weight room.

In the kitchen, there were no dishes in the sink and the telephone was disconnected from the wall.

"Michael?"

The murk of the back hallway swallowed her voice.

There were two rooms on this end of the trailer, Michael's bedroom, the other converted into his weight room. Reese peeked into his bedroom first. Three years ago—the first time he'd invited her over— she shared a kiss with him on the bare mattress. An old quilt with frayed edges lay across the sweat-stained bed. They had played UNO that night, and when she caught him intentionally losing, she playfully nudged his shoulder. He leaned in, planting a kiss on her cheek. Then she let him move to her lips. It wasn't like the first kisses she'd seen on her mom's soap opera, *General Hospital,* or even the kisses on *Saved by the Bell.* It was nothing like TV at all. It was simple, sweet, and innocent, not complicated like the bloody kiss she gave him the night before to keep him from having a breakdown. Everything was complicated now.

She stepped in front of his weight room, took a steadying breath, and held it, hoping she wouldn't lose what little courage she had by exhaling. She opened the door to see Michael lying on the bench, pressing more weight than she'd ever seen him lift. His mother's religious candles of Jesus and Mary were lit, surrounding him on the floor like some strange weight-lifting séance.

Reese pressed stop on the boom box setting on the table near the door, and the music quit.

Michael lowered the bar onto the rack. Weights were stacked on each side of the bar.

He sat up, smiling. "Did you see that?"

Though it was dark in the room and his injuries were obscured in shadow, she could tell the swelling on his face had decreased significantly. She stepped closer to get a better look. The laceration across his face was almost completely healed. No more than a pink indentation marred his face.

"That's 350 pounds! That's all my weights. I took the ones off the dumbbells, and I pulled out the shitty ones from my dad's old things."

"What is happening?"

He lay down on the bench and placed his hands on the bar. "Come here and lay on this. I think I can lift more."

"Michael, we have to talk."

"Come here! You're like 140, right? Lay on the bar."

"How are you better already?"

"I told you I didn't need no doctors. Took out the stitches myself with a pair of scissors." He sat up, energized, more alive than she'd seen him in a long time. The way he used to look in the middle of a football game, or more recently, the way he looked right before a fight, like a rod ready to electrocute.

"I'm glad you're feeling better, but …" Reese fidgeted with her keys. "I really need to talk to you."

Michael smiled. "Same. Come here." He patted the bench for her to have a seat. "I wanna show you something."

Chapter Fourteen

Reese

"A what?" Reese asked. He was worse than she'd imagined. Delusional. Hallucinatory?

"That's what Trevor said."

"Trevor … the vampire?"

"You think I'm making this up."

Reese rubbed her temples, every imaginable thing she could possibly say zooming through her mind at the speed of light: *You're insane; this alone enough for me to break up with you; you need to see a doctor; your brain is broken.*

"Look at this!" Michael bent at the waist and lifted the 350 pounds with one arm. He grunted and struggled with it, but he managed to swing it up and press it over his head. "He said I'd be stronger. Faster, too. The sun is down, so that's good."

"And the sun needs to be down, because …"

"Because the sunlight hurts."

Reese couldn't hold back the sour expression on her face. "Do you think, maybe, the lights hurt your eyes because of a concussion or something?"

Concern grew about a brain injury. Adrenaline could've been coursing through him, allowing him to lift the excessive weight. So many reasonable thoughts ran through her head to explain Michael's symptoms, but his healed wounds were a head-scratcher.

He gestured to his body. "I felt like garbage last night and worse this morning, but this afternoon, I woke up recharged." Michael was manic, eyes wide and body rigid with electric tension. "My wounds healed. Like a miracle! Then Trevor explained what happened, and it all came back to me. The accident. Him in the road … I veered the truck to avoid hitting him."

"That's weird. You know, I heard a guy screaming yesterday, over where Halsey meets Centerville."

"When did you hear that?" Michael's eyes narrowed. "Actually, I've been meaning to ask. Where were you last night?"

She concocted a believable lie about dropping off her part of the homework assignment to Sebastian.

"You went to Sebastian Belinski's?"

"Yes. It was either I drop off my part of the project or stay and work on it with him. So, I dropped off the work and left."

Michael scowled. "That kid's a prick. His whole rich family are pricks too. I hate that I used to mow their yard. I bet they love looking down on poor people like us."

Reese shrugged off the comment to avoid an argument. "You should call your mom and let her know you're okay. She's been calling me all day."

"And where were you today?"

"At work." Confidence took over her voice. This needed to be the end of being the overly nice best friend. The girl who put up with his bullshit. This was the time to take a stand and stop accepting his behavior.

Michael was silent, but the tension in his body told her he was holding back. All the choler and potential energy within him condensing to a point and he was about to explode.

"Michael." She sighed, moved to the door, and put a hand on knob. "I have a few things I need to say. First, I plugged the phone back into the wall. You should call your mom, or at least answer when she calls."

"Okay."

"And I think you should get checked out by a doctor."

"No doctors. I'm all good now."

"But there can be something underlying making you—"

"I told you!" Michael's fists clenched and he charged a few steps closer. "There's been a miracle and you're acting like I'm insane."

"You're scaring me." It was the first time she'd ever said it aloud.

An incredulous expression crossed his face. "What the fuck are you scared of?"

"I'm scared of you!" She turned the doorknob, but Michael's reflex was too fast.

He grabbed her wrist and squeezed. "Why would you be afraid of me?" He released her and spoke through clenched teeth. "I love you more than anyone."

"You've already left bruises on my wrist before."

He grimaced. "No, I didn't! When?"

"Look, it doesn't matter now because—"

Michael winced, hands going to his mouth as he dropped to his knees.

He held his fingers below his nose. "Something hurts." He stood with a growl, tilted his head back and curled his lip. "There's something in there."

"Michael—"

"Will you look at my gums and tell me what's up there? They feel weird."

"No. You're changing the subject."

"Please. I'm serious. Just look under my lip."

"It's too dark in here."

"Well, I can't turn on the light!" He screamed so loud the plates on the bench press rattled, subtly clinking together. "It hurts so much."

"Go see a doctor."

"Just look in my damn mouth!" Michael pinned her to the door. His chest heaved, hands clenched on her shoulders.

Reese sucked in a breath and closed her eyes.

Michael let go of her. "Oh my God, I'm sorry. I'm so sorry."

The thumping of her heart clogged her throat, making it difficult to speak. "I have to go."

"Not yet." He shifted his body weight from one foot to the other, keeping one hand pressed against the door so she couldn't open it. Then, he took a step back with his palms up in surrender and bent down to pick up a candle. "Please, just take a look, then I'll go see the doctor." He sat on the weight bench.

Uncertain how he'd react if she refused, Reese asked, "What am I looking for?"

He raised the candle near his lips and she took it from his grasp. His fingers were cool to the touch.

"You're freezing."

She used her thumb and forefinger to peel up his lip and look beneath. Dry, pale gums were tacky to the touch. "I don't see any—" She stopped herself as she spotted a glimpse of something deep under the lip. Beyond the gumline of the canine tooth was an inflamed and cavernous pocket of tissue. "There's a gash or something up in there. Both sides."

Michael remained silent with his head tilted back. He slurred through peeled-back gums, trying to say, "What is it?"

Angling the candlelight revealed something else within the cavity. A white, bony structure that moved toward the opening then retracted back like cat claws.

Reese pulled away, bringing Michael's face into full view. His eyes had blackened. Not like the dilated pupils from the night before, but the entire eyeball turned ink black. Not a strip of white sclera was visible. No caramel-brown iris. Shadow had filled his eyes and all that looked back was Reese's reflection within the obsidian orb.

She jolted off the bench and Michael moved in sync, grabbing her elbows and thrusting her against the wall so hard she grunted from the blow. He pressed his body against hers, and Reese dropped the candle. The flame snuffed out before it hit the floor. His chest swelled as he nuzzled his face into her hair. His icy breath slithered through her locks, finding her flesh. Michael grew within his pants, grinding against her pelvis.

"Stop." She pushed, but he didn't release her. Reese wedged her hands between their bodies and pressed on his ribs. "Stop!"

Michael obeyed, taking a step away, and turning his back to her. Face in his hands, he mumbled, "I'm sorry."

Nostrils flaring, jaw clenched, and fighting the tears that wanted to form, she struggled to get the words out.

Say what needs to be said and go.

"Call your mom." Her voice shook. "I care about you. I really do. And I love you." It'd be easier if that part about loving him wasn't true. Her chin quivered as she opened the weight room door. "But I can't—"

"Please don't do this." Michael put his hands on top of his head; his eyes were no longer blackened like she thought she'd seen a moment ago. They were back to their original caramel brown color, desperate, saddened.

"I can't be your girlfriend anymore. This is over." The second she said it, she tore open the door and hurried down the hall, through the kitchen, and out the door. Behind her, she left a trail of memories and pain. She imagined if she looked back, she'd see blood-soaked footprints in her wake, made after stomping all over Michael Braxton's heart.

The sun had already set and darkness surrounded her as she ran to her car.

Buster barked, pulling on his chain, hoping she'd take him with her, but there was no time to stop. She tried not to look at the poor dog in the floodlight, who'd likely never go for a walk again. Saying goodbye to her old friend wasn't an option though, because Michael tore open the door to his trailer. It smashed against the aluminum siding. He held up an arm to the glaring floodlight.

Reese jumped in her car and locked the door. The engine started without a hitch and she kicked into reverse before putting on her seatbelt. Michael ran toward her, barefoot through the snow, faster than she'd ever seen him move.

"Reese, wait!"

She backed into the road without fully checking for oncoming traffic.

"Reese!" Michael's voice trailed into silence and his figure faded in the red glow of her taillights.

She drove away with a hook in her back. His claws were deep under her skin, clinging, refusing to let go. This wouldn't be the end of it.

Chapter Fifteen

Michael

His vision was blurred, but Michael managed to run to the end of the driveway. Her taillights disappeared and he roared into the darkness, infuriated that he'd lost control. Something predatory within him wanted to chase her down, make her listen, make her obey, make her hurt. These feelings kept him from chasing after. No matter how instinctive Trevor said this condition was, Michael would not permit it to control him.

Buster's barking pulled Michael's attention away and his eyesight improved. He held a hand up to the blinding floodlight on the garage and headed toward Buster. "Shut up!"

The dog lowered his head and backed toward the dog house, growling.

"What the fuck are you afraid of?" Michael laughed, dampening the anger within. Trying not to think about how royally he'd screwed his chances with Reese. He shrugged off the tension building in his shoulders and knelt beside Buster, who finally seemed to recognize him. Buster sat with his ears tucked back. As he pet the greasy fur, warmth radiated off Buster's body. A hundred degrees of pulsing blood flowed under the surface. On his knees in the snow, Michael nuzzled Buster for a hug. "Good boy."

Michael's tongue brushed against something sharp in his mouth. Bony protrusions had extended beyond his canine teeth. The tip of his tongue explored razor sharp points, then he traced the structure with his finger, following them to the swollen pockets under his lip. They were about as thick as a porcupine quill, but rock hard, preparing to cut into their first meal.

He jerked away from Buster, falling to his butt and backpedaling away.

Buster began barking again, and Michael rose to his feet, fighting the urge to snap his head clean off.

Mom's headlights hit the gravel driveway, saving him from an impulsive decision. Clenching his teeth made the sharp protrusions stick into his lower lip, so he relaxed his jaw and focused on breathing. He took deep, calming breaths and pictured Reese's hand resting on his heart. The sharp, fanglike things retracted back into the swollen pockets.

"See," Michael whispered to Buster. "I have complete control."

***

Michael took a shower, avoiding the inevitable task of telling his mother what happened to him. He stepped into another pair of sweatpants and a clean T-shirt, psyching himself up in the mirror before facing her. When he came out of the bathroom, mom was puttering around the kitchen.

He asked her to sit in the recliner because he had something to tell her. He paced the living room, kicking himself for not practicing what he was going to say. Candles cast an orange glow on the old stained carpet. He hated that carpet. Too many bloodstains and bad memories were locked into its fibers, impossible to scrub clean even with the strongest bleach.

The lights irritated his eyes, but candles weren't so bad. Michael had told her the power went out, but soon she'd know the truth.

"If you're going to say something, say it!" Mom said. "Otherwise, I'm going to bed. It's been a long day."

"Okay, here goes …" He knelt before his mom, who wore jeans that reeked of the plastic factory. That loud cement box of a job, clickity clacking of the injection molding presses … He'd worked there with his mom since he graduated and hated every day. She must've heard by now that he'd quit right before his accident, but Mom didn't mention it.

Her teased hair stood as tall and coiffed as it had when he was little. A gold cross hung around her neck. She fidgeted with it, rubbing it between her thumb and forefinger.

"I woke up this morning with a … a gift."

"Oh?"

Michael looked to the heavens, but his view was shrouded by the water-stained ceiling. He reached for his mother's cross pendant, stealing it from her fingers and clutching it in his fist.

"Michael," Mom said, inches from his face. "Are you alright?"

"It's a gift from God, Mom," he whispered. "It has to be, right?"

"Yes." She smiled with glassy eyes, then wrapped her arms around him and squeezed. "Life is a gift. We prayed that He'd let you live. We prayed so hard, and here you are. The doctor said—"

"Mom."

"—you wouldn't make it, but they were wrong. God gave you a second chance."

"Mom."

"So now you gotta decide what to do with it."

"Mom!"

She silenced herself. Black mascara clumped in bold lashes that made her big brown eyes look alien. They were hopeful, the eyes of someone who trusted in the will of her Savior, unflinchingly. Michael wasn't as trusting, but delivering this news to her would land softly if she believed it was God's will.

"Yes. I have the gift of life, but it's more." Michael couldn't figure out how to say it. Whether to use the word *vampire* or to show her his newfound strength and speed. He took her hands into his. Her hot, throbbing palms were like warming packs against his flesh.

"Honey, you're so cold." She tried to pull away, but Michael held tight.

He closed his stinging eyes; they needed to cry, but nothing came out. "Mom?" Her pulse thrummed against him. The blood in her veins ran just beneath his touch. So close, he could feel it. Her blood—*his* blood. But did they share the same blood any longer? After being drained by Trevor, he wasn't sure any of Mom's blood still flowed in his veins. Could they even be considered family any more if they were no longer blood-related? His lips parted and he opened his eyes to look at the woman who raised him. The woman who once connected herself to him through the womb and fed him with her own oxygen, her nutrients, her own *blood*.

Mom's eyes widened. Her chest inflated as she slowly backed deeper into the recliner. Her feet scrambled to climb into the chair with the rest of her.

Michael's vision failed. Everything was dark and foggy. Mom's outline against the chair slowly came back into focus as he stood. By the time his eyesight returned, she'd started screaming.

"Your eyes!" Her hands held tight over her mouth, muffling her voice.

"Mom! It's okay." He held up his hands.

"Get out! Devil!" She pointed to the door, clutching her cross in the other hand. "Get out!"

Her banshee shrieks pierced his ears. Tears dragged mascara down her cheeks. Saliva strung from her lips. She grabbed a Bible from the end table and backed into the kitchen, repeating the Lord's Prayer with a quaking voice.

"Mom? It's not like that—"

"Devil!"

Michael fought to catch his gasping breaths as he stumbled backward out of the house. His mother's cries bled through the walls as he stood, helplessly misunderstood, barefoot in the snow without a coat.

He fell into the snow onto his ass, and stared at the closed door until the snow soaked his pants all the way through. His house was never a home. Many years ago, when Michael was ten years old, he'd been in this same position, gazing upon the house he'd been kicked out of. That's what he got for trying to do something good. He'd tried to protect his mom from his father's fury, and his scrawny body got knocked backward out the door of the trailer. He'd fallen on his ass in the dirt that day. Locked out of the house for the night, Michael climbed into the bed of the truck and lay on his back, letting the walls of the truck bed hide him from whatever lurked in the surrounding darkness. He never would've admitted he was scared of the dark back then. That he lay there, crying, wishing Mom would come out and take him away from their life.

He'd stared into the sky, upon a gazillion stars, and prayed that his mom and he could have a better life. All night long, he swatted at mosquitoes as they feasted from his body. He cried and swung at them for hours, until he lost the energy and fell asleep.

The following day, after Mom saw the mosquito bites covering Michael's body, she laid into Dad with some yelling, but Michael covered his ears to block the noise. Dad knocked her around so hard that morning, she ended up in the hospital.

Then jail. Then rehab. Then jail again. Last Michael heard, he was in some kind of psychiatric hospital. *Good riddance, you son of a bitch.*

Michael paced the driveway, seething. Had she forgotten about that night almost a decade ago? Mom's stuttering sobs continued to seep through the thin walls. Every time he knocked at the door, it only made her scream louder. He could break the door down and force her to see he wasn't a threat, but he didn't want to scare her any more than he already had. He wasn't sure he could even look her in the eyes after this betrayal. Her refusal to see him as anything other than her son cut deeper than any wound. It sucked the life out of him, bled him dry, more so than that swarm of mosquitoes when he was a boy, and more than any vampire ever could.

Chapter Sixteen

Trevor

He found Jean's Market in town and dropped a quarter into the payphone. Jensen's phone number had been committed to memory weeks earlier, despite refusing to call it until now.

"I'm ready to accept your help," Trevor said.

"Well, well, well … Look who came crawling back!"

Trevor could picture Jensen on the other end, sinister grin from ear to ear.

"There's a kid. He needs blood."

"You finally did it?" Jensen's voice lowered. "Do you need the cleaners?"

"No." Trevor abstained from telling Jensen to lose the arrogant prick act. "I turned him. But he needs blood."

"So get him someone."

"Not this one."

"And why not?"

"He's the religious type."

"Oh, Jesus fucking Christ!"

"And he's young."

"How young?"

"Nineteen."

"Alter boy type, huh?" Jensen laughed. "Wonder how many priest dicks he's had in his mouth?"

"Can I get some fucking blood or not?"

"Chill out, dude. Tell me where the kid is."

"I'm at Jean's Market in Byron. About half an hour west of Syracuse. There's only one fucking stoplight in this town. And that's where you can find me."

Trevor waited under the tree on a picnic table by a hot dog stand that was closed for the season. Several hours passed and the sun lowered in the sky. As twilight took over, he was about to give up on Jensen sending help. Then a vehicle pulled up and its headlights flicked off upon entering the parking lot.

Jensen stepped out in stone-washed jeans, tight rolled around the ankles. High top Air Jordans on his feet. His hypercolor coat changed from purple to blue. He snapped his pasty white fingers and a woman with dark brown hair exited the car as well. She wore a tight minidress, pale white skin showcased bruising around her wrists, the crook of her elbow, and on her neck. She was sullen and gaunt, like a heroin addict.

She carried something and handed it to Jensen, but Trevor couldn't tell what it was.

"Wait in the car," Jensen said. She smiled at Trevor with hungry eyes, begging for him to feed on her, before she slid into the passenger seat of Jensen's car.

"She's fun," Jensen said, licking his lips under a thin mustache. "If you stuck around for a while, maybe you wouldn't have had to eat your own family."

Trevor shriveled inward but refused to show any sign of emotion.

Jensen held up a black grocery bag. "This should hold the boy over until he can feed properly."

Trevor reached for it but Jensen pulled it away. "You feel stronger now, don't you?"

Trevor gave an acknowledging tilt of his head.

"Immortality, my man." He punched Trevor's shoulder.

"I tried to kill myself."

"I told you, you can't do that."

"I didn't think you meant that literally."

"How'd you try to do it? If you say you slit your wrists, I'll bitch slap you right now." Jensen laughed.

"I tried to drive a stake through my own heart."

"Shit, man. That's fucked up." Jensen's brows pinched together. "Fucking psycho, aren't you?"

"Well, it didn't work."

"It would've worked if someone else tried to stab you. But like I said, you can't kill yourself. I don't know how that shit makes sense, but it is what it is." Jensen smacked Trevor's shoulder. "Hey man! But now that you've turned someone, so *nothin'* can kill you."

"Nothing?"

"Absolutely nothing. You're in this life for the long haul, motherfucker!" Jensen threw his head back and his thin, greasy mustache glistened in the parking lot lights.

He handed over the black plastic bag.

Trevor opened it to see two IV bags of blood inside. "Thank you."

Jensen grimaced. "You should've been saying 'thank you' all along!"

Trevor didn't respond to this. Jensen was a man who couldn't be trusted, but right now, he needed his help. "What's that?" He gestured toward the object in his hand.

Jensen handed him a cellphone. "It's a Trac-phone. You ever use one?"

Trevor shook his head, flipping it open. The screen glowed blue as it loaded.

"Remember all the cleanup I had to do when you first turned? The mess you made?"

Trevor clenched his jaw, trying not to recall the blood from their bodies.

"If the kid does anything stupid, all the numbers you need are in the phone under the contacts. Call, and someone will come."

"Understood. I'm bringing him back to the city with me, just after he feeds."

"If he's smart, he won't refuse to feed like you did. We all know what happens when the holier-than-thou types deny the instinct to hunt." Jensen curled his upper lip like a snarling dog. "And if it happens with that boy, that will be more blood on *your* hands, not mine."

CHAPTER SEVENTEEN

REESE

The clock on her dash read 8:12 PM. Sebastian's invite for pizza was for six o'clock. With her eyes puffy from crying, shaking from Michael's violent outburst, she drove home instead. She couldn't show up at Sebastian's over two hours late, sniveling and sobbing from a breakup. Who was she kidding? Michael, as awful of a person as he'd become, had been her best friend for three years, her *only* friend since her childhood friend Sara moved away a year ago. Sara and Reese had exchanged postcards and letters, and occasionally shared a chainmail email on AOL. But within a couple of months, communication stopped. Michael had been the only person in her life other than her mom.

When Reese pulled into the driveway, a white sports car sat alongside her mother's Camry. She parked behind the two vehicles, blocking her mom's car so the stranger could leave. Reese headed to the garage door, and slipped into the side entrance. Upon walking in the house from the garage, she could turn right into the kitchen, or go straight down the steps to the basement, where her finished bedroom sat at the base of the stairs.

"You're home," Mom said, greeting her at the door before she could sneak downstairs. "Where've you been?"

Reese looked over Mom's shoulder to see Quivering Quentin standing behind her at the stove, with an apron on and a pot holder in hand. Something sizzled on the burner.

He waved with a smile. "She's a teenage girl. My guess is the mall."

Mom rolled her eyes. "More likely the library, this one."

"Really?" Quentin paused like he was sizing her up. "I think we're gonna get along. Well, *hopefully* we can get along after." He raised his hand in the air to simulate a stabbing motion.

"Quentin told me you two already met earlier." Mom put her hands on her hips.

"It was my fault, Tammy." Quentin waved a hand airily. "I should've left earlier in the day."

"You okay?" Mom asked.

"I'm fine." Reese looked away, the solitude of her basement room calling her. She needed time to process everything.

"I forgot to ask." Mom put her hand to her mouth as if she were in shock. "I haven't seen you since last night. How's Michael? Is he home from the hospital?"

"He went home last night."

"See! Nothing to worry about. He was fine."

"Actually, he was pretty beat up. It was bad."

"It couldn't have been that bad if they let him go home."

Reese didn't have the energy to explain. She pictured telling her mother everything. About Michael leaving against the doctor's advice. How she had to chase him down. That he was delusional and got aggressive. And that she broke up with him. It all felt like too much, so she kept it inside. At least for now.

"But he's home, right?"

"Yeah, but—"

"Want some steak?" Quentin lifted a sizzling hunk of meat from a pan.

Mom sighed. "She probably already ate at work."

*∗∗

Reese slinked away downstairs and closed herself in her room. She sat on her bed and watched the peaceful movements of the neon tetras in her aquarium. A photo of her and Michael was tucked under the frame of her full-length mirror. They'd been on a field trip when it was taken. He sat next to her on the bus and they couldn't stop talking. She was the honor student and he was the C-student football star. What they lacked in commonality, they made up for with an undeniably strong friendship. For the longest time, she believed they were soul mates. When things went sideways, they were there for each other.

She plucked the photo from the mirror and wanted to burn it, but instead, she mourned the loss of her best friend. There were no friends anymore. Even before Sara moved, they'd already started to drift apart due to Michael's incessant need to be with Reese all the time.

She turned off her overhead light and sat on her bed in the glow of the aquarium, leaning into the corner against two cinderblock walls painted navy blue with splatters of white and yellow, like a starry sky. She'd painted it herself last year. The other two walls of her room were white drywall, holding posters of celestial objects—the Orion Nebula and the Andromeda Galaxy. She'd loved looking at the stars for as long as she could remember. She loved them more than she'd ever loved anything. And now, she could go learn all about them. She didn't need to paint stars on her walls any longer. With Michael out of the picture, she had a universe of possibilities stretched before her.

Michael had made her feel guilty for wanting to go to college. Begging her to give up all of her dreams, because, *if she really loved him, she wouldn't want to leave*. Michael's delusions started long before the accident.

People you love aren't supposed to ask so much of you, and Michael asked for it all. He demanded it all.

As her newfound sense of independence waxed, her confidence in how she broke up with Michael waned.

She tossed and turned for hours, her waking moments haunted with worry. Worried for his physical and mental health. Worried about his delusions or hallucinations. Worried whether he'd hurt himself.

As her eyes grew heavy and her mind slipped in and out of dream states, a tapping sound jarred her from rest. She jerked upright. The sound came from the small basement window near the ceiling of her room. The snow had been brushed away, and a face stared through the glass. She gasped and whipped the blanket from her body, but quickly realized it was Michael.

He tapped at the glass and gestured for her to let him in.

She stood on her bed and gripped the cinderblock windowsill with her fingertips. "What are you doing?" She tried to talk loud enough for her voice to make it through the glass, but without waking her mom upstairs.

His gaunt features made him nearly unrecognizable.

"Let me in." Michael lay on his belly in the snow, resting his chin on his hands. He was in a T-shirt and no coat. "Mom kicked me out." He pressed his hand against the glass. His lips were a sickly blue. "Please, Reese?"

"The window is frozen shut."

"So, open the door!" His voice rattled the glass and she staggered a step back.

If she left him out there, would he give up and go home? She pictured Michael lying there all night in a fetal position, shivering like the poor dead squirrel, eyes crusting over in ice, face glued to her window, lifeless. Forever trying to soak up her warmth because he could never make it without her.

"I can't."

"Fine. I'll knock on the door and ask your mom." Michael backed away.

Reese panicked. She didn't want her mother inviting Michael in without knowing everything that had happened. She ran to her door and sprinted as quietly as she could up the basement stairs. The side entrance opened without a sound.

If Mom got involved, it'd be a huge, embarrassing ordeal. Better to deal with him herself.

Cold concrete sent sharp chills through her feet as she crossed the empty garage to the outside door.

Michael beat her to the first words as she unlocked the door and opened it. "I have nowhere to go." Sad, brown eyes were red around the lids like he'd been crying.

A thousand arguments went through her head at once.

Not my problem.

That's what you get.

Get out of my life!

But she looked at him, sick, pale, deranged, and in need of medical attention, maybe some psychological help, too. In need of shelter for one night. If she left him out there, he'd probably fall asleep against her window and die from exposure on a night that wasn't supposed to be any warmer than seven degrees Fahrenheit.

Her heart quaked, her stomach turned inside out as if her entire body was screaming and laughing at her: *Sucker!*

Reese stepped to the side and gestured for him to come in.

Chapter Eighteen

Reese

Soft blue aquarium light filled her room. Reese sat at the edge of her bed, knees drawn up to her chest, while Michael reclined in the black bean bag chair on the floor, twisting his fist in the palm of his hand. "She got home from work, took one look at me," Michael said. "You should've seen her face."

He leaned forward, resting his elbows on his knees, skin pale, eyes sunken, but every gash on his face was healed as if the accident never happened. "I can't believe she kicked me out."

Reese sat silently on her bed, wishing she could take back her invitation, wishing he would go home, while Michael stared at her as if waiting for her to say something.

"You can stay here just for tonight."

Michael's head fell back in defeat, looking to the drop-leaf ceiling, his hands trembling. "I thought she'd be more understanding."

"Of what?"

"What do you think? I'm sitting there believing God has blessed me with some amazing gift, then Mom calls me the Devil and kicks me out."

"The *gift* you told me about earlier?"

Michael rubbed his face in his palms and leapt to his feet with a snarl. He kicked the bean bag chair across the room and it smacked into the aquarium.

Neon tetras scattered.

"Hey!" Reese ran to the tank to check on the fish.

"Sorry," Michael said. "I just don't know what I'm gonna do."

With her back to Michael, she gritted her teeth. She wanted him out of her house. Instead, she remained calm and patient with him. "Is there someone you can talk to about this?"

"I'm talking to *you*." His voice rose.

"What about your pastor?"

"What's that guy going to do?"

"I don't know. Maybe he can talk to your mom or offer you a place to stay."

"Am I that big of an inconvenience? I guess I'll just go sleep in the fucking street."

Reese turned to face him. "I said you could stay here for a night. I meant, why don't you go talk to Dan Delgado in the morning and see if he can help you?"

"Will you go with me?" He approached her, placing his ice cold hands on her elbows. "Please?"

"I have to work, but I can give you a ride, drop you off early."

"I don't deserve you." He rubbed his eyes, chin quivering. "I think I'm crying, but nothing is coming out. Everything is all dry."

"You're probably dehydrated." She slipped away from him to feed her fish. "They said you didn't get enough blood."

Michael closed the gap again, grabbing her hand as she set the container of fish flakes down. "Why are you pulling away?"

All she had to do was let him stay one night without incident, so she didn't bring up the violent outburst he'd exhibited earlier. "You're freezing. Your circulation is terrible, and you're turning blue. I really think you should go back to the hospital." She rubbed her thumbs on the back of his hands, warming them. Any little thing might help him at this point.

He closed his eyes. "Dear God. I want to first thank you for this gift you've given me."

Reese cringed, watching his blue lips move as he prayed aloud.

"Help me, God. I don't know what to do. My mom … she … I did nothing wrong and …" His voice broke. "I didn't do nothing wrong!" His grip tightened on her fingers. "Just help my mom see that this is a blessing. This is your doing, right?"

With each word, Reese wanted to pull back. What she'd give to float away from him, drift up, gaining distance until she couldn't be in his reach any longer. She wondered how far she'd have to float. Florida? All the way to Berkeley in California?

He'd find her. Maybe she should aim for the stars. Her body could float out the door, up the stairs and into the sky. Rising in perpetuity until she drifted among those stars which always brought her peace. She'd hide there for eternity.

As he prayed and she imagined herself ascending away from reality, his cool touch brought her back. The loss of blood and poor circulation was messing with his head and she worried it could cause issues in the brain. He was already showing signs of being delusional.

"… Amen."

She whispered *Amen* out of respect, and knew she was only one who'd heard his prayer. She was the only one who ever listened.

She relaxed her hands, but Michael held his grip as she tried to reclaim them. Michael squeezed and her metacarpal bones rolled over each other. "Ow!"

"Sorry." He released.

Reese crawled into bed and pulled the blanket over herself. She turned her back to him, facing the starry cement wall, and forced her eyes shut.

No more than five seconds passed before Michael spoke. "I'm hungry."

"There's probably leftovers in the fridge."

"I feel empty inside, like when I had to drop pounds for wrestling. I'd eat nothing all day and felt drained. That's how I feel all over. Like I need to eat, but I have no appetite."

Reese stayed facing the wall.

"Is there room in the bed for me?"

"I don't feel comfort—"

Michael crawled onto the mattress. Reese held her breath. He lay with his head at the foot of the bed, curled into the fetal position. "I'll just lay down here by your feet like a dog."

Reese tucked her pillow under her neck and pressed herself close to the wall to give him room and, eventually, Michael stopped talking and exhaustion took over.

***

Reese woke to piercing pain in her right wrist. The stinging sensation was like her arm had fallen asleep. It was heavy and paralyzed. As she came to and the light from the aquarium brought her vision into focus, she saw a body hovering over her. Two strong hands held her forearm. Her wrist was pressed against Michael's face.

She pulled, but he gripped tighter, keeping her in place. His mouth was latched onto her, a sharp stabbing sensation deep in her arm.

Her pulse jumped to a sprint and the shock felt like a truck had fallen on her chest, knocking the wind out of her. There was a sensation of suction at her wrist and the sharpness of needles in her veins. Reese yanked, but his bite tugged at her flesh.

"Stop." She pushed on his head with her free hand. "Stop it!" She pounded him with her palm.

Michael's head popped up, mouth agape, two long, needle-like fangs sliding from her arm, dripping blood from the tips onto her arm and her bed.

Michael's pupils had dilated beyond the white, and a tenebrous sheen of black covered everything. Ribbons of blood drooled down his chin, and he pulled in a gasp that resonated like a hiss of a venomous snake.

She yanked her arm away, pressing her palm into the puncture holes in her wrist. A guttural reaction erupted from her core, stifled by shock at first, but it made its way up her throat and out in a scream. The kind of terror that couldn't be replicated even in the finest slasher film. An animalistic sound that echoed off the walls of her room.

She scrambled backward, up against the wall. Michael's black eyes slowly restricted, and the white reappeared. The long fangs withdrew behind his upper lip.

Upstairs, the sound of footsteps hurried down the hall.

Michael leapt to his feet and backed into the closet. Eyes panicked. "I'm sorry. I didn't mean to!"

Reese stayed pressed against her wall, trembling.

"Don't tell them!" His eyes were desperate and voice panicked.

Footsteps clamored down the basement stairs.

Michael leaned forward from within the closet. Voice gritty, eyes piercing, he said, "Don't say a fucking word or I'll kill her."

The bedroom door swung open. The light switch flicked on. Reese flung the blanket over, concealing the blood from view.

Michael turned his back to the light and sank deep into the closet, beyond Reese's clothes.

She squinted in the light, keeping her hands under the blanket. "Sorry! Bad dream." A wooziness flushed over her, and her vision tunneled like she was about to pass out.

Mom stood in the doorway and Quentin was over her shoulder with a baseball bat.

"You good, kiddo?" Quentin asked, peering into the room.

Teeth chattering, eyes burning with tears Reese wouldn't allow to form, she fought the temptation to tell. She steadied herself and let the nausea wash over, swallowing her sickness deep inside. She should run. Blast out of bed and get away from Michael—or whatever the hell he'd become. But he was so fast and strong; she'd seen it earlier, but didn't believe it until now. He'd catch her. And if she did escape, Mom would be at risk. She didn't know if Michael was bluffing about the death threat, but she couldn't risk it.

"Bad dream." She forced a laugh and smile.

"Man," Quentin said. "I was hoping to clobber someone with this thing." He twirled the bat by his side.

"Maybe next time, darling." Mom patted Quentin on the back and looked back to Reese. "If you didn't watch scary movies, this wouldn't happen."

Quentin grabbed the knob on the way out and poked his head back in. "You sure there aren't any monsters under the bed that I can beat with this thing?" He grinned.

Michael stepped forward in the closet, eyes meeting with hers.

"No. Everything's fine."

Quentin flipped the switch and closed the door, leaving Reese and the monster alone in the dark.

CHAPTER NINETEEN

REESE

She wanted to run down the hallway, shake her mother awake, and beg her to leave, but the possibility of Michael living up to his word kept Reese from action. She didn't want to believe he would actually kill her mother, or anyone, but the threat was enough to deter her from any impulsive decisions. Navigating the next several hours with caution was vital.

Michael had apologized profusely, claiming he didn't mean to. *It just happened.* After applying pressure, she fled to the bathroom to clean her wrist, examining where he'd bitten her. Two small puncture marks, like she'd been stuck with needles, were surrounded by dark blue bruising similar to the marks on Michael after the accident. Even though the bleeding had stopped, Reese bandaged her forearm with some stretch gauze to hide the bruising and followed Michael back to her bedroom.

"I didn't mean to," he repeated, and plopped into the beanbag chair on the floor.

Last year, during junior prom, he forced her down the hallway by her elbow. Reese faked a smile so as not to make a scene. He'd held so tight it left a bruise the next day, which he refused to admit he'd caused. He'd offered no apology then, and took no blame. *You were pulling too hard away and bruised yourself.* Eventually, she got an "I didn't mean to" for that incident as well.

Reese spent the rest of the predawn hours curled into a ball in her bed, haunted by the image of Michael's inhuman appearance. There had to be an explanation. Some scientific reason why Michael suddenly had retractable fangs. Something evolutionary, a mutation of some sort. Some reason for his eyes to dilate so much they turned completely black. And some reason for increased strength and speed. Something other than *vampires.*

Her arm ached as she imagined an infection spreading through her body. Whatever caused Michael's symptoms could be infectious. If so, it would only be a matter of time before Reese's eyes darkened like his, before her gums sprouted new teeth. She rubbed the tip of her tongue over her canine tooth, hoping whatever he did to her wouldn't turn her into the freak show he'd become. But Reese didn't believe in nonsense. Keeping her sensibility would be the only way out of this situation. Trauma in the eyeballs? Pressure in the brain from bleeding, causing the eyes to go dark? Adrenaline still coursing through his body? Broken bone fragments or something coming from his jaw?

Michael was disturbed and dangerous, that was clear, but he was just a guy who needed serious medical help. Nothing more.

The clock finally read 4:30 AM and Reese slipped out of bed.

"Where are you going?" he asked as she opened the door to her bedroom. He stood outside her closet.

She flipped the light switch and Michael hissed with a hand shielding his eyes.

"I'm going to the bathroom. Is that okay?" She struggled to stifle her anger and fear.

He shrugged. "Of course." Michael kept his hand up as a blinder and turned his back to the lamp. He looked to the tiny basement window. "What time does the sun come up?"

"Not for another hour or so." Reese tiptoed upstairs where Quentin stood at the kitchen sink in a track suit, drinking a glass of water.

"Hey, kiddo!"

She pulled her long sleeve down over her bandaged wrist.

"Do you run?" He jogged in place, throwing Rocky-style punches.

Reese shook her head, but didn't say a word.

"Nightmares keep you up all night? You're up early."

"I have to work." Reese left him behind, heading toward the hall bathroom.

She checked on Mom down the hall, who was still sleeping with one arm hanging over the side of her bed. Polished, French manicured nails touched the floor and last night's mascara smeared on her white pillowcase.

Sometimes she wished her mom was the kind of parent who helped her solve her problems. Her former best friend, Sara, had that kind of parental influence. Whenever something was wrong—bad grade, argument with friends, stuck at a sketchy party—they were always there for her. A crutch to lean on as she grew up. Tammy had always been of the mindset to let Reese figure things out for herself, and Reese valued that independence and empowerment, at least until recently.

This was a turning point in her life, and now she was legally an adult, it was time to act like one and continue to handle things herself. Mom didn't need the added stress.

It was simple. Reese needed Michael out of her life, and she needed someone to make sure he was okay. So what if she couldn't explain what happened last night? She didn't need to.

Quentin had left, jogging down the street for an early morning run in the dark, and Reese went to the phone in the kitchen. Instead of calling Michael's mother, Eleanor, who'd be inconsolable and irrational according to Michael, she pulled out the business card for Dan Delgado, pastor of Grace Cross Church.

His sleepy voice answered.

"Hi. Sorry it's so early, but ..." Reese paused, wondering how to word the following. "This is Reese ... um ... Reese Perkins."

"Hi, Reese. Is everything okay?"

"Yeah. It's just ... well, no."

"Is it Michael?"

"Yes." She sighed, trying to get a grip on her words. "Michael is at my house right now because his mom kicked him out. He really needs to see a doctor but he won't listen to me."

"Do you think he'd meet me at the church? I can be there in fifteen, and then I'll talk him into going back to the hospital."

"Maybe." She felt her voice shaking and she tried to pull her emotions together.

"Reese," Dan said. "Do you think you're in danger?"

"No." Reese didn't understand why she was covering for him any longer. "It's just that he ... he bit me."

"He bit you?" Dan's voice raised an octave. "Hon, do you need me to call the police?"

In the following few seconds, she considered if that would be a good plan. She thought about the police at her home, questioning her. Michael playing it off as nothing, or worse, getting so angry he'd attack them. Things would get out of hand, and she didn't want to be anywhere around him when that happened. "I'm leaving for work soon, so I can drop him off at the church."

"Okay. I'll make sure he gets the help he needs, dear. I'm getting dressed and I'll be there in a jif."

"Just be careful. He's not himself."

***

Michael sat in the front seat of Reese's car, fidgeting with his hands in his lap. "Thank you for giving me a ride."

Reese nodded as she pulled out of the driveway. "I'm taking you to Grace Cross."

"What?" He whipped his head toward her, but she refused to look at him.

"Dan Delgado is going to talk to your mom." Reese rubbed her bandaged wrist. The sensation of Michael's teeth in her veins remained, sucking the life from her little by little.

Michael settled back into his seat.

She pulled into the parking lot under a purple-gray sky on Sunday morning. Dan stepped out of his vehicle, yawning with a steaming mug in one hand.

Michael exited the car and Reese stayed in the driver seat with one hand on the shifter, ready to back out.

Michael leaned into the car from the passenger side. "Aren't you coming?"

"I told you I have to work."

Dan stood behind him. "Good morning, Michael. How are you feeling?"

Michael's jaw clenched. "Great." He forged a smile only Reese could see. "See you tonight?"

Reese gripped the wheel so hard her knuckles went white. "I can't."

"Why not?"

She whispered to stay out of earshot of Dan who stood directly behind Michael. "We broke up."

"What are you talking about?"

Dan reached for Michael's shoulder, but Michael yanked away from his touch.

"Give us a sec!"

Dan held his palms up and backed away a few steps.

Reese lowered her voice. "I told you—"

"Told me what?"

"I told you at your house yesterday, after you attacked me."

"What attack?" He laughed, shaking his head.

Perhaps she'd confused Michael by giving him a place to stay last night. She looked at the clock. 5:47AM. She was already late for work.

"Please, just talk with Dan. You need to talk to someone."

"That's what I have you for."

Reese released a breath, shaking. *We broke up.*

"Come on, Michael. Let's rap." Dan clapped his hands together, diverting Michael from the car.

Michael backed away with a seething rage in his eyes. The kind of look that meant their relationship would not ever be over unless he said so.

CHAPTER TWENTY

MICHAEL

Michael sat in the back office of Grace Cross Church on a floral sofa that smelled like dust. He wore the same sweatpants and T-shirt he'd worn the day before, and a pair of Reese's flip-flops two sizes too small, leaving his heels hanging over the edge. He'd showered yesterday, and normally he'd be due for another by now. But his hair hadn't turned greasy. His T-shirt hadn't yet soaked up a sweaty stench. In fact, his pits hadn't even developed the onion like aroma he'd typically have after only a few hours without deodorant.

Dan Delgado wore a blue polo tucked into high-waist khaki pants with a black belt. He slipped out of his tweed coat and hung it on the back of the office chair behind his desk.

"I called your mother this morning. She's on her way in." He sat beside Michael on the couch, crossed his legs, and folded his hands over his knee. The stench of rust replaced the musty smell of the couch.

"You talked to my mom?"

"You gave her a real scare." He tilted his head. "And it sure seems like you scared Reese, too." A patch of stubbled skin at his jaw flexed and relaxed. "Wanna rap about what's going on?"

"I don't rap," Michael said.

"Well, do you talk?" Dan smiled. "What happened with your mother last night?"

"I …" Michael was about to explain, but a soft thrumming distracted him. The muscles in Dan's jaw flexed again and, with a tilt of his head, he'd exposed a large artery in his neck. The stench of iron plumed, not from the couch, but from Dan. The vessels bulged along Dan's neck, in the crook of his elbow, and beneath the delicate skin of his wrists. Michael felt his pulse quicken, as if syncing with Dan's.

Vision darkened around his periphery. It was the same issue with his eyes that had happened when his mother called him the Devil. The same shadowed vision that had taken over when he woke with Reese's arm in his mouth.

He covered his eyes and pinched his nostrils together. "Please, don't sit next to me."

Dan stood from the sofa and moved to the office chair behind the large desk in the center of the room. "Is this better?"

Once Dan was far away, Michael pulled his hands from his face, vision restored.

"Do I make you nervous, Michael?" Dan eased into the rolling chair.

"I don't know what will happen. I don't want to hurt you."

"Why do you think you'd hurt me? Is it because you bit Reese?"

"What? I don't know what she told you but—"

"She said you bit her, and that she's very worried about your health."

"I wish everyone would stop worrying about my health."

"Your mom is scared too."

"What did *she* tell you?"

"She told me a little." Dan leaned forward, resting his chin on folded hands. "She thinks she saw a demon, son, and that worries me."

"Jesus Christ."

Dan's eyebrows raised at his response, creating deep, judgmental lines in his forehead.

"Sorry," Michael said.

"Your mother works a lot. She's stressed. And she almost lost you." Dan puffed out his cheeks with a long exhale.

"But she didn't," Michael argued.

"It's a lot to deal with for a mother, don't you think? Stress can make us act differently. Fear can make us see things … I think she saw something in your eyes last night. Maybe something that wasn't really there."

"She *did* see something. But it wasn't a demon."

Dan adjusted himself in the chair. "Then what?"

"During the accident, something happened. It changed me."

"Life and death situations have a—"

"No. This was different. I was *dead*. I think God gave me a gift."

Dan looked like he was trying to understand.

"You saw my face after the accident. How do you explain this healing?"

Dan massaged the stubble along his jaw. "I don't know."

"A miracle, maybe?"

Dan sighed. "I won't deny that miracles are possible, but often there is another explanation."

"Come on, Pastor Dan!" Michael stood and approached the desk faster than he'd ever moved. He slammed both hands down on the surface, the air cracking with the sound.

Dan flinched backward, pushing his wheeled office chair away from the desk.

Michael leaned over the desk and took in the aroma of the blood pulsing beneath Dan's flesh. Instead of denying it, he let his eyes darken and his long teeth extend.

Though his sight was clouded, he could make out the shape of Dan backing away as a blurred silhouette, staggering chaotically along the bookshelf.

The sound of objects falling from the shelves cut through the darkness and helped Michael follow Dan through the office.

Dan whispered a prayer almost too quietly to hear as Michael closed in. The words were muffled behind his other senses. Michael gained control of his body and let the darkness fade.

Dan side-stepped away from Michael, arms haphazardly knocking knickknacks and loose papers from the shelves as he neared the door. A Bible thumped against the hardwood.

"Michael." His voice trembled. "Your eyes."

Michael drank in the fear emanating from his pastor. He didn't need his blood to feel powerful. To feel respected.

Dan stumbled, reaching for the door knob. "You mustn't embrace this. This is the work of something dark—"

Michael inched closer to Dan. "You have to tell my mom this is a gift."

Dan squeezed his eyes shut and a tear dribbled out between lashes. "We can get you help."

Tension gathered in his shoulders, rippling down his spine. "You can help by convincing them they don't have to be afraid of me."

Dan opened his eyes, assuming the pugnacious posture of a brave man, but he spoke through tremoring lips. "We can get you there, Michael. But right now, there is something inside of you and we need to get it out. I'll have to do some research, but whatever it is, you're in the house of God now, and we can help you. Properly help you, if I can just make some phone calls."

If Michael had hackles, he felt them raise to attention. He grinded his teeth together as the spindly fangs descended, digging into his lower lip, cutting. He focused on the sensation as Dan continued.

"Maybe, Michael … son …" Dan's heart raced into a sprint as he placed a hand on Michael's shoulder, the other hand remaining firmly on the door knob.

The smell of blood and sweat and fear was intoxicating.

Dan's chin quivered. "Maybe you are so desperate to embrace this darkness because sometimes it feels like there's no hope for you."

No hope for you. A sentiment he'd heard before from his teachers, from his dad. From the asshole foreman, Harry, at work. Nobody had ever seen potential in Michael Braxton. Collectively, all of the faces of the naysayers took the place of Dan Delgado. He stood there with his ever-deepening judgmental lines in his forehead, labeling Michael evil, bad, no good.

Tears burned at the corners of his eyes and the room went black. His body took control, leaving all the sensible parts of his conscience in the dark. All senses blurred and he didn't know which direction was up; he lost the feeling of the floor under his feet. The only sensation was his mouth latched onto Dan's throat. Hollow teeth drew in blood like two syringes, piping hot blood into his body. The warm fluid passed by his sinuses, rushed into his veins, and traveled to his heart, his brain, his toes. He felt every drop as it coursed through his body.

Dan squirmed beneath him, but Michael held him down without effort. The night before, when he'd woken from his trance, feeding on Reese's tiny vessels, it was nothing like this. The jugular was a hose nozzle set to jet. Every fingertip and nerve ending sparked alive with the touch of blood within. The soles of his feet tickled, and an erection grew under his sweats as every inch of him filled with blood. He may have lost control and jumped Dan, but he could pull away any moment if he really wanted to. The problem was he had no desire to stop.

Chapter Twenty-One

Michael

His mother was expected to arrive soon, and shortly after, the entire congregation would be pouring in for Sunday services. Dan lay drained and limp on the couch in the back office and Michael feared he'd killed him, but a gut instinct told him that, despite the blue color of his lips, Dan was not really dead.

"What do I do, what do I do, what do I do?" He rubbed his hands together and started by wiping the blood from his chin. A new sense of power pumped through his body, like he'd injected himself with a massive load of steroids. Electric currents burst like fireworks at his nerve endings, and he was bulging at the seams with the strength to do anything and everything.

Michael used a finger to look at the color of Dan's gums, sticky and tinged blue. He pried open his lip further to reveal a peculiar swelling over the canine teeth, similar to his own.

"What do I do?" He grabbed the collar of Dan's polo and shook him.

After Trevor had drained Michael, he received blood from the hospital. Without that little bit of blood, he wouldn't have come back at all. And without taking more from Reese then from Dan, Michael would never have survived. Dan needed blood before it was too late.

But who?

Knocking from out front drew his attention away from Dan's lifeless body.

Michael poked his head out of the office. Across the main gathering hall, morning light poured through the glass doors. Mom pressed her face to the glass with her palms shielding the outside light.

***

Michael had never seen his mother cry so hard. Not when his father beat the shit out of her, not even the night Michael had been knocked backward out the front door and left in the elements as a meal for the mosquitoes. She knelt before Dan on the couch, sobbing, clutching his arms, breath hitching and gasping for air like she'd lost her own son. He wondered if she cried that hard when she thought he was dying in a hospital bed.

"Mom?"

"You stay away from me!" Snot drooled from her left nostril and over her lip. She wiped it away with her sleeve.

A long, breathy whine escaped Dan's lips. It was the first sign of life since Michael had drained his body. Mom dove in closer to inspect the pastor. She eased her ear to his mouth, and Michael imagined Dan waking from his comatose state, fangs drawing down on his mother's neck.

"Mom, don't do that." Michael grabbed her arm.

She thrashed in his grip. Even though he could throw her against the opposite wall if he needed to, Michael put his boiling frustration on the back burner and opted to let her go. "He might be dangerous."

Her wild eyes seemed to search for an answer. They moved to the desk, where she probably considered using the phone to call for help. Then to the door. She sprung to her feet and took a single step toward it, but Michael was too fast for her. He blocked her exit. "Mom, if you want him to live, you need to listen to me."

"No—"

"I know how to save him."

She mumbled a prayer, eyes closed, squeezing out tears. Spit dribbled from between her chattering teeth.

"God damn it, Mom!"

Her arm raised to backhand him, but an inch before impact, Michael grabbed her wrist and squeezed, sending Eleanor to her knees. Tears streamed, and her makeup smeared. The power to control these moments was a huge responsibility for Michael and he needed to be careful not to let his anger get the better of him. He let go of his mother and stepped back.

"We have to get him out of here before people start showing up," he said.

On her knees, face smeared with makeup, Mom may as well have spat the words. "I'm not going anywhere with you."

"You want him to die?"

"*You* did this."

"Maybe. And I have to live with that. But it'll be *your* fault if he doesn't make it. Because *you* refused to listen to me. I can help him."

His mother shook her head, tears falling in a deluge.

"What kind of person doesn't help a man of God in his most desperate time of need?"

"Don't put this on me." She bared her teeth like a cornered dog.

Michael considered his years of Bible school and Sunday sermons. "We must help the weak. In this way, we remember the Lord."

"Ephesians 4:27: 'Neither give place to the devil!'" Mom squinted with a kind of hatred Michael had never seen. A spitefulness so caustic, it burned his heart and turned his emotions into ash.

He couldn't win a battle of the scripture with his mother, but he knew her well enough to know she wouldn't let anything bad happen to Dan.

He softened his stance, then knelt to the floor beside her. With a gentle tone, he pleaded with her. "I don't want to be like this, but I can't help it now. I didn't *choose* this. And I didn't mean to hurt him. You have to believe that."

She sniffled, eyes finally finding their way to his.

"But we can save him. *You* can save him. You can save both of us." He pulled her keys from her purse and put them in her shaking hands. "Mom, will you help us? Help *save* us?"

She whispered through clenched teeth, "Let him know that he who turn a sinner from the error of his way will save a soul from death."

"That's right, Mom." Michael's heart paused in anticipation of regaining his mother's love. "Save us from the error of our ways. There are going to be a lot of people here soon. A lot of people in the house of God. Get us out of here before they arrive. You can save them all."

***

A note stating the church would be closed due to a family emergency was taped to the front doors. Michael donned a pair of sunglasses and wrapped Dan from head to toe in a large blanket pulled from the donation box.

Upon stepping outside with Dan draped over his arms, the sun roasted Michael's skin. The sound of hissing, burning flesh was enough to drive him mad, but he fought through the scorching pain and tossed Dan into the car, climbing in on top to shelter him from the sun.

Michael covered himself with a second blanket to keep the sunlight off his neck.

Mom stared from the front seat, eyes crazed, still pouring tears, likely unable to look at her son with loving eyes ever again.

It was only a few minutes from the church downtown to their trailer on Halsey Road, but the drive, while shrouded beneath a blanket, felt like an eternity. Mom's whimpers and stuttering sobs were pins under Michael's skin. Worse than the itchy blisters from the sun, which were already healing on his face. He didn't mean to drain so much out of Dan. He didn't mean to do a lot of things. All he could do now was try to make things right with Dan, with his mom, and with Reese.

Gravel crunched under the tires and the car came to a stop. Buster barked at the end of his chain, dancing circles and pacing as his he saw his people were home. The towering trees shaded the path to the house, which would make the walk from the car to the house more bearable. Michael lifted Dan and ran toward the front door. It'd been a couple hours since he'd been drained now. A pale, bloodless arm dropped from the blanket by the time he got to the door. Michael didn't understand much about what needed to be done, but he knew without a doubt that Dan needed blood. He only needed a little to bring him back, but he wasn't about to offer his mother up as Sunday brunch. He needed someone to donate ... or *something*.

He called back to Mom, who hadn't stepped out of the car yet, "Mom! Bring Buster inside."

***

He lay Dan down on his mother's bed and closed all the curtains, darkening the room. If he was going to make this right, he needed Buster's blood immediately.

"Mom!" he called, wondering why she hadn't brought the damn dog inside yet.

Michael shielded his eyes, adjusting to the glaring light outside as he peeked through the gap in the curtain. His vision struggled to adjust. He strained to look toward the dog house, where Mom unhooked Buster's chain and held him by the collar. Buster's barking intensified and he began lunging as a man approached his mother. He was dressed in a black windbreaker, face covered with a scarf and polarized glasses. His threatening stance made his mom appear frail and helpless. Michael bolted toward the door, flung it open, and darted through the snow toward him, eyes blinded by the treacherous light. He blocked his vision, but the glare was too much to bear. The sun had slipped behind a cloud, but still managed to irritate his skin.

"Mom! Get away from him!" Michael shouted, swinging blindly at what he could see through his narrowed eyes.

"It's me, Trevor!"

Michael closed his eyes and pulled his hands into his sleeves to protect them from the light.

"Let's get inside," Trevor said.

"Forget Buster, Mom! Just get inside."

"Who is this?" she asked.

"Get inside!" His savage snarl made her jump.

She hooked the barking dog back to the chain and hurried away.

"We need to talk." Trevor headed toward the trailer.

Michael raced to cut him off. "You're not going anywhere near my mom."

Trevor sighed. "Fine. Get in the car out of the light." He opened the door to the Chevette and slid into the driver seat. Michael joined him, easing into the passenger side.

"You get used to it after a while." Trevor adjusted his glasses. "Still hurts like a bitch, but the pain becomes part of you."

Michael rubbed his eyes. "What do you want?"

"What do *I* want? I want to know where the hell you've been? I came back last night looking for you but you weren't here. I've been waiting all night for you to show up."

Michael cringed. "Stalker."

"I brought you blood." He pulled two IV bags from his coat and set them in Michael's lap. "Or should I assume you've already fed?" Trevor gestured toward the house.

The scent from the bag was enticing. The tips of his teeth scraped under his lip, begging to come out. Michael controlled his desire.

"Was that a dead body you carried inside?"

"What are you talking about?"

"Don't play stupid. My guess is you accidentally killed your little girlfriend."

"See, you don't know shit."

Trevor cocked his head. "So, who is it then?"

"Mind your own business."

"You are my business now! Which is why I need to know who that is and if I need to call for someone to clean up your mess."

"Fuck you, dude."

Trevor grabbed Michael's throat and slammed him backward against the passenger window. Spiderweb cracks fanned from the impact.

Michael pushed back, matching his strength, then launched across the seat and squeezed Trevor's neck. Soft tissue gave beneath his strong fingers. If he squeezed hard enough, could he rip his throat out? If he wanted to, he could kill Trevor right now. He had the strength to kill *anyone* he wanted, if necessary. The power invigorated him, but paralyzed him with fear of what he could become.

Trevor relaxed under his grip and grabbed hold of one of the blood bags, shaking it at him. Michael released him.

Trevor adjusted his collar on his coat. "All I'm saying is that if there's a dead body, the police will come looking. We have people that will come here first and take care of it for us. Get the police off your scent."

Michael reached for the blood bags and held one to his nose. "There's no body."

Trevor squinted, clearly not convinced.

"I'll use this blood." Michael opened the passenger door. "Thanks." He got out of the vehicle, letting the indirect daylight sting his flesh.

Trevor met him around the front of the car and stopped him from heading toward the house. Michael's vision was shot from the light, but he held strong. "What do you want? I'm taking the stupid blood!"

"About your mom and your girlfriend-"

"Leave them out of this!" Michael lunged at Trevor, grabbed his jacket and felt so much fury he thought he could rip the man apart. He tossed him out of the way, his body flying like a doll through the air. Trevor smacked against the windshield, and a thousand cracks webbed across the glass.

Trevor rolled off the hood of the Chevette and prepared to defend himself. But Michael was too stunned by his show of impossible strength. Something had changed inside of him since feeding from Dan. Something that maybe he didn't have a handle on yet.

"Perhaps you don't need those blood bags after all," Trevor said. "But you do need help. You shouldn't try to navigate this situation alone."

Michael laughed at Trevor's ignorance. People who had never struggled in life always said that: *You can't handle it alone*. But Michael had been alone for a long time. He could handle anything. Now, with his new abilities, he'd handle everything.

Trevor looked to the trailer with knowing eyes. "Be careful, Michael, or your mom and that girlfriend of yours—if she's even alive—are going to get hurt."

Michael lunged, but Trevor was ready and grabbed hold of his shirt, ripping it from Michael's body. His pale skin felt like fire in the light. Michael crouched and tucked himself against the vehicle in its shadow. "You stay away from them!"

"I'm not the one you have to worry about."

Chapter Twenty-Two

Reese

"Nice of you to show up." Theresa stood a foot shorter than Reese but commanded respect as the morning shift manager at Fat Joe's.

"Sorry." Reese punched her card into the time clock and snagged an apron from the rack.

Theresa put a hand on her hip. "You've been working here for a year and a half and never once called in sick or came in late. I think we can let it slide this time."

Reese pulled the strings of her apron around her back and tied them. She didn't know what else to say.

Theresa grimaced. "You okay?"

"Yeah, I just slept in." Reese pulled her hair into a ponytail.

"What happened to your arm?" She nodded to the bandage.

There hadn't been enough time to think of an excuse, but it rolled off her tongue with ease. "Grease burn."

"From here? You gotta report that. I don't need OSHA on my ass."

"No. From home. It's fine."

Reese took her position at the drive-thru window, but couldn't focus all morning. Multiple times, she had to ask customers to repeat their orders because she kept drifting into a nightmare, envisioning Michael's spit traveling through her veins. A malignancy, spreading death and disease through her body.

"Reese?" Theresa's voice became clear.

She snapped back to her reality at Fat Joe's, realizing that Theresa had repeated her name at least three times. A customer sat outside the drive-thru window, waiting.

"I'm sorry." She reached to open the window, but Theresa blocked her.

"Go home."

"But—"

"You're not in trouble," Theresa said, lifting the headset from Reese's head. "But you're not here today. You're off in La La Land or something."

"I'm sorry—"

"Oh my God. Stop being sorry! It's okay. Everyone has a bad day. Just go home and come back tomorrow ready to work."

"I'm off tomorrow, then I leave for Florida on Tuesday." Saying the words aloud brought her some relief. There was comfort in the definitiveness of her already-paid-for ticket out of her fucked-up situation.

"That's right." Theresa's face changed. She took money from the next customer at the window and closed the register. "I almost forgot. No wonder you can't focus." Theresa laughed and handed a bag of food to the people waiting outside. "You're dreaming about palm trees and beaches!"

"There's a lot going on," Reese said. Maybe if she hinted at the real problem, Theresa would pry for information, and in turn, if someone prodded for information, she'd actually speak up and say something.

"Daydreaming about sunshine and palm trees is a lot for a teenager to handle." Theresa laughed.

Reese forced a smile.

"Have a great trip, Reese." Theresa gave an exaggerated goodbye wave. "And next week, when you get back, be *here* to work. Not in La La Land, got it?"

Reese agreed.

"You are coming back, right?"

"Of course."

***

When Reese arrived home, Mom sat at the kitchen table with her floral pink luggage bags beside her.

"You're home early," Mom said.

"We had too many people on the schedule."

"Lucky you!"

Reese couldn't figure out why she wouldn't open her mouth and say what was going on, but the longer she held it back, the more she felt the need to hold onto it. What Michael had done was beyond the realm of reality, beyond her ability to explain rationally. The more hours that passed, the more she questioned whether his eyes had really turned black or if it was a trick of the lighting in her room. And what of those punctures in her arm? Reasonable thinking told her it had to be something else.

"What happened to your arm?" Mom asked.

"I burned myself." The lies kept popping out uncontrollably, for no reason other than Reese's inability to explain what was going on without sounding insane. *Say something!*

"If you got burned at work—"

"No, I didn't." She couldn't say it was a grease burn like she'd told Theresa. "I was checking my oil. The engine was still hot."

"Ouch! I've done that." Mom shrugged. "But you're tough." Mom nudged her. "Just like me."

Mom was tougher than any woman she'd ever known. She'd been through so much. She'd dealt with a deadbeat dad. She'd lived through poverty, taking care of her kid all by herself in the 80s and into the 90s on a waitress's salary until she became a manager.

Mom would've flipped if she found out that Michael had become a controlling asshole. Then Reese's reason for keeping her secret came crashing in like the Kool-Aid man in the commercials. Mom was a fighter, a survivor, and for Reese to cry when things got tough just meant one more thing to add to Mom's plate.

Reese eyed the luggage. "Are you coming to Florida with me?"

"God, no." Mom bit her lip. "I'm happy you get to meet your father, but I don't need to see him again. That's some old baggage that can stay in Florida."

She eyed the bags again, waiting for an explanation.

"Quentin is taking me to the Poconos for a week!"

"When?"

"We leave today. Brenda is covering invoices and the schedule at work and the team is splitting my hours. We wanted to get on the road sooner, but I decided to wait until you got home from work."

Before Reese could protest, Mom butted in. "I know it's sudden. I know you need to be at the airport Tuesday morning. That's not a problem. You can leave your car in the long-term parking lot. There's cash in an envelope—the one with the plane tickets—to pay for parking and whatever else you might need." She rapid-fired faster than Reese could absorb. "It's only two nights alone at the house, Sunday and Monday, then you're in Florida for a week with your father. And Quentin and I will be back before you, so we can welcome you home at the airport!"

Reese got hung up somewhere back when Mom said she'd be home alone for two nights. She'd spent nights alone before, but now there was the threat of Michael coming back.

Her mom's eyes were bright and hopeful. They were *happy* for once.

"The Poconos! We're getting one of those champagne flute Jacuzzis. Horseback riding …" Mom finally paused. "I don't *have* to go. We can reschedule it for sometime after graduation, but Quentin found a great deal, so he grabbed it."

"No," Reese said. "I'll be fine." She put on a reassuring face and buried all the self-doubt and fear.

Mom rambled off specific instructions on how to get to the airport and left the phone number to the hotel by the kitchen phone. "Don't forget your tickets when you leave Wednesday morning!" Mom picked them up. "As a matter of fact, I'm going to put them in your car right now. They'll be in the glove box, then you can't forget them."

Mom was a whirlwind of excitement and Reese watched silently as she panic-packed and prepped the house for Reese to be alone. With each passing second, Reese's chance to say something, to speak up, to cry for help … it all disintegrated. She tried to convince herself she could handle the situation.

No matter what Reese thought she'd seen last night, it didn't matter, because it most definitely could not be anything supernatural. She could deal with the break-up without ruining her mom's chance to go on a vacation for the first time in years. She hadn't even told her mom yet that she'd broken up with Michael. Mom would ask why, and Reese didn't have a reason that wouldn't disappoint her. The entire conversation and potential tangents played in her head and she didn't want to talk about any of it. What would she say, anyway?

My ex-boyfriend, who you love like a son, has been an abusive control freak and now he might be a vampire?

Her arm itched, and she imagined an infection spreading through her veins, transforming her into some strange mutation of herself. She'd learned about genetic mutations, jumps in evolution, but whatever happened to Michael didn't make sense. That wasn't how evolution worked. She considered infections, cancers, anything that could rationalize his sickness. Her thoughts turned to a tangled mess in her head; his delusions seemed to be rubbing off on her.

She steadied her racing mind and almost laughed out loud at how she let her thoughts spiral. Michael was simply sick, mentally and physically. But he was in good hands now. Dan Delgado would get him the help he needed.

Mom would go to the Poconos. Michael would go to the hospital. And Reese would be hopping on a plane Tuesday morning. Two nights. Michael was out of her hair and Reese would be fine.

Everything's going to be fine.

CHAPTER TWENTY-THREE

MICHAEL

Michael put on a sweatshirt and stood in the doorway to Mom's bedroom as she placed the back of her hand on Dan's forehead.

"He's freezing." Her voice was soft and steady. "He barely has a pulse."

Mom wouldn't look away from the pastor, as if meeting eyes with her own son would be sacrilegious. God forbid Mom ever face reality and look life in the eyes, accept it, fight it. No. She'd always been the one to cower, turning to God instead of helping herself. Michael's heart splintered as she gazed lovingly upon Dan Delgado. He knew they'd been getting closer, but now it was clear their relationship had gone farther than he'd realized.

He swallowed his spite and held out the IV bag of blood. "This will help him."

Mom refused to look. Instead, she reached across Dan to grab the corner of the comforter and dragged it across his chest, tucking him in. "He needs a doctor." She turned away from Dan to face Michael, but still did not look him in the eyes.

"So did I, Mom!" Michael said. "I needed more blood at the hospital and you let me go."

"Don't you put this on me."

Dan's eyes opened while her back was turned. He lifted his head from the pillow and faced Michael's mom. A black film coated his eyes.

What if Michael didn't intervene? What if he let Dan bite into her? What if he let his mother squirm under his grip? Maybe if Mom became like him, she could see life from his newfound point of view. Teach her a lesson. She'd have no right to judge him. Dan's debilitated state kept him from moving quickly, but he eased closer.

"Mom!" Michael sped to her side and shoved Dan's chest, forcing him down while his feeble arms reached for her.

Mom covered her mouth, containing a squeal, body gyrating as Michael led her to the door.

"Wait out there, Mom."

She backed through the bedroom door, tears filling her eyes. Mouth wide open but unable to scream.

"And don't go outside!" Michael closed the door.

Alone with Dan, Michael tossed the bag of blood into Dan's lap. There were no needles to give an IV, not that Michael would know how.

Dan's body wavered as if every muscle had turned to jelly, sickly and incompetent, but the proximity of blood woke him. The darkness in his eyes focused as his hands brought the bag close to his face. White teeth extended, piercing into the bag. Dan drew from the IV bag, laying back on the bed, groaning.

There was something exciting about it. The sensual sound of Dan's voice, the pleasure of drawing in life, someone else's life force becoming his own. Michael reminisced the moment his mouth was on Reese's wrist, when his hollow teeth siphoned blood, and when Dan's jugular exploded through his veins. Curious about the bagged blood, Michael held the second bag to his nose and smelled the faint metallic aroma through the plastic.

These were the instincts Trevor had talked about. Heightened senses which could seek out blood, when necessary. Michael had fed fully this morning, and didn't have the need, but his vision darkened with his curiosity.

He pierced the bag and drew in the room temperature blood, which felt much cooler in his veins than the fresh sustenance he'd taken in earlier. The rush of the stranger's donated blood coursed through him. He'd had enough, but enjoyed the thrill of it. Michael settled down to the floor, squirming with intoxication. He wanted more of Reese. He wanted to place his lips on her neck and have the sweet nectar of her being coursing through him again. He wanted her to be part of him, and himself part of her.

He sat up, willfully allowing his teeth to recede. His vision returned to see he'd drained the entire bag, and Dan was no longer in the bedroom.

CHAPTER TWENTY-FOUR

TREVOR

There was a body inside that house, and the fallout would be immense if Trevor didn't call the cleaners. He palmed the folded cell phone in his pocket, but before her could make the call, he needed to get the innocents out of harm's way. The mother and the girlfriend were as good as dead.

It was Jensen's reckless phone call for a cleaner that killed Rebecca. Trevor had held Devon's limp body in his arms while he panic-dialed on the rotary phone for help. Rebecca stood screaming and shaking on the stairwell, while he tried to calm her down. Blood poured from his eyes, and he knelt, blocking her only escape from the house with her baby's corpse in his arms.

Jensen and two others had arrived within minutes, forcibly yanking Devon's destroyed body from his arms. The memory was mottled. He couldn't recall walking down the stairs, or how he got there. He couldn't recall the blood being cleaned from the floor, the walls, the phone. But he recalled the snap of bones at the top of the steps, a cleaner standing before Rebecca as her body went limp, and every thump on the carpeted stairway as her body tumbled down.

Michael could easily do the same, and it was obvious he was going to be a problem, but Trevor understood the importance of allowing time and guidance. Perhaps if Trevor had been allowed the same courtesy, things wouldn't have gone the way they did. Michael had to get used to the new feelings in his body. And come to the understanding that his life could never be like it was before. But he would at least get to *live*.

Trevor climbed through Michael's bedroom window as he'd done the night before and crept down the hall as Michael screamed at his mother not to go outside.

He peeked around the corner to see her backing away from the master bedroom doorway into the living area. She clenched her hands over her belly, folding over with convulsive sobs.

Trevor approached from behind and slipped a hand over her mouth to keep her from screaming. Her eyes bulged and she buckled at the knees. Trevor held a finger over his lips to signal that she should remain silent. Fortunately for both of them, she obeyed.

Trevor whispered, "Did he hurt someone?"

He slowly pulled his hand away from her mouth and she backed toward the wall, nodding.

"Is it the girlfriend?"

"It's"—the mother sucked in a gasping breath—"our pastor."

"Is he dead?"

The mother didn't answer. She only cowered, eyes as wide as the moon as tears created new tracks through old makeup smears.

Trevor took a step away from her and looked to the closed door behind which he knew Michael must be feeding. He continued to whisper. "You have to leave. And anyone that he's close to. That girlfriend of his. Where is she?"

She refused to say.

"Does she live here in town? Do you have a phone number?"

The woman's teeth chattered and she sank to the floor.

Trevor moved to the phone in the kitchen and dug through the papers by the phone to find the woman's address book. Every woman he'd ever known kept a book of phone numbers and addresses. He found the little black faux-leather book and tucked it into his inside jacket pocket with his wooden stake.

It wouldn't be long before Michael would be done in the bedroom. Trevor grabbed the woman and muzzled her mouth again. "Get out of here. Don't come back."

Her eyes seemed to search for a reason why he would be helping, but once she realized he was letting her go, she ran, fished her keys from a plate of junk by the front door, and tucked a coat and purse under her arm. She turned the doorknob slowly and quietly, closing it without making more than a click.

The dog barked again outside.

Trevor guided the woman to the car with the cracked windshield. "Just go. Go somewhere he won't find you. Somewhere he won't think of."

"Under P." She finally spoke. "Reese Perkins in the book. Her number's in there. Don't let anything happen to her."

He thumbed through the pages and found not only Reese Perkins' name and phone number, but also her address. "I'll make sure she gets out of here."

Trevor ran to the end of the driveway and, once he saw Eleanor had begun backing out of the driveway, he took off running toward the town of Byron to find Michael's girlfriend and get her to safety before it was too late.

CHAPTER TWENTY-FIVE

MICHAEL

Michael's senses were alert like they'd never been before. Room temperature blood dripped onto his lip. The shriveled blood bag lay drained on the floor beside him. The sound of tires crunched on the gravel driveway.

Michael sped to the window and threw open the curtains. Daylight blasted against his face and he safeguarded his eyes with a raised arm. The overcast skies had cleaved, creating great fissures of blue. Sunlight poured through their cracks. Though he couldn't see clearly, he could tell the Chevette was gone. Someone was leaving. Michael tore open the bedroom door so fast the flimsy thing ripped from its hinges.

Dan stood between the kitchen and living room, his blue polo dappled with bloodstains as he stared toward the open front door. Michael followed his gaze as the Chevette backed out of the driveway, beyond the tree line at the front of the property and out of his sight.

Michael darted out the door with a speed he didn't know was possible. An Olympian's stride, perhaps even faster. The thrill of it nearly overwhelmed the panic of knowing his mother could be in danger. Sunlight split the clouds and struck the back of his neck and hands. The fiery pain slowed him, but he pushed through until he reached the car and put his hands on the hood before Mom could transition from reverse to drive.

Trevor was nowhere in sight. Mom was alone, eyes as wide as the hole in Michael's heart. She screamed, bringing her manicured hands up to her mouth. He never wanted to scare her like this, and his heart broke knowing he was causing her pain. He remained with his palms on the hood of her car, allowing the sun to beat against the back of his neck, to singe the hair on his hands.

Mom flung open the door and ran to his side, using her hands to block the light from his neck. The tips of his ears felt like fire.

"Honey," Mom said. "Get in the car."

Hunched, he walked to the driver side of the Chevette and slipped in. Mom joined him in the passenger seat.

"Your skin was smoking," she said with her hands covering her mouth, eyes locked on his.

The intense burning sensation on his neck and ears calmed once in the car. His skin itched as the burns began the process of healing.

"My God," his mother said, creating a cross on her chest. "It's a miracle."

"Where'd Trevor go?"

She shrugged, shaking her head.

"Until I know that guy is gone for good, you should stay here where it's safe."

Mom's hands were shaking, and her eyes glassed over with a teary sheen. "What about Dan? What's going to happen to him?"

"He'll be okay. I promise."

Michael ran his fingers over his ear tips, then slid them along the back of his neck where he felt flakes of charred skin break away to healthy skin beneath.

"It healed," Mom gasped. She leaned closer, and he wanted to nuzzle against her warm skin, let her hold him like she used to when he was little. Back when a hug solved all problems. He wanted to feel her heartbeat against his ear, drink from her body, taking from the source that gave him life in the first place. Replenish the blood supply that once flooded his body. Michael leaned away from her and put the car in drive.

His mother wrung her hands together in the passenger seat while Michael pulled the Chevette into the driveway and parked it in front of the garage.

Mom stared out the cracked windshield.

He followed her gaze and looked at the garage through the webbed shards of glass. Each broken piece was a window giving a blurred and skewed view of his home. All the broken pieces stayed together from some invisible force he couldn't understand.

"No matter how bad things get, I won't let it all fall apart," he said.

Mom's voice was no more than a whisper. "It already fell apart."

"Then I'll fix it."

"How?" she raised a shaking hand to her face to wipe away a tear.

"I don't know. But I will. I won't let anything bad happen to you."

"And what about Dan?"

"That was an accident. I swear."

"I know, dear," Mom said through quivering lips.

"Why are you crying?" He feared her answer, but asked anyway.

"I'm scared."

"Of me?"

"I'm scared I'm losing you."

"You won't lose—"

"And losing Dan ... I think I love him, Michael." Tears spilled harder and his mom sniffled, pulling fast food napkins from the glove compartment to wipe her nose.

Her words, though he couldn't understand why, were a betrayal. She gave him time to respond but there was nothing to say.

She twisted in her seat to face him. "I never said I was sorry for what your father put us through. I thought if I could just sweep it all under the rug, maybe you'd forget. Maybe we could pretend it never happened."

Michael felt the remnant feeling of his father's fists on his skin. "It wasn't your fault."

"I'm your mother. I should've—"

"Punched him back?" Michael laughed. "It's not like you could've won in a fight against him. You did all you could."

"I could've left."

Michael shrugged. Repressed feelings scratched at his scars, trying to escape, and it made him want to puke. "I'm not going to be like him, if that's what you're worried about." He hoped she'd deny it, but instead she sat quietly, each second in silence a punch to the face. "I will never hurt you."

"I know."

***

Inside the trailer, with his mother safe by his side, he tried Reese's phone again. She'd been really upset with him that morning when she left him at the church, and he had to make things right. He called more times than he could keep track, both at home and at work, but she wasn't there. Hopefully, he hadn't screwed it up so bad she'd never speak with him again. He needed to see her face-to-face, and even though the sunlight-induced burns on the back of his neck and hands had healed completely, the memory of the pain haunted him, keeping him from stepping foot into the direct sunshine again. He'd wait for the sun to set and go to her, make her understand it was an accident. That he wasn't under full control of his actions because he hadn't had enough blood. But now that he'd fed, now he had enough to sustain him, he was certain he could be around her without hurting her. She needed to know it would never happen again.

Mom sat on the couch next to Dan, holding his hand while he read a passage from the Bible. His sermon-voice was as soothing as a lullaby, and Michael's eyes grew heavy.

CHAPTER TWENTY-SIX

REESE

After Mom and Quentin left for the Poconos, Reese stood before the picture window in the living room, watching the street, expecting Michael would show up at any moment. Even though she'd left Michael in the hands of his church, hoping they'd talk him into getting the help he needed, she wasn't certain anyone would get through to him.

Reese had thrown out the bandage and inspected the puncture marks on her arm. Aside from some bruising, it didn't look too bad. She kept trying to convince herself she didn't really see Michael's eyes turn black, or those long teeth pierce her skin, but the marks on her arm were undeniable proof.

There had to be a reasonable explanation, so Reese did what she always did when she needed information. She went to the local library.

Other than a mom with a toddler in the children's section, there was nobody else in the library this late on a Sunday afternoon. They didn't have much, but it always worked out well enough for school project research. A set of 1943 Encyclopedia Americana sat on the bottom shelf of the non-fiction aisle. If she wanted updated texts, she'd need to go to the well-funded library over in Weeds, where there'd surely be something from the 1990s, or at least a 1980s edition. But for now, she'd start here. She slid Volume 27 from the shelf and flipped to *Vampire*. The article was a single paragraph that took up only a quarter of the page. Reese found an isolated corner of the library and claimed her spot, leaving the book on the table. The card catalogue drawer for V led her to a book on vampires which was supposedly non-fiction. She wrote down the location and found it on the shelf. *Vampires, Burials, and Death,* and she grabbed a few other books on folklore as well.

She flipped to the encyclopedia reference first:

"Vampire, according to a superstition prevalent in many ages and countries, the ghost or spirit of a dead person ... sucks the blood of living persons ..."

"Vampires especially favor their friends and relatives with their visits …

…anyone whose death is caused by a vampire, becomes a vampire …"

Reese scratched at the bruising on her arm and continued reading about how it was believed vampires could be killed.

"… the body may be pierced with a stake cut from a green tree, the head cut off, and the heart burned …"

Reese closed her books and rubbed at her temples. What the hell was she thinking?

Fiction. Folklore. Superstition. Every book was the same. There were plenty of cases of people suspected of being vampires, but no real substantial information to help her. Nothing about real—or supposedly real—vampires.

If she was going to find answers, she'd have to think differently. Scientific studies. Perhaps a book on evolution or human mutations. Or maybe research on animals that fed on blood.

She grabbed another volume of the encyclopedia from the shelf. Volume 19, the letter *M*. But all she learned about the mosquito was on diseases and anatomy, including the word *proboscis*.

"We close in five minutes," the librarian called across the room. The mother and kid had left, and Reese was the only remaining person. More research would have to wait.

***

Perhaps Reese could have some peace of mind if she knew Michael wasn't going to bother her. That he went to the hospital and got the help he needed.

She returned home and stood in her living room with the lights off, staring out the window at the streetlights and woods between her and the main road. Her car, parked alone in the driveway, may as well have been a beacon announcing she was home alone.

Her fear that Michael would return dragged time to a slow, dreadful pace. Each tick of the clock was infinite, waiting for some inevitable disaster. Time, the torture device. *Tick … tick… tick …* waiting for insanity to settle in.

"This is stupid," she said to her reflection in the picture window. "Whatever you think you saw was impossible."

Reese slipped into her mom's rubber boots and coat, opened the front door and trudged into the foot-deep snow to the center of her front yard. The darkness tried to devour her, and she let it, knowing there would always be light above. She craned her neck back to view the stars. Scattered clouds had been moving over the area all day, and now they obscured patches of night sky, but the constellation of Orion shone through. She'd read about a nebula in the Orion constellation. It was a faint glow that could be seen from Earth, and she hadn't taken the time to look for it since she'd read the article. Using her hand to block the streetlight, Reese let her eyes adjust, and spotted the blurry speck of light in the sword region of the constellation.

She felt pride in finding the nebula, and she wondered why she'd wasted so much time on Michael over the past years when she could've been out here under the stars. She could've been viewing more nebulae and galaxies through a telescope. She could've already applied to colleges to study this stuff for real, and discover things that had never been found. In the morning, maybe the clouds would part and she could finally view the comet. The open expanse of stars above was her future, as long as Michael Braxton stayed in the past. So long as she could put whatever happened behind her. "It never happened."

The unmistakable sound of footsteps crunching through snow brought Reese's attention crashing back to earth. Her body tensed, seeking the source of the sound as a man emerged from shadow, wearing a dark jacket and a black and white scarf. Dark skin and a goatee came into light.

"Excuse me," he said. "Are you Reese?"

Chapter Twenty-Seven

Trevor

Trevor sped to Jean's Market in town and asked for directions to Hamilton Street, where Reese Perkins lived. After only a few minutes of running, he was on her street searching for her house number. A row of loosely-spaced single-story homes lined one side of the road. The opposite side was a dense barrier of pines running between Hamilton and Route 31.

He approached the girl from the street, keeping a safe distance so as not to frighten her, but that didn't help. She sprinted toward the house through the foot-deep snow and up the front steps. Trevor caught up behind her with ease before she could place a hand on the door handle. He grabbed her arm to stop her, realizing he shouldn't have chased after her. But instinct kicked in, like a cat that needed to chase whatever ran from it. Trevor regretted grabbing her, and he felt even worse when he had to muzzle her with a strong hand.

He looked over his shoulder to be sure none of the neighbors had seen or heard, but the houses were distant enough he didn't have to worry.

The terror in the girl's eyes was tougher than a stake to his heart. It mirrored the fear in Rebecca's eyes when she'd stepped into the room the night Devon had died. He pressed his finger to his lips to shush Reese, then let her go.

Reese sank, cowering on the porch steps.

"I'm Trevor." He took a step back to give her space.

She was frozen, eyes calculating as he descended to the bottom of the porch steps. Her pulse was fast, the smell of her blood enticing, but he was still sated from turning Michael.

She slowly rose, one hand easing to the door handle.

"I'm not going to hurt you."

Reese was frozen against the iron porch railing. Not a word. Not a movement. Just wide eyes focused on him. The hand on the door subtly adjusted, and her breaths were deep, but steady.

"I'm just here to warn you about Michael."

"He's not here." She turned the handle, opened the door, and put one foot inside. "We broke up."

"I'm worried you're in danger."

"He's getting help. I dropped him off with his pastor this morning."

"That man might be dead now."

The sound of her pulse sped as she drew in a gasp and held it. She hurried into the house and tried to slam the door shut, but Trevor rushed forward and stopped the door from closing.

Reese let out a squeal, and tried to slam the door repetitively on his arm, but Trevor flung the door open wide. He stayed at the threshold, trying to appear as non-threatening as possible.

"He's only going to kill again. And I'm worried he'll hurt someone close to him."

"I broke up with him," she whispered.

"I'm not sure Michael is aware of that." He reached into his inside coat pocket and removed the stake he had carved two days earlier. He tossed it toward her feet. "Do you know what that is?"

From the dark foyer, she glanced down, but didn't move. A deer in headlights—poor kid.

"It's a wooden stake. Do you know what it's for?"

The kid dove for it and held it toward him, hand shaking. Maybe not so much a deer after all.

"That's right," Trevor said, his hands up in surrender. "Do you know what we are?"

"Back off." Her threat came out as a whisper.

Her heart beat strong. Trevor's pulse synced with hers, fast, rhythmic. His vision began to fail, eclipsing to black. The threat sent his instincts into attack mode, but he shut them down. "Honestly, kid, you'd be doing me a favor if you could kill me. If you want to, go ahead."

She held steady, pointed end of the stake toward Trevor.

"Pack your bags and get the hell out of here. At least for a few days, until we can get Michael out of town." Trevor backed away from the door. "If he comes around, if he tries to hurt you, don't hesitate."

***

115

Trevor left the girl alone and sank into the shadows of the trees across the street, watching the house, waiting for the girl to get out. None of the lights flicked on, but he could see the shadowy movements of her body move from one room to another. He pulled the cell phone from his pocket and waited. Once he was certain this girl had left, he could call Jensen for help in extracting Michael from his home.

CHAPTER TWENTY-EIGHT

REESE

Reese was locked in defensive readiness with the front door wide open, allowing the cold January air to penetrate the house long after Trevor took off. His touch from where he'd grabbed her arm lingered on her skin. She could still sense the indentation of his cold hands. The vision of his eyes turning as black like Michael's. She clutched the stake in her hand, recalling the text from the library: *The body may be pierced with a stake.* Just when she thought she could chalk everything she'd experienced up to her wild imagination, further proof came through her front door.

She dialed the number on Dan Delgado's business card to check in, to see how Michael was doing. Maybe Dan would tell her Michael was at the hospital and everything was going to be all right. But the phone rang four times and went to his answering machine.

She hung up and considered dialing Michael's house to speak with his mom, but she couldn't bring herself to do it, knowing Michael may have answered.

For one of the first times in her life, she felt everything falling outside of her control and she needed help. She didn't know what she was going to say to her mom when she called, but she found the number by the phone and dialed the hotel in the Poconos. She asked to connect her to her mother's room, but it was too soon. Mom and Quentin hadn't arrived yet. Reese left a message with the receptionist and hovered a finger over the phone, looking at the emergency numbers written beside it.

She could report what Trevor had said about the pastor, that it was possible Michael had hurt him. But she had no proof other than the words of some deranged man who'd showed up on her doorstep with a wooden stake. The only information she had to give authorities would be deemed one hundred percent batshit crazy.

Evidence of some sort would be necessary for police to take action. She had marks on her wrist to prove Michael had bitten her the day before. But they were more like puncture marks than bites.

She closed the curtains and remained in the dark, sitting on the floor against the cabinets, clutching the stake. Her heart beat so hard she worried it'd give out.

She focused on calming her breaths until the drumming of her pulse quieted within ears. The pressure in her head eased while she inspected the stake. Its surface was bumpy with little nicks and grooves. It was about the length of a ruler, and it fit her palm perfectly, as if it was carved just for her. She wanted to burn the thing—the little piece of evidence that proved she was losing her mind—but there was a chance she might need it. Reese tucked the stake, pointed end up, into her tube sock, and let her wide-legged jeans conceal it.

She might not be fully convinced of everything she'd seen, but one thing was true: *Michael is dangerous.*

She'd known for a long time. She knew when he used to start fights in school. She knew the first time he grabbed her by the arm a little too hard. She knew it and kept hoping he'd get better. And now, it was only a matter of time before Michael, delirious, heartbroken, and possibly inhuman, came to see her, and there was no way in hell Reese planned to be home when he did.

***

She threw on her sneakers and, within minutes, she was at Sebastian's door, uninvited, asking if she could come in to work on the project because, "It could use a little polishing before the presentation tomorrow." The translation was already perfect; it was humorous, smart, and original. Both she and Sebastian knew this, but she needed an excuse to be there.

Her parents invited her to join them at the table for ravioli.

Mr. and Dr. Belinski exchanged obvious glances, the kind of expressions that exposed their knowledge of her state of distress, but they danced around the questions they so obviously wanted to ask.

"What do your parents do for a living?" Mr. Belinski asked.

Reese stabbed at a large piece of ravioli. "My mom is one of the managers at Ray's Diner."

"Oh, I like that place!" Dr. Belinski said, dabbing the corners of her mouth with a napkin.

"Yeah, great burgers," Mr. Belinski said.

Sebastian's parents were kind enough not to ask any prying questions for the rest of the evening. She'd expected Dr. Belinski to say something about Michael and Friday night at the hospital, but she didn't say a word about any of it throughout the entire dinner.

After dinner, she slipped away to use the restroom while Sebastian went to his room. When she came out, Dr. Belinski stood in the hallway.

She looked out the bathroom door and spoke quietly. "How's your friend, Reese?"

She shrugged, looking away. Where was she supposed to even begin? "I don't know."

Dr. Belinski gestured toward her arm. "Are you okay?"

"It's just a …" She stopped herself from saying it was a grease burn. Somehow, she figured Sebastian's mom would see right through her. "I think Michael had some head trauma or something. He's not acting right."

"How do you mean?"

"He bit me."

Dr. Belinski's expression didn't change. She simply waited for more information with the nonreactive expression of a doctor.

Sebastian's door opened down the hall and he peeked out. "Hey. I'm online and found a website about Hamlet's soliloquy."

Dr. Belinski held up a hand to her son. "In a minute. I'm going to check Reese's …"

"Grease burn," Reese said.

"Okay." Sebastian ducked back into his room and shut the door while Dr. Belinski stepped around Reese into the hall bathroom.

Reese unraveled the bandage and showed her the two pinprick marks on her forearm. Purple bruises faded to yellow at the edges.

Dr. Belinski grimaced. "This doesn't look like a bite."

"I know."

"Do you know what it looks like?"

"It's not from doing drugs. I swear." She looked at the bite marks. "Last night, Michael came to my house. He looked better, like he was healing, but he was acting weird. I fell asleep and when I woke up, he was biting me."

"Is it possible he was injecting you with something? Maybe you were still in half a dream?"

She thought back to the night before and supposed it was possible. What if Michael had injected her with something that caused her to see things?

Dr. Belinski took Reese's arm in her hands and inspected the site closely. "There's a lot of bruising, but the puncture holes look clean. No swelling, no redness, no signs of infection. So that's good."

She leaned closer and looked directly into Reese's eyes. "I can do a quick neurological exam to be sure you're okay."

Reese let Dr. Belinski grab her medical bag and she did an exam in the bathroom. She checked her eyes, heart, lungs, reflexes, and after only a few minutes, Dr. Belinski sighed. "Your heart rate is a little fast, but other than that, everything looks okay."

Reese opened the door to the bathroom. "Thank you."

Dr. Belinski stopped her. "Reese. I know there's something you're not telling me, and that's okay. I just want you to know that you're safe here. And if you need anything, just let us know."

She nodded, chewing on her lower lip, and the burning sensation of tears formed behind her eyes.

"All right," Dr. Belinksi said. "Go get your homework done, now."

***

She sat with Sebastian on his bed in his dimly lit bedroom.

"Sorry about my mother," he said. "She can be a lot."

"She's nice. Just wanted to make sure I was okay."

"Are you?"

"Yeah, I'm fine."

Sebastian pulled up a chair to his computer. "You didn't come for pizza last night."

"Something came up."

He clicked on the mouse and a screen with the headline *Hamlet's Soliloquy* appeared in old English font. "It's just weird that you were a no-show last night, and then you show up out of the blue like you're on the lam."

"I can go if you want."

He rolled his eyes. "That's not what I'm getting at."

"I told you. The project."

He sneered. "The project is fine as it is. Do you want to talk about whatever is going on?"

She shook her head and they sat in silence. But Sebastian didn't pry. He simply sat next to her, staring at the screen.

"Sooo," he said. "I guess we can do something else."

Reese looked toward the screen. "Do you wanna research genetic mutations?"

He fought a grin. "If you're wondering if I evolved an ability to glow in the dark yet, I haven't."

Her face twisted into a smile, working muscles she hadn't used in days. "Maybe someone else out there has."

Sebastian closed the window to the website and opened *Ask Jeeves*.

He read aloud while typing: *Are there any glow-in-the-dark people in the world?*

The search results were scarce. Glow in the dark toys, dolls, one website for a glow-in-the-dark blow-up doll.

"The internet is a wasteland of insanity," Sebastian said. "In a few years though, as more and more people and business start embracing the world wide web, there'll be loads of information on here. I'll be able to Ask Jeeves to show me bioluminescent people and there'll be someone, somewhere that has loaded that information."

"Ask Jeeves about modern day human genetic mutations."

Sebastian seemed intrigued and began to type.

"Like, say if a dog was fed only really tough meat and its teeth couldn't cut through it, could he grow new teeth?"

There was a knock and the door suddenly opened. Sebastian's dad leaned into the room. "Are you almost done online? I need the phone, kiddo."

"Aww." Sebastian mocked a childish whine. "But we were about to ask the net how to get superhuman powers."

"The greater good will have to wait. I have a phone call to make."

His dad shut the door and Sebastian disconnected from the internet.

"What do you think?" Reese said.

"About what?"

"Do you think an animal could grow the type of teeth it needed in a survival situation?"

"I don't think it works that way."

"I know. But hypothetically, a dog could adapt a trait to help it cut through the meat, right?"

"Theoretically." He shrugged. "I guess? But even if it did adopt the trait of being able to tear through this super-meat, the trait would evolve over time, over generations. He wouldn't just suddenly have pointier teeth."

She fiddled with the hem of her shirt while Sebastian sat beside her.

"Do you believe in supernatural stuff?"

He threw his head back, laughing. "You're really avoiding talking about whatever is going on with you."

She shrugged. "Supernatural things. You know, like, ghosts and werewolves …" She shot him a side-eye. "Vampires?"

"I don't know about all that, but I believe if there is supernatural stuff, it's really just science we can't explain yet."

"I could get behind that. Vampires, for example. Who's to say they don't really exist? Maybe they do, but it's not like the TV vampires. They're just a genetic mutation or something."

"Are you okay?" Sebastian's brow furrowed. "I mean, I'm cool talking science and supernatural 'til the sun comes up, but I think maybe there's something else you're avoiding?"

Sebastian was too smart and sympathetic to her situation for her to continue hiding things. There was so much to say, but she had to be careful which parts she divulged.

She'd start with the simplest part. "I broke up with my boyfriend last night."

Sebastian leaned back, his eyes widened, taking in the bomb she'd just dropped. "Last night?"

"We were together for a few years. He was a real jerk, you know? And so, after I broke it off, he came by the house and it was kind of scary and I was worried he'd come by again tonight, so I came here."

"Do you mean Michael Braxton? You two are still together?" He dragged his hair back from his forehead with both hands. "He's gonna kick my ass, isn't he?"

"I broke up with him."

"But not until *last night*. Friday, you were here with *me* but still his girlfriend?"

"I'm sorry—"

"Don't be sorry to *me*."

"Well, I'm sure as hell not going to be sorry to *him*." The words spewed from her with so much spite, she worried Sebastian would be angry.

But he looked more terrified than anything. "No, you're right. You shouldn't be sorry for any of it. I'm just a little shocked is all."

She released a sigh which held all the bad memories and bottled emotions, and fell backward onto Sebastian's bed with a frustrated grumble.

The room was silent for several seconds before Sebastian said, "Are you saying *I'm* the reason for you breaking up with him?"

"No." Reese smiled. "I mean, you helped. But I knew for a long time."

"Nope. That's all I needed to hear. Sebastian Belinski's ruggish good looks broke up a relationship." He smirked, lying on his side, elbow bent, head propped on one hand. "I didn't think you two were a thing anymore. I mean, you never talked about him."

"Maybe there's a reason for that."

"Well, damn. I don't know what to say."

"I'd say …" Reese stared toward the ceiling as if she could see through it to her future, and she broke out Hamlet, using her best English accent. "…*'who would fardles bear to grunt and sweat under a weary life?'*"

"Not you!" Sebastian held up a hand for a high five.

She smacked his palm. "Nope. Fardles can fuck off."

Sebastian laughed. She loved his genuine nature. His kindness. His fawn brown eyes and the way he looked at her like she was the answer to all equations, the bioluminescence in the dark places. Or maybe that's how she felt about *him*.

The Belinskis offered her the futon in the office upstairs so she wouldn't have to be home alone for the evening. Sebastian stopped in before bed to say goodnight. He didn't hesitate or count down from five like he did on Friday night. His hand slid tenderly behind her ear, and he kissed her. It was a kiss of confidence, of healing, a promise of better days to come.

He pulled away with sparks in his eyes, leaving Reese standing, more enamored than ever. Her arm hairs prickled to attention, sending a shiver down her back. She took a deep breath to ease the excitement, but it persisted. Reese leaned in for more. Sebastian shut the door to the office and she wasn't sure if she was leading him or the other way around, but they were moving across the floor toward the futon, kissing the entire way. Sebastian, walking backwards, bumped into the edge of the futon and sat, bringing Reese with him. She climbed on, straddling his lap and holding his face in her hands. His hands ran down her back and to her waist, then slid around her hips, outer thighs, and to her calves. The wooden stake pressed into her leg.

"What's that?" He pulled back, looking toward her leg.

Reese climbed off quickly, adjusting her pant leg. "What?"

"You got a baseball bat under there?" He laughed.

"Something like that." She gave a flirtatious grin, heart pounding from the excitement of kissing him and the nerves of him finding her concealed weapon.

A knock at the door pulled Sebastian to a stance. His mom peeked in. "Good night."

"Good night," Reese said, standing soldier-straight.

She eyed Sebastian with a steely glare.

"Ma." He rolled his eyes. "I'm going to my room in a minute."

"Okay." Dr. Belinski left the door open and exited the room.

Before Sebastian returned to his bedroom for the evening, she stopped him at the office door and gave him one more gentle kiss. "Thank you for letting me crash here for the night."

The lights went out and Reese lay on the futon, a bar pressing into her back. The room was void-black until her eyes adjusted, picking up faint, blue-gray shapes. Though she was safer here than in her house, she still feared Michael would come looking for her.

She dreamed of walking alone down a back road. It was so dark she couldn't see anything but the shapes of trees where their tops met the sky. Not a star to be seen. As if every light in the universe had blinked out, and there was nothing but this road in the middle of nowhere, in a vast empty expanse of a starless existence. On the road behind her stood a tall, shadowy figure. A ghostlike man, draped in black. She hurried her pace to get ahead, but each time she looked back, he was closer. Her legs couldn't move fast enough to run, and the harder she tried, the slower she moved. Legs turned to rubber, and she crawled across the paved road, down the double-solid yellow lines, but the shadow-man closed in. He was at her ankles, reaching.

Her kicks were weak, her screams no more than a whisper.

Reese jolted awake as headlights from the distant road dragged shadows of branches across the window. Reese sat up straight, heart in her throat, sweat clinging to her brow. Out the window, she expected to see Michael, hanging from the window sill. But he wouldn't be desperately clinging to the glass for warmth like the dying squirrel. He'd be waiting to drag her out into the cold, down the desolate road under a starless sky.

Chapter Twenty-Nine

Michael

Michael woke in his dimly lit living room. The range hood light in the kitchen was on, but the rest of the house was in darkness. Mom stood at the window with the curtain parted, hands tented over her mouth.

Without saying a word, he approached from behind, and Mom flung an arm up to block some imagined attack. He'd never shown her any reason to be afraid of him, yet she flinched in his presence.

Outside, Dan knelt beside Buster, who sat with his ears pinned back, panting.

Michael hurried outside, barefoot in the snow. The cold wasn't sharp and stabbing, but cool like a natural spring. He supposed his body wouldn't be so sensitive to a lot of things now that he was different.

"What are you doing?" he asked Dan.

"I had to step outside for some fresh air." He extended a hand toward Buster, who growled and backed up. "I'm not strong enough. I felt like I might hurt someone."

"But you didn't," Michael said. "You chose not to."

Dan tilted his head back and looked to the heavens. "Just know that I understand. I forgive you."

"I swear, I didn't mean to do it."

"I know, son." Dan placed a hand on his shoulder, then knelt eye-level with Buster. "After I came outside, Buster began barking, so I came over to pet him …" Dan's pupils grew, extending beyond the iris. Capillaries blackened and reached inward from the corners of his eyes.

Michael said, "You can't eat our dog."

Dan squinted against the flood light and turned his back. "The thought shamefully crossed my mind. The bag of blood you gave me earlier. Can you get more?"

"No. That was it."

Buster wouldn't be safe here so long as he and Dan were around. He needed a plan, not only for Buster's safety, but for his future. Now that he was satiated, it was time for Michael to start thinking about what he was going to do long term. Before, his only plan was to work and be with Reese. Now, with more power than ever before—more power than *anyone* before—his future would be different. No more shit jobs working the injection molding line. No more roofing jobs or landscaping. He could do anything he wanted if he played his cards right. But the first thing to do was to take care of Dan before the guy killed someone. How hard could it be to find blood from a willing donor? He could park in the Tessa Plastics lot and wait for Harry the Horrendous Foreman to eat lunch in his truck like he did every night. It seemed too risky being out in the open like that, though.

Michael needed to be smart. To find someone who might not be missed for a few days if they disappeared. Someone like a drug dealer or a prostitute, or someone who didn't care what they did with their body.

"I know someone you can get blood from," he said.

"Who?"

Michael unhooked the dog from his house and walked him across the snowy yard to the Chevette.

Mom opened the front door. "What are you doing?"

"I'm taking Buster somewhere safe," he said. "Lock the doors and don't answer if anyone knocks."

Mom slammed the door shut immediately.

"Come on, Dan."

Buster jumped into the back seat of the car. Dan sat in the passenger seat while Michael drove the back roads toward Reese's house.

"I hope you know how to flirt." Michael laughed.

Dan turned to face him, but didn't say anything. It was a silent acknowledgement that he knew what needed to be done.

When he pulled into the vacant driveway, dark windows greeted him. Buster panted and paced the backseat while Dan clenched his fist into tight balls.

"She's not here, is she?" Dan asked.

"They should be home." Michael went to the door and knocked, but there was no answer. He stomped through the snow and lowered himself to the basement window, cupping his hands around his eyes to look inside. The aquarium light was on, casting a blue glow on Reese's furniture, but she wasn't in there.

By the time he climbed to his feet, Dan was out of the car and approaching.

"I'm not gonna last much longer," Dan said. "I feel sick."

"Come on." Michael headed to the garage door, but it was locked. They only locked it before going to bed, and it was far too early for that. He headed to the front entrance—the one they rarely used—and spotted fresh disturbance in the snow. He climbed the steps and rang the bell, hoping Tammy would come to the door, but the house was silent.

"I've never felt this terrible," Dan said, hunched over like he was about to hurl.

"Where the hell is she?" Michael pounded on the front door, rattling the adjacent windows.

"She was pretty shaken up," Dan said. "Maybe you should give her some space."

The pastor's advice was a cheap jab. Michael faced him. "Why don't you stay out of it?"

Buster barked from the vehicle. On the road, a couple in winter coats and scarves strolled casually with a golden retriever on the end of a leash. The man lifted a hand to wave and Dan returned the gesture. He stared at the couple as they continued past the house. Michael could sense it too—hot blood pumping strong through their bodies. Dan's body became statuesque, eyes squinting against the darkness growing within him.

It wasn't as strong in Michael because he'd had enough, but Dan was still recovering. His desire must've been intense. Part of Michael wanted to watch it happen. He wanted to see his pastor sprint across the front yard and leap onto the couple, attacking like an animal.

"Get me out of here," Dan whispered. "Please."

"Fine." Michael headed to the vehicle with Dan following close behind.

"There has to be another way," Dan said. "I can't be responsible for hurting anyone."

He opened the back door. "Get in."

"Back there? Why?" Dan leaned down and looked at Buster as he backed against the opposite door.

"I think you know why."

Michael backed out of the driveway. He would've liked to have driven around searching for Reese. He wanted to know if she was all right. If she took off with her mother because of what he'd done. Perhaps the two of them left for Florida early. His heart plummeted to his gut at the thought of her leaving, especially after things ended the way they did. They could still have the life he'd imagined for them, so long as he could prove to her he wasn't some sort of monster.

Buster growled in the backseat as Dan closed in. Michael fought the urge to look in the rearview mirror. He struggled against every voice within him wanting to tell Dan to stop, because this was the only way to get through this. The growling abruptly ended with a high pitched yip, and Michael's heart shattered.

The frozen earth would not allow the proper burial for Buster, so Michael carried him to his dog house and placed him inside. He positioned his body like he was resting peacefully. Dan stood behind him mumbling a prayer, while Michael sat beside at the dog house opening and pet Buster's body.

Tears spilled down his cheeks, and when he wiped them away, it was nothing but blood on the back of his hand. This didn't have to happen. If Reese were home, she could have given Buster a safe home. She could've helped him. That's what people in relationships do; they help each other. This was the one time in his life that he needed her more than ever, and she was gone.

His sadness evaporated and the void left behind was filled with anger.

CHAPTER THIRTY

MICHAEL

By morning, Mom and Dan were hand-in-hand again. She leaned her head on his shoulder while she slept. Dan seemed content for the time being. He slipped out from under Eleanor and lay her head to rest on the couch.

"Michael." Dan approached Michael in the kitchen, where Michael had been dialing for Reese all night. "What are we doing here?"

"What do you mean?"

"Maybe we should get help."

"There's no help for us!" Michael hung up the phone.

"You need to let her go," Dan said.

The words were a knife to his heart, but Michael kept his lips tight, afraid he'd let his rage spill over.

Dan continued. "I love your mother. I do." He rubbed his face in the palms of his hands. "But every second I'm with her is torture, and I don't think I can control this feeling for very long."

"That's the difference between you and me. I've been with Reese a lot longer than your little crush on my mom."

"What I have for your mother is more than some school-boy crush! Can't you see that?"

"I will never hurt Reese."

"You already have!"

"What are you talking about?"

"She said you bit her."

"And you believe that?"

"Then where is she? It's a Monday. A school day, right? She should've been home last night, doing homework, getting to bed early for the next day. But she wasn't. Why do you think that is?"

"I don't know!" Michael paced the kitchen, fists clenched in balls. "Maybe she worked another shift. Or maybe she left for Florida early—"

"You said the tickets were already purchased."

"Then maybe she was doing homework somewhere else. The library? Or …" Michael thought about her project with Sebastian Belinski. The thought of her with him made his blood curdle. "I don't know where she was last night. It doesn't matter. But I bet she'll be at school today. She has a project due."

***

The clouds were thick overhead, bulging and ready to spill their snowy guts everywhere. Michael bundled up, covering most of his skin and protecting his eyes with a pair of shades, and he walked into town. He left the Chevette home in the driveway; the shattered windshield was damn-near impossible to see through anyway.

He approached the back entrance of the school from the senior parking lot and stepped through the doors. A banner stretched across the ceiling. *Class of '97: Go Panthers!* She'd graduate in a few months, and they'd finally be able to begin their lives together. But everything would be different now.

Michael climbed the steps near the back entrance, the ones he used to run up and down with his football team. He bounded up the steps with ease and would've liked to show his old coach and the scouts how much they fucked up by not giving him the scholarship. He could only imagine how his new skills would playout on the field.

One student walked the science hallway upstairs. Their back was to Michael as he lurked behind. Classroom doors were closed and students sat inside, oblivious to the threat just outside. He navigated to the end of the hall and turned down the wing where he knew her advanced English class would be. Mrs. Winters stood at the front of room 204. He found the back of Reese's head. Her wild, dark blonde hair was easy to spot. Beside her, Sebastian Belinski leaned in and whispered something. Reese turned her head and laughed at whatever he'd said.

Michael imagined crashing through the door and tackling Sebastian to the floor. He pictured the kids screaming as he moved lightning speed through the classroom, tearing out the throats of anyone who made a noise, or anyone who came between Michaael and the only person who had ever mattered to him.

Chapter Thirty-One

Trevor

After watching Reese drive away the night before, a blanket of relief washed over him. More than anything, he wanted to call Jensen, or one of the emergency numbers in his phone, and let them know of Michael's whereabouts. He could ditch the phone and continue on to his pa's old cabin north of Byron. He could sneak into the woods and never been seen again, scraping by on wildlife and living in solitude.

While he stood between the trees across the road from Reese's home, he'd imagined a thousand scenarios that allowed him to be free from the trouble he'd gotten himself into. But he couldn't run away again. He couldn't back down from his responsibilities. He needed to follow through no matter how uncomfortable it became. So, he found Jensen's number in the phone and called. Within an hour, a vehicle picked him up, but Jensen was not with the driver.

The pale, bruised woman drove Trevor into Syracuse, rather than to Michael's house.

He exited the sedan and walked through the alley behind a bar on West Fayette Street, where Jensen was waiting for him. He led Trevor inside to room with velvet curtains as a door. There was woman draped across a chaise lounge—a sensual, dark-skinned beauty who stood and greeted him with her scarlet lips parted, inviting. She was so high she looked like she might topple from a slight breeze. He wanted nothing more than to put his lips on her pulsing jugular; the remainder of the evening was a blackout.

Trevor woke in the early afternoon under the fog of whatever drugs were in that woman's bloodstream. Bleary eyed, he dropped his heavy feet to the floor of Jensen's Syracuse apartment. The curtains were drawn, and he staggered into the open-concept kitchen. Reminiscent of the day he'd woken here weeks ago, it took him a moment to find his bearings and recall what had happened the night before.

Jensen stood at the refrigerator with the door wide open. "I keep it in case I need to store blood." He was shirtless, wearing purple parachute pants. A cross was tattooed on his chest.

"What the hell happened last night?"

"You and that Elsie chick, bro! She's a trip."

"I called because I needed help with the kid," Trevor said, head swimming from drugs still in his system.

"You needed to get laid, my man." Jensen threw his head back, laughing.

"The kid is dangerous. He won't listen to me."

"Well, ain't Karma a bitch?" Jensen's face turned sour.

"I think he killed someone. Maybe even turned them. He's strong and he won't come with me."

Jensen ran his fingers along a row of keys hanging on a rack by the door. He plucked one from a hook and tossed it to Trevor. "That's for the black Honda parked in the garage downstairs. Take it."

"You're not coming?"

"You just fed. You're stronger than ever. Go wrangle that kid and put him in his place."

"And if I can't?"

"Then, boom! Stab the kid in the heart. I don't give a fuck, just figure it out!" Jensen's eyes blackened and he gritted his teeth as his fangs descended. "Jesus, man. I can't do everything for you."

***

Trevor pulled the Honda into the kid's driveway, where the mother's Chevette was now parked again. "Damn it."

He stepped out of the vehicle. There were no birds in the clouded sky. No sounds of nature in the trees as everything settled in, preparing for the snow storm. In fact, not even the dog barked. There was a bale of hay blocking the entrance. Trevor approached the house, considering busting through the door and dragging the kid with him. Instead, he opted for the polite route and knocked.

The front door opened. A man with a thick mustache stood facing him. "Yes?"

"I'm … I'm looking for Michael."

"He's not here right now."

Trevor took a step up and leaned into the house, but the man put a hand on his chest, blocking him.

"I said he's not here."

"Go away!" the mother's voice cried from behind the door. She stepped into view, shaking. "You did this. This is all your fault!"

Dan spread his arms, protecting the woman behind him.

"You're the pastor, aren't you?" Trevor said. "You're the dead body I saw."

The pastor's eyes softened but he held his ground.

Trevor put some space between them and stepped down into the snow. "Have you fed yet?"

The pastor's eyes filled with shame as they flicked toward the dog house and back to Trevor.

"I see. That won't be enough," Trevor said.

"I already know that," Dan said. He stepped down and whispered, "I don't know what to do."

"If you care at all about her, you'll tell her to leave. To go somewhere nobody can find her. I tried sending her away yesterday—"

"Like a safehouse?"

"Exactly. Nobody—not even you—can know about it."

"What's going to happen to my son?" Eleanor said, drawing closer to the doorway.

"I won't let anything happen to him," Trevor said. "We just have to watch him for a few weeks and help him get through the hard part. We make sure he doesn't accidentally kill anyone, or *turn* anyone … else."

Eleanor wiped her eyes and held her chin up. "He went to find Reese."

Trevor had watched the girl drive away the night before. Surely she wasn't so stupid as to return home after he'd warned her? "She was leaving town."

"Not until tomorrow," Eleanor said, covering her mouth with her hands. "My Lord, is he going to do this to her, too?"

Dan held Eleanor's hands clasped within his, and bent to rest his forehead against hers. The two prayed quietly, while Trevor stood guard, waiting for Dan's eyes to blacken. Waiting for him to give into his animal instincts, but he didn't. He kissed the woman he loved, then let her go, watching her back the Chevette out of the driveway.

"Wait for me here," Trevor said. "I'll go get Michael, and the three of us will get the help I should have accepted weeks ago."

CHAPTER THIRTY-TWO

REESE

Before Sebastian woke up, Reese tucked the wooden stake into her tube sock and snuck downstairs to leave. Mr. Belinski stood in the kitchen as she tried to go by unnoticed. He offered her a bagel with cream cheese and asked why she was running away. The comment seemed more of a joke than a real question, but Reese stood there with nothing to say other than some made-up thing about having to get an early start.

She stopped home and sat in the driveway with the door locked. As the minutes passed, the idea of skipping school and heading straight to the airport a day early felt more appealing. She watched the corners of the house, the wooded patch across the street, and the hedges along the yard for any sign of Michael or Trevor. At first sight of either of them, Reese planned to kick the vehicle into reverse and get out.

She'd already lingered too long. She flung open the car door and moved quickly.

Navigating her empty home felt like a scene out of slasher movie, as if at any moment a masked murderer would jump out from hiding and jab a blade in her gut. She dialed the hotel in the Poconos. It was only seven o'clock, so Mom was certain to still be in her room. She got the receptionist and asked for her mom's room.

"I'm sorry. They've asked for a *Do Not Disturb* until nine AM. I can leave a message."

"It's an emergency. This is her daughter."

"Okay. I'll see what I can do. Can you hold?"

Her gut twisted, wondering what she'd tell her mom. But all she had to say was that Michael hurt her, or that she was in danger, and Mom would be home in a heartbeat. Or at least by the end of the school day. The wait was excruciating, but finally there was a click.

"Miss?" the receptionist said. "There's no answer in their room. They might be out. But I'll leave a message that you called, okay?"

Reese nodded, but nothing came out.

"Do you have someone else you can call?"

Speechlessness overcame her.

"Honey, you okay? Do you need me to call someone?"

"I'm okay." Reese hung up.

You got this.

All she had to do was avoid running into Michael. Once she was on her way to the airport in the morning, Reese would be untouchable for at least a week. A week away would give her time to figure it out, so long as she could get through the next twenty-four hours without seeing Michael.

***

School was a blur. As faces passed her in the hall, she wondered if any of them suspected anything. Could they see the torment behind her stoic expression? Could they see the anguish and worry? The fear? Did they suspect she had a weapon in her pantleg in case Michael showed up? Why would they? They'd never seen past her façade before, or they never cared to.

Sebastian was her island in the sea of craziness. Her light in the abyss of darkness. They'd presented their Hamlet translation to the class, Sebastian putting forth his best dramatic effort. Reese fell short, losing her place on the page multiple times.

All she wanted to do leave town.

The three o'clock bell couldn't come fast enough, and Reese speed-walked to her car in the senior parking lot. Sebastian stopped her before she could unlock the door.

"Are you okay today?"

She bundled her winter coat as it began to snow.

He tilted his head to draw her eyes toward his. "You're wearing the same clothes you wore yesterday."

Reese looked at her outfit and shrugged. "I was in a hurry."

"You seem like you're somewhere else today."

She quoted Hamlet, "Off in some undiscovered country, from whose bourn no traveler returns?"

"I hope not!" Sebastian said. "That would mean you're dead."

The snow fell fast. Hefty, wet flakes coated the pavement.

"Forecast says there's a big storm coming through," Sebastian said.

A storm could ruin her chances of leaving tomorrow.

"Hey!" He waved a hand over her face.

She plastered a huge smile across her lips and came back to him. "I'm good. I've just got a lot going on right now."

"You wanna talk about it?" He placed a hand on her arm and rubbed her elbow.

Reese checked over her shoulder as other students walked by or drove off. She looked to the street, checking for watching eyes and scanning the field between the lot and the stadium. "Do you think your parents would let me stay just one more night?"

"I'll ask."

"I leave for Florida in the morning, but I don't want to be home alone tonight."

"Because of Michael? Is he bothering you?"

Reese's eyes flooded, but she harnessed her tears so they couldn't fall.

Sebastian tilted his head. "Hey. Yeah. I'm sure it's fine. Just grab your stuff and come over. I'll talk to my parents."

"Thanks."

"Are you gonna be okay?"

"I'm fine." She'd said it so often, sometimes she believed it.

Sebastian leaned over and kissed her softly. A brief kiss, consoling and tender. She leaned into him, burying herself in his arms. If she could zip him up in her luggage and take him with her, she would.

"Okay." The corner of his mouth turned up. "I'll go home now and let them know you're coming."

Reese got in the car and started the engine. Her vehicle faced the snowy field leading to the football stands. A person stood near the bleachers, wearing a bulky coat with blue and silver. It was too far away to tell, but she knew the stature all too well. Bulky and tall. Cowboys' colors. A double-take made him vanish.

A gaping black hole formed in her chest. It crushed her heart and her lungs, stopping her breath. It pulled at every cell, collapsing inward. Her entire body imploded as she realized Michael had just seen her with Sebastian.

She didn't spot the Chevette, so he must've been on foot. She hurried home faster than she should have been driving, but she had to beat him there, so she could grab her things and get out. She banged her hand on the steering wheel, infuriated that she didn't have the foresight to load her luggage into her car when she'd stopped home in the morning.

Reese came to an abrupt stop in the driveway and hurried to her bedroom. She hauled her luggage up the steps and parked the bags in the garage before running back into the kitchen for her list of phone numbers.

As she reached for the list, she stopped so quickly her hair whiplashed forward. Michael sat at the kitchen table. A gray scarf was wrapped so high around his neck it covered his chin, lips, and ears. Sunglasses shielded his eyes from the muted gray light coming in the window. Both hands pressed into the table as he stood up, chair scraping the linoleum.

He swayed side to side. Fists were knotted into balls. "Who was that?"

"Who was who?"

"Don't play dumb!"

Lies failed to formulate, and Reese stood in stunned silence.

"I saw you kiss him."

Reese backed away, plotting her escape. Sprinting toward the garage door, away from Michael, was the first option. Ducking around him and going for the front entrance would be closer, but she knew she couldn't outrun him.

"Did you walk here?" She tried to keep her voice calm as she craned her neck to look out the kitchen window for a vehicle she already knew wouldn't be there.

"Yeah. I took the shortcut through the field." He removed the scarf from his neck and set it on the counter, keeping in step with her as she backed toward the garage door. "You know the field where we sat under the stars and fell in love?"

He moved two steps closer for every step she'd taken back. His chest heaved. Knuckles turned pasty white. His jaw was clenched and his body swayed like a giant tree bending to powerful winds. "So, were you just lying to me that night you said you loved me?"

She shook her head.

"Are you in love with *him*?"

"It was nothing."

Michael took off his sunglasses and squinted. A darkness swam within his brown eyes.

She stood her ground, but Michael grabbed her by the coat at her sternum and walked her backward until she was pressed into the refrigerator. He grabbed a fistful of material and lifted her with one hand. Gravity tried to pull her body through the coat, but Michael had a firm grip and pressed his clenched fist into her neck. Her feet scrambled to find the floor.

She wheezed, gasping to get a breath, and when she opened her eyes, his obsidian, marble-like eyes reflected the image of a pathetic girl. The girl who was supposed to be strong and independent quivered under the grip of a monster. One she might've been able to overcome if she ever actually tried. But with each passing second, those opportunities disappeared with her failing breath.

She stretched one arm toward the stake in her boot in a final attempt to fight back.

Michael's face distorted with furious indignation.

"You're so fucking stupid! You think you can trust that guy?" He screamed about her naivety and lack of common sense. He screamed and raved and Reese focused simply on breathing. Wheezing breath in, coughing and gagging out. Each time she coughed, Michael eased his grip enough for her to catch a life-sustaining breath, then returned to applying pressure. Long spindly fangs extended from under his lip and Reese braced for the inevitable.

"I can't believe you're fucking cheating on me!" His voice turned to an animalistic bellow while blood seeped from the corners of his eyes.

Reese raised her knee, tugging at the bottom of her jeans to get her fingers on the stake, but her vision tunneled and she was about to pass out.

"Fuuuuuuck!" Michael's face was a cobra, mouth unhinged and ready to strike.

As she failed to reach the stake in her sock, she braced for impact.

Michael put both hands on her shoulders, allowing her to take in another breath, but before she could expel a single cough, he shoved her against the refrigerator. Her shoulder blades struck hard, and her body fell to the ground, ragdoll legs bent beneath her. A roll of paper towels fell from the top, followed by something hard that crashed on her head. An empty glass cannister shattered in pieces around her.

Michael lunged at her, fangs inches from her face, black starless eyes narrowed to vengeful slits. "Do you love him?"

"No." It spilled out of her uncontrollably. Her teeth chattered, but no tears fell.

"Belinski?" Michael rubbed his face, pacing the kitchen. "Revenge of the Nerds Belinski?" He laughed. "That doesn't make any sense!"

She stayed on the floor, one hand wrapped around the stake, concealed by the leg folded beneath her.

With his eyes returning to normal and his fangs retreating, Michael bit his lower lip and filled his chest with a breath. He gathered his scarf and sunglasses while Reese lay shattered on the floor among the broken glass.

Get up and do something!

But with each second, the window of opportunity shrank.

He attacked her, and she had a gash on her head to prove it. If she plunged the stake into his heart, her defense would be justified. But now he was calming down, would it still be seen as self-defense? Or just rageful vengeance? If she attacked now, and she wasn't quick enough, she didn't know what he'd do in return.

He wiped the blood from his eyes with the back of his hand. His tone changed to something more solemn. "I can't look at you right now."

Every second was an eternity. Each heartbeat a moment upon which she could not act fast enough. She'd always thought she'd be the girl who would handle these situations with strength and tenacity. She'd be the *take-no-shit* kind of girl who'd stand up for herself. But fear—real fear—made her behave against her will. It made her cower and tremble when she wanted to fight.

Michael left the house, the front door wide open, allowing in the wintry air. Shaking, Reese stood up, avoiding the broken glass. Mindlessly, she grabbed a broom and began sweeping. She should've been planning what to do next, but nothing was happening inside her head other than what she assumed was shock. He'd never been so violent before and she was certain if he came back, she wouldn't survive his next outburst. This was the part where she should call the police, report the attack, but she stared at the phone. All the fear and turmoil had reached its point of singularity and it finally burst inside of her into a silent killer. It slaughtered all of her emotions. There was no more fear. No more anger. There was absolutely nothing but a desolate wasteland in her heart. Her tears were dried. Her heart calm. All she wanted now was to go away and never look back.

She didn't bother calling her mom again.

Reese shook some shards of broken glass from her hair and ran her fingers over the front of her neck where she still felt the remnant touch of Michael's grip.

"Reese?"

The sound of his voice petrified her. She was rooted to the kitchen floor, unable to turn.

"Reese? Is he here?"

She turned gradually, keeping a palm on the counter by the phone. Trapped in the kitchen table cove, she eyed the Ginsu knives nearby, which would be easier to get to than the stake in her pantleg. Trevor stood with his palms up.

"Did he hurt you?" He gestured toward her forehead, closing in.

Reese placed her fingers on her head. It was wet where the cannister had hit her. Her fingers were coated in blood. She shook her head, trying to break whatever trance had taken hold since Michael left. Regaining her sense, she bent down for the stake and pulled it from her pantleg, fumbling with the material until she got both hands around it. The pointed end aimed at Trevor.

"I'm here for Michael. Where did he go?"

She shrugged.

"He hurt the pastor, and he'll hurt you and everyone he knows."

Reese adjusted the grip of the stake in her hands, edging out of the cove and into the open, where she could run for the door if she needed to.

Trevor kept two hands up. "Did he go home?"

"I don't know."

She hadn't thought about it since he left, but when the immediate veil of trauma started to pull back from her eyes, she knew exactly where Michael would've gone. The dried-up heart within cracked in two. "Sebastian."

"Who's Sebastian?"

"A kid from school." Vomit climbed her throat, but she fought to keep it down. "Is Dan going to be okay?"

"No."

Guilt and worry and torment and every terrifying emotion flooded her body again. Whatever was left in her heart had torn open, spilling into her belly. The fact she'd put Sebastian in danger weighed so heavy she couldn't move. Michael was probably already over there, banging on Sebastian's door, trying to start a fight, or worse.

Reese kept the point of the stake lazily toward the man before her. "I have to warn Sebastian." She picked up the phone, frantically searching for his number in the rolodex, but she hadn't memorized it.

"Where does he live?"

"Not too far."

"He might already be there by now."

Trevor reached for the folded county map by the phone and opened it. "Show me!"

Reese found Sebastian's road on the map and described his house. Trevor pulled his sunglasses over his eyes. "Can you leave town?"

"I'm leaving the state tomorrow."

"Leave *now*. What about your parents?"

"My mom's on vacation."

Trevor backed toward the door. "Get your things and get out. I'll take care of Michael."

"What are you going to do to him?" It shouldn't have mattered, but there was still something in her that worried for him.

"I'm gonna help him. But if anyone finds out you know about him, about me … they'll kill you. Whatever you do, don't come back to this house."

Chapter Thirty-Three

Michael

Several stop signs bent under the wrath of Michael's fists along the way. The thought of her with another man ignited a fury in his gut. It singed the walls of his abdomen and burned his lungs.

Cars sped by and Michael kept his head down, blocking the brightness of their headlights, which wasn't as abusive on this snowy day. He took his journey slowly, keeping to the roads rather than speeding over there hot-headed. He tried to quell the storm within, reminding himself there was no way Reese would cheat on him. Of all the guys in the world lined up to be with her, what would she see in Sebastian Belinski? There had to be a reasonable explanation. The first thing he needed to do, though, was to convince Sebastian to back off. And he needed a cool head for that.

If he didn't get out Reese's house when he did, he would have hurt her, and he would do everything in his power to avoid turning into his father. The people he loved would never have to fear him, but it sure seemed that lately, those people had no problem hurting *him*.

By the time he reached the Belinski's place, it was getting dark. Michael had calmed down enough to have a civil conversation, man-to-man.

Two cars sat in the driveway, gathering snow. The split-level was lit with a warm glow, like some kind of damned Hallmark family home. Maybe that's what drew Reese to this guy. A little bit of normalcy. He had a family that had Thanksgiving dinner on real plates, and they probably held hands while saying grace, and laughed about whatever made happy families laugh. Sebastian had something Michael could never give her: a big, happy family.

Reese had said she'd broken up with Michael, but she'd said that before too. They always ended up together in the end. Maybe with everything going on, she was confused about what she wanted. But if Michael could take Sebastian out of the equation—talk to him sensibly about things—then he and Reese could get back on track.

On his doorstep, Michael summoned some Christ-like patience and pressed the doorbell.

He removed his scarf and put his sunglasses in his pocket. The overcast sky and the porch roof gave enough protection from the twilight. Within seconds, the door opened to Sebastian *fucking* Belinski. That stupid face asked to be punched, but Michael swallowed the sudden urge to throw fists. The light inside was glaringly bright and Michael fought the irritation.

Sebastian's eyes were skeptical. "Can I help you?"

"Do you know who I am?"

"Yeah. We went to school together."

"I'm Reese Perkins' boyfriend." Michael held eye contact. A predator within wanted to rip the kid apart, but he held it back, gently rocking from side to side. He clenched his fists tight to keep from swinging them.

"Yeah, I remember, but ..." Sebastian tilted his head. "Look—"

"And I'd like to know why you had your tongue down my girlfriend's throat." The thrill of trapping the son of a bitch was one he hadn't felt in a long time. The exhilaration before a fight. Heart thundering, muscles tensing. Eager to swing, but he withheld. As Christ-like as he wanted to be, nothing made him feel more alive than righteous violent justice. The agony of holding back was punishment enough for considering hurting this guy.

Sebastian's hands went up. "Reese said you broke up."

"Well, we didn't." The sharp point of his fangs teased the back of his lip, ready to help. "Reese and I have been together for years, so this is what you're going to do ..." Michael rubbed his hands together, attempting to warm them with his breath, but the air from his lungs couldn't do the job. He placed one hand on the door frame, leaning in. "You're going to leave her alone, or else."

"I'll leave that up to Reese." His voice trembled.

Michael swung without thinking, but arched to the side of Sebastian and punched the door frame. The wood snapped. "What the fuck does that mean?"

Sebastian eyes filled with fear as they shifted to the cracked wood under Michael's fist. He took a step back. "It means I can see why she dumped you." He slammed the door shut.

Michael didn't try to hold back the rage this time.

He rammed the door with his shoulder, busting it from the hinges and splitting the wood frame. The door crashed to the floor and the thrill of it invigorated him.

Sebastian's arms stiffened and his face flinched up tight like he'd shit his pants; Michael hated his face now more than ever. He hated everything about the kid. He hated that he'd touched Reese. He hated his stupid, two-story fancy house that looked like a painting. He hated his perfect family and his perfect book-smarts. But most of all, he hated that Reese liked him back.

"That was really fucking rude." Michael broadened his shoulders. "I just wanted to talk to you."

"You need to leave."

"*I* need to leave?"

The audacity of this little shit was almost funny. If he didn't want to pound his skull in so badly, he might have let his brief chuckle turn into full-fledged laughter. "*You* need to leave Reese alone."

"Fine, man. Whatever." Sebastian continued to back up until he was pressed against the wall, family photos all around him. "My parents probably heard that and called the police."

"Do you think I fucking care?" Michael kept his lip from curling up, exposing his teeth, exposing what he was. All he needed to do was send a message, remind Sebastian that Reese was not up for grabs. He let out a steadying sigh. "I've been with her for years. Did you know that? *I* was there for her through everything. *I* put in the time. *I* love her. Not you!" The heartache and fury balled up inside, gravitating to his core, swirling together in a storm that had to be released from his body or it'd tear him up on this inside. He let it go, curling his fingers tight, clenching his fist and cocking it back. "*I* love her!"

Michael swung. His fist plunged into Sebastian's right eye, crushing bone. A crunch, followed by a *squish*, as if his fist had punched through a sheet of frozen snow and then sank into the softness beneath. *Crunch, squish.*

Michael pulled his fist back. The indentation in the guy's face was like a crater. At the center, a ruptured eyeball oozed. Blood and brain matter seeped through broken skin. Sebastian was held upright only by the back of his skull, lodged into the drywall.

When the brief moment of excitement passed, Michael realized what he'd done.

"Shit."

"Hey, what's going on?" A woman's voice approached from the other side of a door in the house. It swung open to Sebastian's mother, Dr. Belinski, with a cordless phone pressed to her ear. Michael rushed toward her before she had a chance to say anything to the person on the other line.

She only had time to squeak out a gasp before Michael ripped the phone from her fingers and smashed it against the wall. He covered her mouth with a hand, shushing her, but she fought in his grip. Her eyes broke his heart. Michael glimpsed the dreadful expression of a mother who'd lost her son, then he wrapped his arm around her neck and placed another hand over her mouth to shut her up.

He wanted to calm her down, let her grieve, let her bury her kid, but none of that was possible now. Unsure what to do to, he squeezed tighter, keeping her body turned away from Sebastian. But Dr. Belinski kept fighting.

"Stop it," he whispered in desperation. "It was an accident. I don't want to hurt anyone."

She twisted her body, bringing a foot up to kick in a fruitless attempt at escape. Michael gave a swift jerk of his arm, to remind her to stay still. A snap came from her neck. It popped under his arm and Dr. Belinski fell limp. Her full weight collapsed in his grip. Michael stood with his arm locked around her neck, frozen, hoping he didn't accidentally kill her. Sebastian was one thing, but *her … What did she do?*

All Michael could think to do in the moment was close his eyes and wait for a miracle. Wait for God to reverse his actions. Wait for himself to wake up from the nightmare.

"Please," he begged, giving her body a shake, but when he released, she didn't snap back to consciousness. Her body dropped to the floor with a hefty thud, legs bent unnaturally beneath her.

"Pizza's ready!" a man's voice yelled from somewhere on the other side of the house. "It's cold out there." His voice neared, closing in on the door from the kitchen.

All the options rushed through his head. The front door lay on the floor, open to a darkening sky. If Michael ran now, there'd be footprints. Fingerprints on the bodies. Evidence. Though it was snowing, he wasn't sure his tracks would be covered completely for a while.

Think!

The kitchen door swung open, leaving Michael no time to consider his options. All he could do was act on instinct. He lunged at the man before giving him a chance to see his family dead on the floor. Michael leapt upon him, eyes blackened and fangs extended, pushing him back through the swinging door to the kitchen. It was the kindest thing to do. The most compassionate act. No man could live after seeing his family like this. Michael's actions were a service. A necessary evil. Instead of letting his teeth seek a vein, he swept the sharp protrusions across Mr. Belinski's neck, slicing it open. Needlelike teeth instinctively soaked up some of the blood as the guy fell to his knees in the kitchen. A blackened curtain fell over Michale's eyes as the door swung behind. If his vision was clear, he'd see the bodies of mother and son on the other side. It was as if his new abilities could protect him from the trauma he'd just experienced. To blind him to the awful things he'd gone through.

Michael held his hands on Belinski's neck, shushing him as he choked and gurgled on his own blood. The swinging door gradually slowed, in time with Mr. Belinski's failing pulse.

CHAPTER THIRTY-FOUR

TREVOR

Trevor sped on slick roads to get to Michael before the kid did something he'd regret. His cellular flip phone jostled in his upper right pocket as he ran.

Trevor made it to the address Reese had given him. A long driveway through pines led to a quaint home. It was the kind of place he and Rebecca had always dreamed of buying, but they could never seem to get far enough away from the city with their jobs. He pictured the two of them, Christmas morning by a fireplace, waiting for the kids to come down the stairs. But that image of stairs only brought back the memory of Rebecca trying to wrestle Devon from Trevor's arms. The weight of Devon's body sat heavy like a ghost in his empty arms. The image of their bodies was seared into his mind and would haunt him forever.

Time seemed to slow as Trevor neared the front door of the Belinski's, which been torn clear off the hinges. Inside, a body lay on the floor against a wall. Half of the guy's face had been bludgeoned into a pulp. The sight of skull fragments, pink connective tissues, and a ruptured eyeball made Trevor gag. A woman lay on the floor as well. Trevor knelt beside her, pressing his fingers against her wrist, but he couldn't feel a pulse.

The sound of movement behind a white door drew his eyes upward. Trevor eased through the swinging door, to reveal Michael hovering over the body of a third victim. Instead of anger, Trevor only felt sorry for Michael.

"Michael, stop."

Michael jumped to his feet. Black eyes struggled to find where Trevor stood. A steady stream of blood poured from each of Michael's fangs, pooling on the hardwood floors.

Michael staggered to the side and fell against the wall, pulling his knees to his chest. "I'm sorry, I'm sorry, I'm sorry ..." Blood seeped from the corners of his eyes and fell down his cheeks.

The kid was so full of blood he couldn't contain it. It leaked from his fangs and eyes, beaded on his skin at his pores.

Trevor remained in the doorway. "You took too much."

"I didn't mean to."

"I believe you." He pulled out his cell phone from his jacket pocket, opened it, and dialed Jensen.

Jensen answered.

"That kid I told you about?"

"Yeah?" His gravelly voice sounded irritated.

"We need a house cleaning."

"Son of a bitch."

"I told you I needed help—"

"This is on you!" Jensen snarled over the phone and paused for a moment. "You were reckless."

"If someone doesn't get out here and clean this up, then this is going to end up on the nightly news."

Jensen remained silent.

"It's bad."

Trevor sent him an address, closed the phone, and slid it into his pocket. The smell of hot pizza suddenly met his nose. The pie sat on the counter over the body of the Belinski father, lying in a puddle of his own blood. The aroma of hot pepperoni melded with the irresistible scent of blood.

Still curled tight against the wall, eyes returning to normal, Michael sniffled and used his sleeve to wipe away what should have been snot. Blood spilled from his nose, instead.

"They're coming to clean this up. It'll be like it never happened. People can't know we exist, or we're all exposed."

Michael climbed to his feet. "So what if we're exposed?"

"So what?"

"What does it matter if people know we exist?"

"What do you think they would do if they found out we existed?"

"They'd be afraid. They'd fear us. *Respect* us."

"There's a big difference between respect and fear, kid."

Maybe it was the adrenaline rush of the kill, but whatever it was, Trevor was cautious with how he responded to Michael.

"We keep a low profile so as not to end up at war with people."

Michael put his hands on his head and began to pace the kitchen. "I gotta get out of here."

"You need to stay."

"I have to see Reese."

Trevor grabbed his shoulder, stopping him from walking through the kitchen door to the living room. The kid stiffened under his grip, then slowly turned to face him. He squared his shoulders to Trevor.

"Don't touch me."

Trevor released. "You're a danger to her. Can't you get that through your skull?" He gestured to the man's body.

"I won't hurt *her*."

"You just *accidentally* killed three people."

Michael leaned in, face snarling. "Two were an accident."

"And the third? Was that the boy you were jealous of?" Trevor blocked Michael from leaving. "You think you have the right beat someone to death because … what? Your girlfriend liked him back?"

"He knew she was mine!"

Trevor had known some jealous men in his lifetime. Jealous men were small men, no matter how big they appeared. But they were dangerous when they felt they didn't have control. And right now, Michael was losing control.

"I didn't mean to," Michael said.

Trevor calmed his tone to try to help Michael see some common sense. "You'll kill her. Maybe not today, but it *will* happen. You'll kill everyone that you love." Trevor's eyes burned with the need to let tears fall, but he fought the pain.

Michael shoved Trevor against the wall. The drywall cracked under the blow, but Trevor refrained from fighting. "I know you don't want to hurt her, but—"

"I just want to talk to her." Michael ran his fingers through his hair. "I gotta know."

"You gotta know what?"

"If it was just a kiss, or if she was screwing him too!" Michael charged out of the kitchen, leaving the door swinging behind.

Chapter Thirty-Five

Reese

Before she left the house, Reese called Sebastian's number to warn him that Michael was coming to confront him. His mom had answered, but there was a clamoring sound in the background that cut Dr. Belinski short. "Hang on, sweetie," she'd said, followed by a short gasp and a crackle.

The phone cut out.

Reese had no clue what she'd do when she got there, but she felt responsible for putting the Belinskis in Michael's path.

Centerville Road grew dark as night fell. She struggled to see beyond the dense snowfall, but she kept focused, and eyed the sharp wood stake in the passenger seat.

The more rational person within her told her she was overreacting, but there was no denying what she'd seen in Michael's face this time. The reasonable side of her said things like vampires didn't exist, and if they did, the lore attached to them might not be true at all. Despite her skepticism, the carved wooden stake that Trevor had left with her was now on the passenger seat of her Corolla. No matter what, vampire or not, driving a sharp object through the chest of anyone should stop them dead in their tracks.

As she neared the crest of the small hill before Sebastian's place, a figure came into view. A man in a silver coat caught the beams of her headlights. His stature was unmistakable as he raised an arm to block her headlights.

She slowed to a near-stop, rolling alongside him, and his facial features came into focus. Blood covered his face and hands. It was smeared over his Cowboys jacket, but she couldn't spot any injuries.

Michael leaned over to look through the window, then signaled for her to roll it down.

Everything within her screamed to hit the accelerator, but she was so petrified, she couldn't seem to lift her foot from the brake.

Out of the darkness behind Michael, another man sprinted into the headlights' glow. Trevor plowed into Michael. Their bodies smashed into her car and rocked the vehicle. Metal crunched from the blow. With his arms in a bear hug around Michael, Trevor dragged him over the snow bank and beyond her view. The two disappeared into the blackness of the rearview mirror.

Pulse thumping between her ears, Reese lifted her foot from the brake, but was stopped abruptly by Trevor as he smacked both hands against the driver side window.

Reese smashed her foot on the brake and came to a sliding stop on the slick road.

He yelled through the glass, "He killed them. They're all dead!"

Michael reappeared like a phantom from the darkness and grabbed Trevor by the collar. He yanked him away from the vehicle.

"Run!" Trevor screamed as Michael hurtled a fist into his face, smashing him into the road so hard that Reese imagined him exploding on impact.

She lifted her heavy leg from the brake and hit the gas. Tires spun in the snow. Her back end fishtailed until the tread found its grip. Reese couldn't turn around on this narrow patch of back road without getting stuck in a snowy ditch, so she drove forward, over and down the hill, leaving the violent fight behind her.

Reese slowed at the entrance to Sebastian's driveway. The house lights were on, but the front door was wide open.

She needed to see for herself if it were true. She needed to walk inside and confirm what Trevor had said was a lie. She needed the Belinskis to be okay.

She pulled in and let her car roll to a stop behind their vehicles, which had at least half an inch of snow piled on top. The front door wasn't simply open, but removed.

Reese opened the car door and edged closer to the front porch.

"Sebastian?" The crippling fear within her wouldn't allow her voice to raise above a mousy squeak.

She reached the bottom of the porch steps to see someone's legs on the floor behind the sofa. Blood covered the floor beneath the body. Violent shaking took over her body while she climbed the porch steps, and every tremoring inch of her body ceased the moment she heard screaming coming from the woods behind her. Primal, angry, and wild screams as Michael and Trevor fought.

Reese turned on her heels, instinct for survival taking over all else. There was no time to process, or cry, or even *think* about anything other than getting as far away from him as possible.

Run.

CHAPTER THIRTY-SIX

TREVOR

Michael bludgeoned Trevor's face so hard that blood filled his eyes. Trevor managed to roll away, only to collapse onto his back in the snow.

"Why would you tell her I killed them?" Michael towered above, a silhouette against the clouds with nickel-sized snowflakes falling around him.

Trevor's right eye refused to open. Blood flooded his mouth, and his syringe-like teeth worked to siphon it back into his body. He coughed, and crimson spray collided with the snow. His wounds were itchy as they worked to heal him. "You don't want to go down this path. I've been there—"

Michael dove onto him, straddling his torso, fists wailing with hurricane force. He pummeled his chest, his arms, his face. Michael destroyed Trevor's body in a vehement fury, creating new wounds faster than the others could heal. Eyes black and teeth extended, the animal in Michael controlled him now.

Maybe this was Trevor's punishment. To look the monster in the eyes at his death with the same terror his baby boy had.

Michael climbed off, disappearing from view, denying Trevor the courtesy of being tortured for what he'd done. But as much as Trevor wanted to expire here in the snow—to finally rest—he couldn't let Michael go after that girl. He used what strength he had left to get to his feet. As he pressed into the ground, his left arm snapped at a fracture he hadn't noticed until now. Trevor staggered after Michael, down the embankment.

Trevor mumbled between swollen lips. "I killed my own son. And my wife is dead now, too, because of me."

Michael stopped with a hand resting against a tree. He hung his head. "I'm not like you."

"No," Trevor said. "You're worse." He staggered closer, hugging his broken arm as bone regenerated within. "Let her go."

Michael snapped a branch the size of a baseball bat from the tree. With its jagged end, he aimed at Trevor. "I will *never* let her go."

"Then you'll kill her." Trevor struggled to remain standing as his wounds began stitching shut. "Then they will have to kill *you* for being too unpredictable. I know. I'm already on their shit list because of—"

Michael lunged before Trevor could react. A sharp, sudden pressure in his chest sent him to his knees. Sparks shot up his legs as he impacted the ground. The large, pointed branch lodged into his heart. He grabbed it, wanting to pull it free, but he was too frail. It burned like the sun. Blistering, searing pain in his chest. Jensen had said he wasn't supposed to die from a stake to the heart.

He fell to his back, legs bending beneath.

Michael left him.

The tingling sensation of healing ceased. Wounds remained. Bits of his own flesh swam into his mouth. A reflexive cough sent chunks of his insides misting against the backdrop of the clouds, while snowflakes drifted down and clung to him.

Maybe it was finally his time to go. He could go to sleep, then wake to meet his wife and son in Heaven, if there was such a place. But Trevor was a man who'd done such terrible things, there'd be no pearly gate for him. He feared if he closed his eyes, fire and brimstone awaited, and he was ready to accept it rather than live like this any longer. As the snow piled on, his vision faded. If he slept, maybe he'd be so lucky as to never wake up to anything.

A vehicle's engine could be heard in the distance. Soon after, Trevor saw headlights pass by. He heard voices and flashlights. He tried to signal, but his body failed to respond. Whatever hope was left in the world disappeared as the darkness cloaked him.

Chapter Thirty-Seven

Michael

He gathered snow in his hands, rubbing, washing away the stains and the memory of Dr. Belinski's face, but it refused to leave. The fear in her expression, the moment before death was imprinted on the back of his eyelids.

Trevor lay lifeless on the icy bank. Michael was covered in blood and he couldn't tell which smears and splatters were from Trevor, and which were from Sebastian and his parents. The palms of his hands were foreign to him, like they'd taken on a mind of their own. Like they'd become weapons used by a creature within himself he'd previously been able to keep contained.

Headlights cut through the darkness in the distance, and Michael fled across the field through calf-deep snow. He sprinted through fields and woods until he was back in the woods at the edge of his home.

Arms folded across his belly, he dropped to his knees. Scarlet gore oozed from his sockets, dripping into the snow as he cried over the lives he'd taken. Four lives extinguished in a single evening, and as he watched the blood come clean from his hands, he realized how this was all his fault. However, even though Mr. and Dr. Belinski—and maybe even Sebastian—didn't deserve to die, *Trevor* got what was coming to him.

The blood pouring from his body wasn't his own, it was Mr. Belinski. It was Dan Delgado and the anonymous donor from the blood bag. Like Trevor had said, it was too much, and now it overflowed from his tear ducts, desperate to leave his tortured soul.

This was how Michael would pay the price for losing control.

"Help me," Michael hissed through clenched teeth, praying to God. "If there was ever gonna be a time you step up and help, do it now. Pleeeease." His chin trembled, fighting the pain. He raised his attention to the Heavens, and the clouded sky turned red from the blood in his eyes.

There was no reply from above. Only the howl of wind between the trees. Branches clacked together as the storm intensified.

The sound reminded him of the night he'd slept in the back of the pickup. He'd lain there, shaking as the wind picked up and rustled the leaves and pine needles. He'd wondered if Dad would come out and deliver the rest of his beating. Wondered if Mom would be dead in the morning when he reentered the house.

And now he was that child again, standing at the threshold of his own home and praying he didn't step inside to find his mother in a pool of blood. Leaving her alone with Dan was a mistake, but he had needed to find Reese. He needed to sort out the mess that his life was becoming. The Chevette was gone from the driveway and the trailer lights had all been shut off. He turned the knob on the door and stepped inside to his abandoned home. The darkness swallowed him whole. He'd never felt so alone or lost in the vastness of the world.

The uncertainty of his mother's well-being crushed him. Dan's whereabouts and whether they'd run off together haunted his thoughts. That had to be what had happened. She'd fallen for him so quickly, fawned over his health condition, holding his hand and caring for him, when only hours earlier, she'd cast her own son out the door with barely a shirt on his back.

The only person Michael had left was Reese, and the string that connected them was threadbare. All that mattered now was reeling that thread in and never letting go.

Chapter Thirty-Eight

Reese

He killed them all. The sound of Trevor's voice lingered in her skull. As aggressive as she'd known Michael could be, she'd never guess he'd go this far. It was all hot-headed talk. It didn't make sense that a person with the capacity for so much love could also be filled with so much hatred. It didn't make sense when Michael began to act jealous. It didn't make sense that he hurt her. And it didn't make sense that the man she'd considered spending her life with would turn out to be a monster. But she couldn't deny her own eyes any longer.

The little car struggled in the white-out conditions, battling the back road hills like icy mountains, back end of the vehicle losing purchase of the road and sliding sideways. She coasted down the hills with caution, checking the rearview mirror often. There were few cars out on the road tonight and Reese was lucky enough to get behind a snow plow on I-90 for the drive to Syracuse.

She pulled into the long term parking garage at the airport and backed into a space nestled between among other vehicles, and she waited. In the silence, with nothing but her own breath to be heard, she stared out the windshield across the garage, waiting for him to appear. Shadows turned to lurking figures in the corner of her eyes. Their faces were obscured by shadow, but she sensed them watching her every move.

She climbed into the backseat where the rear windows were slightly tinted, and she curled into a ball on the seat. Hunger signals finally kicked in, reminding her she hadn't eaten all day.

The night was fraught with wide-eyed paranoia. Jumping awake because every movement of light and shadow in the garage could've been him. Every sound and click of a car door could have been his approach. What little sleep Reese got was tormented by nightmares of being chased. Her feet were stuck to the floor, some inexplicable force kept her legs from running away and the dark figures closed in around her.

She startled awake at dawn as a family unloaded a minivan across from her.

As they fumbled with luggage and whining children, Reese got out of her car and stretched. In just over an hour, she'd be safe on the plane. Her heart thumped so hard it made her sick to her stomach, but having nothing to eat in nearly a full day didn't help either.

She scanned the lot for any signs of Michael, crossed the parking garage with haste and moved through the sliding glass doors into the airport, where she grabbed a Snickers from a vending machine and stood in line for Delta.

While families and business people shuffled forward in line, dreaming of their upcoming vacations, or fretting over whatever business deals they had coming up, Reese thought about Michael, bloodied and delirious, as she had seen him on the side of the road. She pictured the body—*was it Sebastian's?*—and hated herself for not going inside and checking on them. Maybe he was still alive. Maybe he needed help.

He killed them all.

To avoid suspicious glances, Reese held her chin up, casually picked at her fingernails, and pretended to be as normal as possible. She tugged on a piece of dead skin at the corner of her fingernail and convinced herself that everything would be okay, eventually, so long as she kept running.

She stepped up to the desk when it was her turn and pushed her ticket across the counter.

"ID?" The clerk's badge read *Belinda*. Her mile-high Aqua Net hair reminded Reese of Eleanor's dated style.

Reese fished her driver's license from her pocket and handed it over as the clerk Belinda typed her information into a computer.

She scowled and typed again, looking to Reese, then back to the computer. "Ummm."

Reese waited, yanking the skin from her fingernail. A dab of blood bloomed to the surface and she hid it in her pocket.

Belinda leaned over to another woman beside her and asked her to check the system.

She pointed and shook her head at the screen. "It's been refunded."

Reese must've looked like a deer in headlights as she stood with her mouth hanging open, because the woman next to Belinda arched her pencil thin brows and clarified directly to Reese. "That means you can't use it."

Belinda rolled her eyes at the woman then looked back to Reese. "Sorry, the ticket isn't any good."

"Could it be a mistake?"

The woman—Valerie was on her name tag—picked up the ticket and tore it in half. "If you get a refund, that means the ticket doesn't work anymore, sweetheart."

Reese felt all hope shatter into pieces and fall to the floor with the halves of her ticket out of there. "I didn't refund it. My father bought it for me."

"Is it possible that he got the refund and didn't tell you?" Belinda asked. "Here, let me check if there's another flight booked to your name."

The woman beside Belinda shrugged and went back to tending to her own passengers.

Belinda cringed. "I'm not finding anything, but we can get you on the next flight to Orlando at ten-o-eight."

"How much is that?"

"One way is $130."

If Reese had a hundred and thirty dollars on her, she'd spend it on a one-way ticket to anywhere. But all she had was a few twenties. "I have to make a phone call."

Belinda pointed to a row of payphones under the baggage claim sign.

Reese carried her luggage to the phones and set her bags by a bench. Morning sun crept over the horizon and through the window, casting a yellow glow on the floor. She dug out her father's phone number and dialed.

It rang for what felt like an eternity before she hung up, retrieved the quarter from the return slot, and dialed again. Nothing.

With each passing second, she could feel the shadow figures from her nightmare closing in. They devoured the air, making each breath more labored than the last. Reese steadied those panicked breaths and tried the backup number, the secondary phone number Mom insisted she have. Bio-dad's sister Charlene.

The phone rang, and Reese kept her back to the airport, facing the phone and pleading quietly for someone to help her. "Come on."

Aunt Charlene's line rang four times and a groggy voice answered. "Hello?"

"Hi. This is Reese. George's daughter."

"Oh, hey sweetie!" Her voice was raspy, tired.

"I've been trying to reach him, but he's not answering."

There was a long pause before Aunt Charlene spoke again. Several seconds. Enough time for Reese to debate whether to ask if she was still there.

Charlene cleared her throat. "Sweetie, I can't get ahold of him either lately. He's been AWOL again."

"Oh. But I was supposed to fly in today to see him."

"That was today? Lordy, this is terrible timing. He hasn't been to work or nothin'. He does this sometimes, falls off the wagon, you know. It's a disease, it is."

"Is he okay?"

"Well, that's debatable, and neither here nor there. What matters is that you're okay. Did you make it in safe? Need a ride from the airport or somethin'?"

"No. I'm in New York still. They said the ticket he sent me was refunded and no good."

Again, Charlene had such a long pause, Reese worried she'd hung up. Then, she sighed deeply. "I am so sorry. You know this has nothing to do with you, right? He wasn't working, so he probably needed the cash for, well, you're old enough to understand."

Tears nipped the inside of her lids. She tightened her quivering lips, locked her jaw from chattering, and kept those tears from falling. "Yeah."

"It's a disease," she repeated.

"I know." Her voice broke.

"I can't believe he did this to you!"

"It's okay." She shrugged, but it wasn't okay. Nothing about any of this was okay.

After Reese got off the phone, she kept the receiver clenched in her palm and sat on the bench with the sun on her back. She called the number her mom had left for the hotel in the Poconos and left another message with the receptionist at the front desk.

"Can you tell her …" Reese paused. "Can you let her know I'm coming there?"

"Oh. Okay. I will do that. Do you need an address?"

"Yes, please."

Reese jotted down the address in the notes section of her wallet with a new plan in mind. The Poconos were only a few hours away, maybe longer in the snow. She could grab a map on her way out. As the shock of last night's incidents wore down, and more calculated rational thinking took over, she realized she couldn't continue to run without first contacting the police. Even without concrete evidence, she could make an anonymous call from the airport payphone and ask them to check on the Belinskis. Her heart burned, worried the authorities would plague her with prying questions, but it was the right thing to do. She stood, holding the phone between her ear and her shoulder, sunrise pouring through the window to her left, and imagined the comet out there, now washed out by sunlight.

She flipped open the cover of the payphone's book, and found the local emergency numbers listed at the front. As she practiced in her head what she'd say—*I'd like to report a potential violent crime at 369 Centerville*—she considered whether to disguise her voice.

She wondered if the shop in the airport sold maps and whether she'd need to stop for gas on her way to the mountains. She'd figure it all out because she had to.

Everything will be okay.

A hand landed on her upper back. It sped in out of nowhere and struck her like an asteroid impact, destroying all hope. He squeezed her shoulder, as her fingers hovered over the phone's buttons. Her skin shriveled, and any prospect of continuing to run turned to dust upon hearing his voice.

"Hey," he said.

Everything in the universe froze. Her earth stopped spinning, the sun died on the horizon. If Reese were to close her eyes and fall backward, the world and the stars and the galaxies would all shatter to pieces. And his hand would remain on her shoulder, anchoring himself to her through the end of all things.

"Who you calling?" Michael stepped forward to stand on the other side of her, where the wall blocked direct sunlight. His face was wrapped in a scarf. Sunglasses protected his eyes. His heavy gloved hand remained cupped, but firmly locked on her shoulder like he'd trapped a baby bird beneath.

Reese hung up the receiver and turned to face him. "George."

"I thought I missed you." Michael's face was pale blue, but a flush of pink bit at his cheeks. His jacket and jeans were soaked, and melted snow dripped on the floor beneath him. There was no blood soaking his clothes, or smeared on his hands and face. "I ran here to catch you before you left, but the board said your flight was already leaving."

Reese sidestepped into the sunlight, then sat on the bench, bathing the back of her neck in its yellow glow. Michael stayed in the shadow a foot away.

"Why didn't you go?" he asked.

"He refunded the ticket."

Michael's jaw dropped and he shook his head. "What an asshole." He took a step closer, but retracted when his boot met the beam of sunlight from the window. "Come here."

Reese crossed her arms and kept her head down, safe for now within the sun's embrace. Here, he supposedly couldn't touch her, but Michael defied the rules and stepped into the light. He sat on the bench beside her, putting an arm around her back. Reese tensed as he scooched closer enough that their hips touched. He rested a wet gloved hand on her knee. "I'm sorry."

His breaths were labored, and the subtle sound of sizzling drew her eyes behind him. A strip of exposed skin on Michael's neck blistered. The stench of burning skin and hair hit her nose and she jerked to a stance, stepping out of the sun.

"How'd you and me get the worst dads ever, huh?" Michael joined her in the shadow in front of the phone and took her hand. "Come on. Let's go home."

Everything within her fell inward. Every drop of blood, every cell, every hope and dream she'd ever had, crushed down to a point of singularity. The pressure built and if she didn't let it out, she might puke. Vomit rose into her esophagus, but she swallowed it. "I'm not going home."

"Where are you going?"

"None of your business?"

Michael's relaxed demeanor stiffened; his face subtly shifted, muscles twitching. "Seriously. Where are you gonna go?"

"What does it matter?"

"What kind of question is that?" Michael shifted his weight and leaned in.

His threatening stance forced her into submission. She had no chance against his superior strength and dominance, so she tried not to anger him further. There was no telling what he'd do in a populated place like an airport. He'd let the sun burn him alive as he held onto Reese with all his might. Would he thrash and fight and kill everyone in his path just to be with her? She imagined the carnage that would follow if she screamed and tried to get away from him. Would bullets stop him if she were to alert security, or would they only enrage an impenetrable beast? She couldn't let his wrath unfold here with innocent people—kids and babies—so she bit her tongue and held strong.

"I just mean that lately, not much seems to matter."

Michael leaned in, pulling her chin up to look in her eyes. Her reflection glared back at her from his sunglasses. A distorted image in the lenses that she couldn't recognize as herself.

"*You* matter to me," he said.

Reese counterfeited a grin to appease him, and her tears finally fell.

Michael drew her close, pulling her head into his chest in an embrace. "Don't I matter to you?" His arms were venomous snakes coiling around her body. A boa constrictor squeezing, squeezing, squeezing, so damn hard she couldn't breathe. Reese would eventually run out of air, and fall into a limp, lifeless body for Michael to devour. She wiped her tears away, and grabbed her luggage, which Michael snatched from her.

"I got it." He smiled as he offered his sad attempt at chivalry, then nodded toward the door to the parking garage. "Let's go."

Every face they passed on the walk through the airport was focused on their own business. Reese's eyes tried to desperately meet with someone, anyone. Maybe if she could signal somehow that she didn't want to be with him, someone might take action. But nobody looked. Not a single person noticed her silent pleas behind puffy, red eyes as she walked beside a monster leading her back to his lair.

Chapter Thirty-Nine

Reese

Sliding glass doors to the parking garage opened, and Reese stepped over the event horizon and into the garage with Michael, fear her only motivation. Her speeding pulse hammered through her veins and into her fingertips. Michael kept one hand on her elbow as he dragged her rolling luggage with the other.

"Where are you parked?" Reese struggled to get the words out. If she and Michael could separate long enough in the parking garage, she could speed ahead and lose him.

"I walked."

"That's like thirty miles."

"Yeah, I know."

"In the snow storm?"

"I would walk the entire planet if I had to." He lifted his sunglasses and squinted against the parking garage lights. "I'd walk through Hell to be with you. Don't you know that?"

Reese nodded, tears welling, but she wouldn't allow them to spill over.

"Hey." Michael caressed her arms and tilted his head. "It'll be okay. Forget your loser dad. You're better off without him."

She unlocked her car and the two slid into their seats. An instinct to keep running was under her skin, but she needed to pick the right moment.

Reese kept her hands locked at ten and two o'clock on the drive home. The highways were plowed almost to the pavement, and there were dry tire ruts in which she could maintain a decent speed. Her empty stomach ached, or maybe it ached from the stress of not knowing what was going to happen next. Reese was too nauseated and petrified to say anything, so she kept her eyes on the road and focused on staying alive until the right moment presented itself.

"I'm glad you didn't leave." Michael's voice cracked.

Reese refused to look at him.

"I mean …" He sighed. "I'm not glad about what happened with your dad—"

"I don't care about that."

Michael couldn't have been so delusional as to believe that her behavior was in no way a reaction to what he'd done last night. Was he not going to at least mention something? Would he not try to offer some excuse? Some pathetic attempt at an apology?

"All we have is each other." He sniffled, and out of the corner of her eye she spotted him wiping his face with the back of his glove.

Michael reached across the console and placed his hand on her knee. A quick reflex made her leg twitch and, when she glanced down, she fought her instinct to gasp and knock his hand away, because there was blood smeared on his glove.

"I'm leaking," Michael said. "It just pours out of me sometimes."

Reese kept her eyes ahead, afraid to stare, and afraid to ask any questions.

"Can I stay at your house?"

No words could escape. If she replied *no*, he'd ask *why*. Then Reese would have to tell him that she was so scared she'd rather crawl into a hole and die than be anywhere near him. That he was a murderer. That she didn't love him. If Reese replied with anything but a *yes*, there was no telling how he'd react.

"They know where I live," he said. "It's too dangerous to go back."

As she neared her exit of the highway, there was a tractor trailer headed in the opposite direction in the eastbound lanes. She thought about the night she sat with Michael at the gas station, the night he'd said he'd step in front of a truck like that and end it all. The night he manipulated her into helping him just so he could keep her close.

One jerk of the steering wheel and she could cross the grassy median, head into oncoming traffic. She wasn't sure if an accident of that magnitude would kill him, or if he really needed a stake to the heart like Trevor had said, or a beheading and burning like the book in the library suggested. A fiery crash could be enough to end him. If not, at least Reese would be out of her misery.

So, what if she ended Michael's terror now? What if she veered into the other lanes? Blasting through the snow-covered median would slow her down, but she could get in front of that truck before it stopped. She could aim to have the passenger side hit first. Do the world a favor and rid it of Michael, but in doing so she might die too.

Reese didn't want to die. She wanted to live, to see the comet, to see the stars and the moon and the world. She wanted to laugh with friends and travel. She didn't believe her life was worth ending, but if Michael was stopped, then he couldn't hurt anyone else.

She thought about her mother and her old friend Sara, and realized she'd grown so distant from everyone in her life over the past year that nobody would miss her if she was gone. Nobody other than Michael.

The tractor trailer zipped by, and she was glad she hadn't gone through with it. Who was she to traumatize that truck driver with the death of two young people? Reese stayed safely in her lane, turned on a blinker to exit, and let the opportunity slip away. As she approached town, every chance to escape from his grip evaporated. Every grand idea of dropping him off and driving away, jumping from the vehicle, screaming and running for help … all *enterprises of great pitch and moment turned awry* as Reese Perkins cowardly lost the name of action again.

She pulled into the vacant driveway and put the vehicle in park. She wondered if Trevor was okay after he and Michael had fought. He'd warned her not to return home, yet here she was. Perhaps he'd show up and help get her out of this situation. She wondered if her mom would finally call back, or come home early. And she mostly wondered, if nobody comes to save her, would she have the courage to run or fight?

For now, she'd go into the house, because there was no other option. Any fight or flight response would end with his fury, so she froze. She did exactly as he wanted, moving under his command out of the vehicle and toward the garage door.

If she stepped inside, she felt like she'd never come out, but if she screamed or ran, it would be far worse.

Chapter Forty

Michael

By the way she was behaving, Reese must've seen something last night out on Centerville Road. Something Michael wished she hadn't. Trevor had certainly fucked with her head by telling her Michael had killed the Belinskis. What if she'd gone to their house and found their bodies, or what if she'd backtracked and watched Michael as he drove a branch through Trevor's chest?

All Michael could do now was win her trust back.

Crying was something of a nightmare now, leaving tracks of bloodstains down his cheeks. Proof he was weak, and he didn't want to show that side of himself to Reese, even if she was the only person in the world who'd ever allowed him the right to cry. He washed the blood from his face with more vigor than he had the night before. He'd gone home last night after leaving Trevor dead on the side of the road. Mom and Dan were gone and he worried whether Dan killed her. He cried last night while showering, hoping he didn't lose his mother, but she'd made it very clear he was a disappointment. She couldn't offer him sanctuary when he needed it most, so maybe he didn't care what had happened to her. He'd burned his bloody clothes before coming to the conclusion he had to go after Reese, even if that meant walking all night in blizzard-like conditions to the airport. Love had no limits. Now he had her back and couldn't blow it. Michael removed his wet clothes and put on a pair of jeans and a T-shirt he'd left at her house a month ago. He dried his face, listening to Reese as she moved around in the kitchen down the hall.

When he came out of the bathroom, she offered him some. She'd always been selfless, to her detriment. She was the girl who would offer the homeless guy on the corner a dollar, even though he didn't deserve it. When going to the movies, she'd smile and say, "Thank you," to the ticket counter guy, not realizing her smile was flirting, and she was fueling his desire to be with her. She might've been book-smart, but she was way too innocent to survive this cruel world. He took a serving of skinny noodles and tried to force it down, but his stomach knotted as it hit bottom.

"You can have it." He pushed the dish across the table toward her.

She nodded, but still hadn't said a word since they got back to the house.

"I'm sorry for everything," he said.

A forkful of noodles went in her mouth, eyes focused on her meal, still refusing to look him in the eye, like she was hiding something from him.

"I'm trying here." His voice raised, but he took a breath to calm his frustration.

Reese pulled her focus from her plate and stopped eating to look at him.

"I went home yesterday after I left your house. I got a little hot-headed, so I'm sorry for that."

Reese sat back from her plate and picked at her fingernails, occasionally glancing up to look at him.

Michael shrugged. "Mom was gone. I'm pretty sure I'll never see her again." Saying the words aloud brought an ache to his chest. He choked back his pain and straightened in his chair. It was time to man up and take control, move on from his mother's abandonment. Reese was still sitting across from him. Reese didn't run away, so that was something.

He reached across the table and took her hand. It was warm and stiff, unmoving.

"I love you," he said.

Seconds passed, and if another one went by, he'd break into a million pieces knowing she didn't love him back.

Fortunately, she whispered, almost inaudibly, "Love you, too."

It may as well have been Cupid's arrow, piercing his heart, restoring hope that he and Reese could be together forever. Even in his condition, she could continue to love him.

"Beauty and the Beast, huh?" He laughed.

But Reese only shoveled more food into her mouth.

"I'm sorry about your dad. That's gotta be tough." He forced a quick smile. "What a dickhead, right?"

Still, she sat unresponsive, dead silent like she was mad or something.

He slammed his hand on the table. "What's going on?"

Reese startled with a flinch. She set her fork down slowly and finally gave him her attention.

He lowered his voice. "I don't know how to make you feel better. What are you thinking? What are you feeling? Give me something?"

She took a deep breath and released it in a long steady exhale. "I'm scared."

"Of what? Me?"

She kept her eyes on her food. "You hurt me."

"When?"

She looked to the refrigerator, where, just the day before, he'd lost his temper. She touched the top of her head.

"What?" Michael stood, and she flinched again. She didn't move much, but it was a subtle twitch in reaction to his movement. He wished he could prove that she didn't need to be afraid of him. He moved closer to look at her scalp, where a miniscule scrape had already begun healing. "What happened here?"

"The glass fell on my head when you pushed me."

"That was nothing. I didn't even touch you. But I'm sorry the refrigerator rattled when you backed against it. I knew something fell, but I didn't know you got hurt. Are you okay?"

He tilted his head and looked down at her as she nodded, picking at dead skin around her fingernails. Her gears were turning in that brain of hers. Always trying to make sense out of things that didn't deserve the time. It was one of the things he loved about her. She could rationalize anything. If he skipped his homework for a game, she used to remind him that his college scholarship potential was in football, not math. And when he skipped too many assignments, she'd say he couldn't get the scholarship without the grades. When he was robbed of his chance for a scholarship, and opted to go straight to work after graduation, she told him exactly what he needed to hear.

He kissed the top of her head, inhaling her scent. Scabbed blood was inches away from his lips. He wanted her, all of her, but Reese was afraid of him. Regaining her trust was a priority, but he couldn't take all the blame here. Reese needed to accept that some fault lay in her own hands. If she hadn't been seeing Sebastian behind his back, none of this would have happened.

He took a step back, leaning against the counter. "I still don't understand why you were with Sebastian. I mean, what did you see in that guy?"

"We were just friends."

Michael's stomach knotted, noodles fighting his new anatomy. "You say that, but I saw you kiss him." He forced a laugh to keep the mood light.

Reese stood up and carried her dish to the kitchen sink.

Michael followed. "Say something!"

"We were just friends," she repeated in an emotionless voice.

The anger building within exacerbated his stomach pain, and he felt like he was about to throw up. Michael turned away and hurried to the hall bathroom. He knelt over the toilet and his stomach lurched. Noodles spewed forth. They came out the same as they went in, barely chewed. Clots of blood clung to the noodles in the bowl. His stomach cramped again, so he sat down, realizing he hadn't used a bathroom since this all happened. There'd been no need until now.

Hot liquid splashed into the bowl. Between his legs, crimson splattered the bowl in the bloodiest diarrhea blowout he'd ever seen. The sight made his stomach churn again, and he vomited gore into the tub beside him.

He recalled the time when he was about seven years old and "Had it coming out both ends," as Mom had so eloquently described. He'd sat on the toilet with a bucket in his lap while Mom waited on the edge of the tub, rubbing his back, while Dad shouted to "Keep it down in there!"

When he finished heaving, he felt the finishing urine trickle out the tip of his penis. But instead of pee, thick scarlet dribbled out, plopping into the water.

He wiped himself clean and looked in the mirror, knowing that the next few days were crucial to gaining control over his emotions and over his thirst, crucial to winning Reese back, and in keeping off the radar of whoever may've come looking for Trevor's killer. His face was foreign to him now. It was the face of a man who had done unspeakable things. Things that had to remain buried. Things he could never speak of to anyone, not even Reese. It was a face hardened by life, a face riddled with traumatic experience, a face whose features became more inhuman the longer he stared at it … a face like his father's.

Michael drove his fist into the mirror and the glass shattered, falling into the sink, before his stomach lurched and more cruor spilled from his guts.

He cleaned up his mess after his body had rid itself of the excess blood. Yet still, his lips and the roots of his teeth ached with the need to latch onto a vein. If he was going to be seeping blood from every orifice every time he took too much, perhaps he'd need to dial it back. Feeding once a week should suffice, according to what Trevor had told him. So, he'd wait a week until he took more, and if it became too difficult, Reese would surely let him take a little to get by.

Chapter Forty-One

Reese

Michael had been in the bathroom for a while, and every second he was away was a second she should've run. All she had to do was get out of the driveway with the car. He wouldn't be able to catch her if she could get that far. She stood in the small foyer space near the front door, listening for Michael down the hall, yet she couldn't seem to propel herself out the door. The blinking of the answering machine caught her attention out of the corner of her eye.

She checked the messages to find three calls from telemarketers, and nothing from her mother. A retching sound came from down the hall, and Reese realized she had more time than she'd thought. She ran to the garage door. Her shoes were set neatly on the mat and her keys were hung above. All she had to do was go.

Go now.

But instead, more seconds passed staring at the keys and her shoes. If he emerged from the bathroom to see her trying to leave, she wasn't sure how bad it would get. But if she stayed for a while, maybe he'd let his guard down and she could slip away without a fight later on.

Her decision was made for her when Michael got out of the bathroom and entered the kitchen, closing blinds and curtains as he moved through the house. Reese meandered back to the kitchen table by the phone.

Michael was glued to the windows all afternoon, peering from behind the curtains whenever a vehicle drove by. Every noise was a threat. After an hour of pacing, he finally settled down on the couch near the big picture window.

Reese moved to the computer at the edge of the living room and sat in front of a blank screen.

She hit the power button.

"Are you waiting for someone?" she asked, voice weak from disuse.

Michael drummed on the arm of the couch, hooking a finger on the edge of the curtain. He smiled. "I'm just looking outside."

Reese clicked the icon to launch AOL and the modem screeched to life. She worried that her mother might try to call while she was using the internet, but if Mom hadn't called by now, it probably wasn't going to happen. She pictured her with Quinten, horseback riding along snowy trails, skiing in matching snowsuits, and warming up by a lodge fire. She pictured her mother *happy*.

"What are you doing?" Michael asked.

"Going online."

"For what?"

"To play a game."

He grabbed the remote and clicked the power, and the 38-inch black box TV turned on. "I'll play Sega with you later, if you want."

She forced the corner of her lip upward in a sad attempt at a grin. "Maybe when I'm done with Minesweeper?"

The conversation was so unnatural, she didn't know if this moment was real. For several seconds she hoped it wasn't. She waited for her eyelids to open, revealing that she'd been asleep on the plane and she was on her way to see her father.

Michael sat at the edge of the couch, with one eye able to peek through the gap in the picture window curtain at the front of the house. He clicked through the cable guide screen and grunted about how it was easier when they just had three channels and the TV Guide book.

Michael didn't have a computer in his house yet. He'd never been on the internet and had no interest in learning when he'd been at her house before. So, he didn't need to know that the games Reese liked to play on the computer—Solitaire and Minesweeper—didn't require dial-up to play. While the modem loaded, she went to the kitchen for some water out of the tap. She waited a few minutes for it to connect. The AOL screen appeared and said, "You've got mail."

Nothing but junk mail filled her inbox. Chain letters from her mom's Aunt Ruth. She supposed she could send an email. An S.O.S to someone in her life, but then what? They'd call the house to see if it were real, speak to Michael, and her intentions would be outed. What Reese needed was SWAT to come barreling through her house and take her away from him.

She pulled up Minesweeper. The window filled the screen, hiding the web window. She started clicking boxes to show the game was in-progress, then she minimized the window.

From the TV, the *Cheers* theme song played and Michael set the remote down to let the show play.

She'd seen movies where people ordered pizzas and even called for help on the internet, but that wasn't something anyone could do around here. Her county had just rolled out the 9-1-1 call system last year, so she was certain there wouldn't be a way to call for help from her computer. And dialing from the phone would be impossible unless she could get some privacy. If Michael heard the call, it'd be too late.

She pulled up *Ask Jeeves* on the computer and typed in a question: *How do I make an anonymous—*

Michael stood, turned off the TV on the first commercial, and Reese maximized her Minesweeper window as he walked behind her to the kitchen. "Wanna go downstairs and play Sega?"

"Yeah. I'll wrap this up and be right down."

He leaned over her shoulder from behind and put his hands on her arms. Michael pressed his face against the side of hers and kissed her cheek. "I love you."

Reese forged another smile. "Love you, too." The words poisoned her lips and she wanted them back.

"Hockey or Mortal Kombat?"

"Surprise me."

Michael leaned in, sincere desperation filled his eyes. "You're acting weird. You okay?"

"I'm fine." She waved him away. "I'll be right down."

Michael smiled. "Okay. I'll give you a sec." He went downstairs, and Reese leaned back in her chair, watching the entrance to the basement across the kitchen. She pulled up the *Ask Jeeves* screen and continued her question: *How do I make an anonymous emergency call?*

She hit enter and waited while the screen turned white, loading up the results. Another thirty seconds went by and footsteps bounded up the basement stairs. Reese scrambled to minimize, but accidentally closed the window.

"Hey," Michael said. "It's not loading."

"I'm coming." She closed Minesweeper and signed off.

"Goodbye," AOL said.

Reese shut down the beige box and pushed her chair in.

"We gotta get an N64. Have you seen those yet?"

"No," she said, following him to the basement.

The descent was a willful walk into a prison sentence. If she made it to the bottom, it'd be even harder to leave this house. She lingered on the final step, then took the leap. Because she had something down in the basement she didn't have upstairs. The sharp wooden stake Trevor had given her was in her bedroom, tucked between the mattresses.

"The N64 is like 3D. Chuck has one," Michael said beneath a dangling bulb light.

He stood in front of a love seat and TV. A place the two of them had made out on more occasions than she could count. A five by seven blue carpet beneath the furniture was an island in the sea of the dark basement. She knelt in front of the TV and picked up the Sega Genesis console. "It's getting old."

Reese blew into the cartridge slot and wiggled the cords in the back. She pushed Mortal Kombat into the slot and powered it on.

Michael sat down behind her and picked up a controller. "Thanks!"

She couldn't understand what was happening in his head. How he could act like any of this was normal. But she didn't have the guts to ask what the hell happened the night before. What the hell was going to happen. So, Reese, until she knew what else to do, picked up a controller, chose Sonya as her character, and played games with Michael like they used to when everything was perfect between them. Michael selected Scorpion as his fighter and they yelled and laughed at the screen for several rounds.

They couldn't avoid talking about what happened forever, but Michael needed time, and she had to regain his trust before making a move. She suppressed her fear, pushed it as deep down as it could possibly go, and played video games with the monster sitting beside her. It was better than the alternative.

Her character Sonya did a series of ultimate moves until Scorpion's health was critical. *Finish Him*, the game said, and she tapped the controller to blow a fire kiss, destroying her opponent.

"Come on!" Michael tossed the controller on the floor. The game music continued, but Reese and Michael were deadly silent.

"Let's do something else." Michael powered down the console and went upstairs, defeated.

She eyed the bedroom door, waiting for him to clear the landing so she could duck inside and grab the weapon, but he stopped and waited for her.

"You coming?"

She joined him, turned on the local evening news, and waited for a report about the Belinskis, but nothing came. Michael was in the kitchen rattling pots and cooking something, and she didn't care to ask what.

He lit some candles and placed them on the kitchen table.

"Reese," he said. "Come here."

By then the news had begun to repeat itself without any mention of a homicide, so she clicked the remote and did as he asked, joining him in the kitchen where a plate of spaghetti noodles, drenched in red sauce, was waiting for her.

"Tada!" He bowed. "I made you dinner, milady."

Reese wasn't hungry, but she sat at the table while Michael helped push her chair in. An empty box of Barilla and a jar of Ragu sat empty on the kitchen counter.

"Thank you," she said, waiting for Michael to stop playing house and start explaining what had happened the night before.

"I made you La Spaghett-ay Ragu Parmesan." He grinned, genuinely proud of himself. "There's no meat or anything."

"That's okay." She picked up a fork to twirl some noodles around. Despite her lack of appetite, Reese ate.

"How is it?" he asked.

"Good." She danced her fork in circles. In the candlelight's glow, the sauce reminded her of blood. "Do you miss eating?"

"Not really." He crossed his arms and leaned back in his chair. "Okay, maybe a little. But it's worth it for the way I feel."

"How is that?"

"Awesome!" He slammed a palm on the table and smiled. "I wish I could show you how this feels."

The conversation was forced and surreal. She didn't care how he felt. She didn't care about if he missed eating. She didn't care to eat his shitty food. "Can I ask you a question?" As soon as the words came out, her heart sprinted into a race. It throbbed in her neck, like it might explode if she said the words, but also like it'd explode if she didn't.

"Of course. I'm an open book." He leaned forward on his elbows, brown eyes sparkling in the dancing flame. He was pale, but for once he looked like himself. He looked like the boy she fell in love with.

"What happened last night?" The question was lobbed onto the table like a dead body. An accusation.

Michael grimaced.

"I mean, will you tell me what happened?"

"What do you mean?"

Something like courage inside her seemed to swell, and as much as she wanted to call him out on everything, to scream at him that he was a murderer, she remained calm and asked, "Did you kill Sebastian? I know you wouldn't on purpose, but—"

"What are you talking about?"

"The Belinskis?"

"What about them? Did I kill Sebastian Belinski? Are you seriously asking me that?"

As he lied to her, it wasn't courage growing within her. It was something less fierce. Something growing unafraid, but not bravery. Something reckless. Something so tired she didn't care how he reacted.

"Did you kill Sebastian and his family?" Her heart caught in her throat. It sat there, barely pulsing, choking her. Part of her didn't want to know, but she needed the truth from him.

Michael squinted in disgust, shaking his head. "You think I'd hurt them because of one stupid kiss?"

Reese looked to her plate of spaghetti.

"It was just one kiss, wasn't it?" he asked.

Two noodles were stuck together and they trapped her focus as she spun her fork; they fought getting tangled in the prongs. Without looking up, she said, "I saw you covered in blood. I saw you last night on Centerville Road. And you saw me."

Michael's jaw dropped and his arms went limp by his sides. "Are you changing the subject?" He laughed, a fake, forced violent outburst. "Pretend the kiss didn't happen. Whatever."

Reese kept her fingers pinched on her fork. She locked eyes with Michael. "You and that guy Trevor were in the road."

"You saw Trevor last night?"

"He said you killed them all."

"This is rich." Michael laughed, standing from his chair. He paced the kitchen, then approached Reese. He towered over her and she wanted to stand, to allow herself a chance to fight or run, but he blocked her in. "And you believed him?"

"I *saw you*—"

"No, you didn't. Remember, yesterday, when you were making out with another guy and I was pissed? Well after I stopped by your house, I went home, where I learned my mother had taken off with our fucking pastor."

"I went to Sebastian's. I saw—"

"Jesus, are you sure you didn't have a bad dream? You have a lot of weird dreams."

"It wasn't a dream."

"Well, damn." He knelt beside her, placing a hand on her knee. "No wonder you've been acting so weird. Whatever you think happened, it didn't."

"I was there."

"Wait a minute. So, then here's a question for you. Why were *you* at Sebastian's?" Michael's eyes were leery as he stood again. His chest inflated. "You know what? I don't want to know. Whatever happened between you and him is over."

Undigested noodles churned in her gut, but she tightened her core. She gently touched the scab on the top of her head, then looked back to her noodles and pushed the plate away. "Okay."

"No," Michael said. "As a matter of fact, it's not okay. I *do* want to know why you were going to Sebastian's house."

"You're right. Probably just a dream, like you said."

Michael remained still. Out of the corner of her eye, he could've been a statue. "Great, now you're dreaming of that guy." Michael's upper lip curled and he smashed a fist into the doorframe, splintering the wood.

The burst made Reese wince, but she held steady, biting the inside of her cheek to feel anything but the panic now coursing through her.

He paced, clenching fists, as Reese thought of the wooden stake now sitting wedged between her mattresses. How she should've tucked it into her pantleg.

She stood before him.

"I can hear your pulse," he said.

She imagined every beat of her heart screaming to him, divulging her secret intentions. That she was not sincere, that she was terrified of what he'd become. But she drew closer to him. "Then you can hear how fast it's going?"

"I do."

Reese placed her hand on his heart. "That's because I'm afraid of you, and I don't want to be."

"Well, don't be." Michael's expression twisted. His jaw clenched and he struggled with the anger growing inside, but she knew him well enough that when she touched him, he softened. "I'll never in a million years hurt you."

She let her eyes fill with tears.

"Do you believe me?"

"I believe you don't want to hurt me." She leaned closer and pressed her head against his chest.

Michael held her in an embrace and her heart sped faster. He pulled away and looked her in the eyes, but they had grown dark again. Black orbs reflected candlelight. Michael lunged forward, taking her head in her hands. She tensed, expecting violence, but he kissed her. A passionate, desperate kiss. It tasted like the icicles pulled from the aluminum eves when she was a kid—metallic. It was a fervent kiss, and his teeth pressed too hard against her mouth, but she let him continue so long as it kept him calm. She let him continue until she felt the sharp prick of a needle against her bottom lip. She jerked away to see Michael's fangs descending and smears of blood on his mouth.

Hands outstretched, he said, "I'm sorry. Did I hurt you?"

Reese wiped a drop of blood from her lip as Michael grappled for purchase on a counter. He blinked rapidly, and crouched on the floor until his eyes returned to normal.

"That was awesome." He tried to step forward for more, but Reese put up her hands.

"Can we wait?" she asked.

His eyes were hungry, but needful of her love. He nodded in agreement. "I will wait an eternity for you."

Chapter Forty-Two

Reese

They fell asleep on the couch in their jeans and T-shirts. Michael sat beside her, holding her hand and talking about how he'd like to live here with her forever. Start a family here. She didn't offer the obvious counterarguments. She let him talk and dream, while she sat waiting for an opportunity to present itself. Nick at Nite quietly played on the TV, running *Threes Company*, *I Love Lucy*, and *Gilligan's Island*.

At three in the morning, Reese realized she had fallen asleep, and Michael was still awake. *Leave It to Beaver* was on the screen and Michael stood in front of the large picture window, stealing a glimpse between the curtains.

"Do you sleep anymore?" she asked.

"Not as much." Michael remained statuesque, staring between the curtains.

"What is it?" Reese asked.

"I thought I heard something."

She jolted forward, all grogginess evaporated in a second.

Michael went to her side and sat on the edge of the couch. He put an arm around her back, and one hand on her knee. His cool breath skimmed her neck as he leaned in for a hug.

She pulled away. "What happens now?"

"I don't know."

"Are they coming for you? Is that why you're watching out the window?"

"I'm worried they'll come for *you*. They don't like other people knowing we exist."

Reese moved away from Michael. "We shouldn't be here. If they're going to come looking for you, you should go into hiding for a while. Go somewhere they can't find you, just until it all blows over."

"I'm not afraid of them."

"I am!"

"That's why I'm not leaving your side." Michael eased closer.

Reese sat on the couch and pulled a large pillow into her lap, pulled up her knees and hugged it closely.

"I like this show," Michael said, joining her on the couch again. June Cleaver was preparing a meal in her kitchen. "I like the idea of simpler times. Just a simple family, with no real problems, you know?"

Reese wet her dry lips. She'd left her lip balm in the car, but she didn't bother to say she needed it. She stared at the screen and remained silent.

Michael sighed. "That'd be nice. That's what we need. We need our own place, where it can be just you and me for a while. Like a cabin in the woods or something. Like you said, go into hiding."

"I can't do that."

"Why not?" He turned to face her, his large frame backlit by the glow of the television.

"I have school."

"School?" Michael laughed. "Really? I think there are bigger problems to worry about."

"It's senior year. I can't just stop going."

"Your life is more important than some stupid piece of paper. That's the plan. That's what we're doing. We'll lay low here for a few days, make sure we aren't being watched or anything, and figure out where to go. I'll clear out my checking account and savings. It's not much. How much do you have?"

She had about three thousand dollars saved. "I don't know. Not much, but what are we supposed to do in the long run? What happens if we find a cabin somewhere. We'll have to go to work someday. And it's not like you'll be able to work, so it'll be me, the person without a diploma job hunting while living in a cabin in the woods? None of this makes sense."

"Don't you see?" Michael grinned, like he had the most exciting secret to tell. "Neither of us will have to work."

She shook her head, trying to make sense of his rationale.

"I can do whatever I have to do to get money."

"So, you're going to, what, become a thief?"

"I don't know what I'll do, but I know we'll figure it out." He knelt before her, taking both hands into his. "I need to protect you from what's out there. Because how are we ever going to have that"—he nodded toward the Cleaver family on the screen—"if I can't at least keep you safe? So, I will do whatever I need to do over the next few days. Trust me."

***

Reese had drifted to sleep again, waking when a vehicle slowed down in front of her house. Headlights shifted the light through the kitchen and living room. Michael was unresponsive on the couch, having fallen asleep, head tilted back. She hurried to the window as a pickup stopped in front of the mailbox at the end of the driveway. The newspaper delivery person left the daily paper in the blue box and drove away. The sky was heavily clouded, but there was the first sign of daylight coming through.

Michael's eyes were closed and his arms rested crossed over his abdomen. Would this be their future if she never left? A life spent in fear of every passing vehicle. A life under the rule of this person whose emotions were so volatile and reactive, she had to handle every conversation with utmost caution. She had to give up her senior year, give up prom and college and parties and friends. Michael had already strained much of it out of her life even before he had become what he was.

Reese made it all the way across the kitchen and slipped her feet into her sneakers. She watched Michael across the house as his chest rose and fell with each breath. The keys didn't make a sound as she lifted them from the hook, because she was careful to palm the entire set firmly so they wouldn't clink together.

The garage door creaked, and in the silence of the morning hours, it was as if someone held a megaphone before her every move. On the other side of the house, Michael hadn't moved from his sleeping position. She slipped into the garage. The door would have to stay open, so as not to risk waking him when it closed. She hurried to the outside garage door, and pulled it open. The early morning chill nipped at her bare arms. The packed snow from the storm had melted the day before, and all that remained was a thin coat of flakes dusting the pavement from an overnight flurry.

"Where you going?" Michael's voice called from behind her.

She reacted swiftly and pretended not to be startled as she looked over her shoulder and continued forward. "To get the paper."

His hand was on her before she could three steps outside. "What the fuck are you doing?" He grabbed her bicep and squeezed, yanking her back. The tendons in her arm rubbed beneath his grip, and she worried he might be able to squeeze so hard, he could rip right through. He pushed her into the garage and surveyed the surroundings.

"I was just getting the paper." Her keys were clenched in her fist and he might not have noticed them yet.

He closed the garage door. "Do you think I'm stupid?" He snatched her hand in his and clenched. Her knuckles rolled and the keys stabbed into her palm. "Were you leaving?"

"No!" She let her hand go limp, caving under his strength.

Michael released.

"I was getting the paper." She rubbed her hand and dangled the keys. "I left my Chapstick in the car overnight. So, I was getting that too." As terrified as she was, she stood her ground and spoke with conviction.

Michael turned to look out the garage door window. "So, are you stupid?"

Reese held firm, grit building between her teeth.

He moved closer, put a palm against her cheek. "Nobody can know we're here. I thought I made that clear."

"I'm sorry! My lips feel like they're going to fall off. I didn't think it'd be a big deal to run out to the car real quick to grab my Chapstick and get the paper."

"Jesus Christ, Reese. How the hell are you an honor student?" He laughed to himself and escorted her back into the house. Michael opened the closet door and dug into his coat pocket, retrieving his lip balm. He handed it to her.

She took it and applied it right away. "Thank you," she whispered.

"I need to be able to trust you, okay?"

"Okay."

***

Michael spent the morning talking about places in the world he'd like to go. Blowing all his money on plane tickets so they could go to some island in the middle of nowhere. Reese nodded along and let him hear whatever she felt he wanted to hear, scheming a plan to get away, but as the hours passed, and as he hovered over her every move, the hope of escape dwindled. He followed her into her bedroom when she fed her fish. He followed her to the computer and sat next her when she played Minesweeper, and he even followed her to the bathroom, waiting outside the door while she relieved herself. He claimed it was so she could alert him if someone came through the small shower window.

By late afternoon, they were on the couch in the basement, playing a few more rounds of Mortal Kombat, then they switched to a movie. Michael popped Caddyshack into the VHS player and Reese began to feel like his prisoner. Life at the end of a chain. A sudden wave of guilt crashed over her as she realized nobody was at Michael's house to take care of the dog.

CHAPTER FORTY-THREE

MICHAEL

She wanted to see Buster, and as much as it killed him to take Reese to see him, it needed to be done. He closed Reese's passenger door and walked around to the driver's side.

Overcast light glared off the snow-suffocated landscape, and Michael squinted through his sunglasses, scanning the neighborhood for any suspicious movement. They'd been at the Reese's house for almost twenty-four hours without an incident. No masked men in black came looking for him. Maybe nobody found Trevor's body. While Michael worried that he might walk into an ambush when he got to his house, he had to give a little when it came to Reese. She'd been through a lot, and if he wanted her trust, he'd have to earn it.

He pulled into his empty driveway a few minutes later.

"I don't see him," she said.

"He's probably curled up keeping warm."

"We should bring him inside for a while." Reese stepped out the car and Michael followed her.

"Buster!" she called, and waited like he was going to trot out of his dog house and greet her. Michael wished it would happen. He wished he could take back a lot of what had happened. Make things right. Especially what he'd done to Dan. But that was all behind him, and all that mattered was moving forward, no matter how hard it was going to get.

Reese approached his dog house. "Why is the hay completely blocking the entrance?" She grabbed the chain where it connected to the house and pulled it free from the deep snow until the end dangled in the air. "Where is he?"

Michael shrugged. "Buster?"

She grabbed the twine binding and lifted the bale out of the way, revealing a curled up, stiff dog inside. "Buster?" Reese knelt to look inside then twisted quickly to face Michael.

"Is he okay?" Michael asked.

She reached in the dog house and nudged his body. Her hand retracted slowly, and she squatted there, silent and still.

"Oh my God, is he okay?" Michael asked.

Reese's shoulders swelled into a hunch and a sob burst forth. She fell onto her butt in the snow and cried.

Michael edged closer. "Maybe Mom thought she was helping by closing him in overnight during the storm."

Reese dried her tears and stared at Buster's body. "He has blood on him."

Michael leaned down to look inside, to see Buster laying exactly as he'd left him, curled into a ball like he was taking a nap. The blood on his fur was stiff.

Reese got to her feet and her eyes moved across the tree line.

"I bet Trevor did this. I bet he came looking for me and I wasn't here, and my mom wasn't here, and he took it out on Buster." He choked on his words, and while it wasn't the truth, he felt with all sincerity that a real injustice had happened. Buster was an innocent bystander, and it broke his heart to lose him. Blood tears filled his eyes. He sat beside his friend in the snow and cried with her.

Chapter Forty-Four

Reese

"Why would he kill a dog?" Sorrow ripped through her body, making it difficult to say anything while Michael drove back to her house.

"Probably needed to … *eat.*"

Her breath was rigid and unsteady, wondering if Trevor had killed Buster, or if Michael was keeping something from her. Either way, she was partly responsible. She should've gotten Buster out of that situation long ago. There were countless times when she could've stood up to Michael, argued with his mother, but she didn't. She stood by and let the mistreatment happen.

Michael drove the car up her short driveway and put it in park. He watched the rearview mirror while Reese sat with her hands her lap.

She didn't want to go inside, but if she fought it, she'd end up like Buster. Blood-soaked and left for dead in the cold. Michael got out of the car and opened her door. She couldn't move. She couldn't place one foot in front of the other. She couldn't willfully walk to her doom.

Michael pried her from the seat. "It's okay," he said. "I got you."

She put up an ineffective attempt at a struggle; she locked her legs, and refused to move, but he bear hugged her.

"It'll be okay. I promise," he said, dragging her toward the door.

The neighbors pulled into their driveway, and it was close enough that if she screamed, they'd hear.

Say something.

But Michael forced her through the garage door and out of sight before she could.

***

She got some privacy in the hall bathroom. She'd told Michael she was going to take a shower and he promised to keep an eye on the door.

186

The shower window was narrow, and it cranked open on a hinge at the top. If she could pop the screen off, she might have been able wedge herself through. But Michael would expect it.

Reese washed and rinsed her hair, and while still nude, cranked open the window. Cold air oozed in and bit at her skin. She'd never tried removing the screen before, and didn't know how. She ran her fingers along the edges to find a way, but it may not have been removable.

A muffled ring pulled her attention to the bathroom door. She poked her head outside the shower curtain to hear Michael say, "Hello."

His voice was difficult to hear over the shower, so she stepped out and placed her ear against the door.

"Yes, she's fine. I'm here with her now."

Reese turned off the water and scrambled to put her clothes on. Jeans fought against her wet skin, but she shimmied into them. "Is that my mom?" she yelled. She cracked the door open and grabbed her shirt. "Michael?"

From the kitchen she heard him laugh. He was using his charming voice. The one she'd fallen in love with. The one she only heard when he was around other people. "I will take good care of her."

"Mom?" Reese wiggled into her T-shirt and ran into the hall. "Is that my mom?"

"Oh hey," Michael said. "Yeah. She's on her way out though and will call back later."

"Why didn't you get me?"

"You were in the shower. I told her about your dad and Florida and Buster passing away … you know, that you needed a minute."

"He didn't *pass away*. And why wouldn't you let me talk to her?"

"So, talk to her!" He threw his hands in the air.

"Was she at their hotel?"

"I don't know. I didn't ask."

She held the receiver and dialed *69 to get back the number that just called but there was no answer.

"Wait," Michael said. "She did say she was calling from a payphone. Maybe that's why."

Reese lowered herself into the chair at the kitchen table.

"She's extending her trip for a few more days. They're going to another hotel."

"What hotel?"

"She didn't say."

"So, she's just not coming back?"

"Not right away." Michael sat in the chair beside her. "But that's good, because now we have more time before we have to figure out where to go."

***

Michael spent the afternoon damn near gleeful that it was just the two of them. He made her a sandwich she didn't have the stomach to eat, and he fetched her water and watched her drink. He asked her to settle down in the basement with him in front of the TV, and he popped his *Caddyshack* VHS tape in again, but neither of them watched it.

Michael opened a map of the county and started picking areas he thought would be a good place to make a home. "There are all sorts of hunting cabins up here."

Her world, for the first time in her life, felt out of her control. Maybe this was her limit. This was the one thing she couldn't suck up and handle all on her own. Wouldn't her mother be so disappointed to know her daughter didn't grow up to be as independent as she'd hoped? She finally needed help with something, and now she had the guts to ask, it was too late. Anyone who might've cared was gone. Sebastian, Dr. Belinski, her own mother …

She stared through the TV screen and everything blurred into light and static. It reminded her of an image she'd seen in Astronomy Magazine of the cosmic microwave background. It was as if she stared all the way back to the beginning of time, and she wished she could be there now. As far as physically possible from her reality.

Michael had stopped talking for a while, but she wasn't sure how long. In her periphery, she caught him staring.

"What?" she said.

"Nothing." Michael rubbed his hands on his knees, shaking his legs nervously. "It's just"—he looked up the stairs—"I think I need to … *eat*."

"Oh."

He got up from the couch, paced as if he wanted her to say something, like he wanted her to find what he needed, then he began to sluggishly ascend the stairs.

"Where are you going?"

"I don't know." Michael stopped and turned. "You know what I mean, right? When I say I need to eat?"

"I think so. That's why I'm asking where you're going. I mean, where do you find … what it is that you're looking for?" It felt ridiculous to say *blood*. To say, *where are you going to find a person to eat?*

"I guess I'll just go outside and start looking."

Reese got up from the couch, ready to charge up the stairs and stop him from leaving. Stop him from doing whatever he was about to do. "What? You can't—"

"You got any better ideas?" Michael sat down on the steps. "The longer I wait, the longer I won't be able to control it. But if I get out there now and find someone, take just a little. I don't know. Maybe that'll work."

"You can't go attacking random people?"

"Why not? That's what happened to *me!*"

"That doesn't make it okay." She crossed her arms, hugging her bruised forearm against her body.

"I know it's not okay, but I also can't starve myself then accidentally kill someone."

"By someone, you mean me?"

"No. It would never be you." He met her at the bottom of the steps. "I would never, ever hurt you. I don't care what my instincts are telling me. I will fight it."

"What are your instincts telling you now?"

He closed the gap between them, pressing his body against hers. "A lot of things."

As his hands slid into hers, interlocking fingers, as his cool breath brushed her temple, she wondered if this would be the moment he lost control. Reese held her breath until Michael pulled away.

"I should leave the house for a while." Michael said, and ran upstairs. He wouldn't have to go far to find someone. The neighbors were likely home. He could pick one of them, or if he stumbled into the wrong room, or crawled through the wrong window, he might find someone's kid, or a baby. An easy target. Or, perhaps, since animals weren't off the menu, he'd find one of the many pets up and down her street, or a kid out sledding. And even if he did pin someone down, take only a little, and let them go, that kid would be traumatized for life.

"Wait!" she said, and regretted it the moment it left her lips.

✳✳✳

She encouraged Michael to return to the basement couch and they sat in front of the TV. She shut it off. "Does it hurt? How you feel?"

"It's uncomfortable. You know that hunger feeling? Or like when you're really thirsty and you have to chug a lot of water? It's like that. But not in my stomach. It's all over. Like I can feel my veins drying up. Every nerve ending is screaming all at once. It's like being really hungry and thirsty and horny and angry all at once, all over your body."

His eyes clouded over with a dark shadow, but he closed them and they returned to their normal color. "Are you sure you're okay with me doing this?"

"I don't know," Reese said. She was one hundred percent against him doing it, but there was no other option. This was the only way to keep people safe.

"It won't hurt," he said.

She glanced to her forearm. "It *did* hurt."

Michael put his lips on her bruise and kissed it. "But that's because you yanked away."

"Well—"

"I know." Michael's hands went up. "I know. But I didn't have much control then."

"And you do now?"

He took her arm into his hands and pulled it close to his mouth. "I do."

Reese tried to tug away, but he entrapped it in an icy grip.

"Trust me," Michael said.

She closed her eyes, allowed her arm to go limp as he drew it to his lips.

His kiss landed on her bruises like a cool compress. Her body stiffened as Michael's eyes met with hers and blackened.

"What's happening?" Reese whispered.

"I'm making sure I do this carefully, so I don't hurt you."

"Your eyes."

"Everything gets kind of dark and blurry. But I feel you." His lips touched her skin as he spoke. "I can feel your pulse on my lips. Are you ready?"

Reese's entire body stiffened while Michael's long, skinny fangs descended.

"Please." The word barely escaped her quivering lips.

"It's okay." He kissed her arm, planting soft lips in steady pulses along her bicep, her shoulder, to her neck. He traversed her exposed skin and moved down her other arm to the crook of her elbow. His jaw opened and the teeth pierced with the precision of a doctor's syringe. The pinch of the bite was momentary.

Michael positioned his body, kneeling before her, drawing blood from her arm.

She closed her eyes again, breathing as calmly as she could, reminding herself that if she didn't do it, it'd have to be someone else. Her arm ached as she tensed under his piercing bite.

"Okay," she said with a wince. She touched his face, giving a soft nudge. "Can you stop?"

She tapped on his broad shoulders, trying to get his attention, but he was unresponsive. Blood continued to be siphoned from her arm. He groaned with what sounded like pleasure.

Panic rose within, but thrashing or fighting would only tear her vessels and hurt like hell, so she pushed on him again.

"Stop," she said. "Michael, please." She scooted her body closer to his and ran her fingers through the back of his hair. "That hurts. You said you wouldn't hurt me." She pushed on his shoulder again, and finally, he pulled away. Michael snarled and threw his head back with an intoxicated smile. Two long, mosquito-like probosces dribbled her blood from the tips. She applied pressure to her arm and tucked her knees up under her while Michael writhed on the floor.

As he came down from the high of feeding on her blood, his eyes returned to normal, and his teeth retracted.

"Did that help?" she asked.

"More than you know." He nuzzled up against her.

She slipped out from under him and stood to leave the room. Lightheaded, she needed a moment to let it pass. Her head swam and her gut went queasy, and she couldn't do anything but sit back down beside him until it the wooziness went away.

"Nobody has come looking for us yet. Maybe this place is safe," Michael said. "Do you think your mom would let you have this place?"

She pictured living here with Michael for the rest of her life, keeping him from being set loose on the world. Maybe this was her path. Not to travel across the country or to discover a comet. Not to have her own place. Maybe Reese's lot in life was to be the person who could keep Michael from unleashing his malice onto the world.

CHAPTER FORTY-FIVE

REESE

Whether it was still Thursday or Friday—*or had Saturday come?*—didn't matter. Every day was the same. She woke, thinking this would be the day she'd make a run for it, but there were few opportunities that felt like the right time. Her appetite dwindled. She occasionally forced down a few bites of Top Ramen or Hamburger Helper, without the hamburger. They played games, watched TV, and Michael had never seemed more content. He posed hypothetical questions about their future, whether or not he could have a family now that his bodily fluids consisted of nothing but blood. He suggested they test it out and claimed he was joking, but Reese didn't laugh.

And whenever he wanted to take from her, she let him.

She was a ghost of herself. So much so she wondered if she'd died days ago, and now she was trapped in a cycle of all the things she'd done leading up to her death. All of this was her version of Hamlet's *undiscovered country, from whose borne no traveler returns.* If she were to die, could death possibly be worse than what she was going through already? Or would she simply fall asleep and be at peace?

Reese lay on her bed, gazing upon the painted stars, dreaming of being among them. Michael lay beside her, and out of nowhere said, "I still don't get what you saw in Sebastian Belinski." His jealousy would never fade away, even if he received some treatment to make his condition disappear, jealousy and rage had always been in his heart. It coalesced into a massive ball of unstable emotions and if Reese didn't say what he needed to hear, he'd go supernova.

"I wasn't thinking."

Michael laughed. "No shit. Why would you even go over in the first place?"

She'd talked about it so much, she didn't know what else to say to him. She scoured her brain for the least incendiary thing she could think of. "He said the project needed improvement, and I believed him. I think—"

"That's the problem!" Michael paced the floor. "You never think."

"I'm sorry." She stood to meet him, getting as close as she could. She reached for his hand.

Michael's nostrils widened for a second before he thrust his hands at her and flung her across the room. Her back smacked against the door and it cracked under her weight. The wind knocked from her lungs, she clawed for air while Michael stood before her, panting. She pulled in a wheezing breath, realizing she'd never get out of this alive. And Michael would never let her go. He would latch onto her and squeeze so hard to keep her, even if it meant her eyeballs popped out of her sockets and her guts ruptured outside her body. She'd be an inside-out disgusting mess of a human, and it would never matter to Michael, as long as she was his.

Reese charged at him and he grabbed her by the arms as she pressed her body against him, kissing his neck, slipping her arms under his and around his back in an embrace. She worked her mouth over his stubbled skin, teasing his earlobe with her tongue. "I'm with you."

His impassioned breaths lengthened and the tension in his shoulders relaxed.

"I'm with you and that's all that matters," she whispered, dragging her lips across his jaw to his lips.

Michael drove forward, using one arm to hold her steady, as he lifted her with the other and carried her to the bed. His free hand explored beneath her shirt, then fumbled with the button on her pants.

The stake was immediately below her, beneath the mattress, near the edge. If she could turn her body and get a free arm, she could get a grip on it.

He slid his hand into her panties and between her thighs, where his fingers were met by a dry, unwelcoming landscape. Rough fingers grazed her delicate skin and she pulled her hips back, drawing away from his touch.

Michael drew back, kneeling over her with one hand down her pants. His eyes had darkened. Slender teeth descended as he lunged at the crook in her elbow, creating new puncture wounds among the dozen she'd already received. She squealed at the sharp sting of his bite, but she continued to stretch her arm, bending it awkwardly to get to the stake.

His fingers wriggled around recklessly until they finally found moisture. She squirmed beneath, shifting her hips away from his touch.

"Please don't."

Michael pulled away from her and sat upright on his knees while his teeth dribbled blood. The puncture wounds on her arms seeped scarlet, and Reese didn't bother to hold pressure on them. She eased closer to the edge of the bed.

"I want you," Michael said. He forced her body away from the edge and centered her on the bed, far out of reach from the stake.

The protest in her heart remained trapped behind frozen lips. Nothing escaped her mouth but stunned silence. Michael went back to placing kisses on her body. He lifted her shirt up and over her head, kissing and licking the blood that he'd spilled on her belly. In her bra and jeans, her arms crossed in a futile attempt to create a barrier, she wished she could close her eyes and be somewhere else. Wake up to a normal day where this was all a nightmare. Instead, Michael lapped his tongue on the spots of blood that had seeped from her arm, then those that smeared on her ribs.

"Please don't."

"It's okay," he whispered.

She shook her head.

Michael smiled. "It's okay." He advanced, peeling away clothes.

Reese whispered, "No," as he pulled her jeans and panties around her hips. Unsure when she stopped whispering *no* aloud, and when it became an internal, inaudible chant in her head, a prayer to the universe to make it stope. She clenched her jaw to control the chattering of her teeth.

"You're shaking." Michael grabbed a blanket and pulled it over his shoulders as he lay his body down against hers. "I'm sorry I don't offer much body heat."

Reese gathered every last bit of courage in her soul to mutter one last stance: "I can't do this."

Michael pet the side of her face. His eyes blackened again. "It'll be okay."

He kissed at her neck as Reese shut her eyes. Her chest heaved, taking in panicked breaths. Then the pinch in her neck forced her eyes wide open. Michael had latched onto her jugular, body writing over hers.

She squeezed his biceps, pushing, but her pathetic attempt to make him stop was unnoticed. If she struggled any more, the sharp teeth could rip through her neck.

Michael forced himself inside, despite her clenching and scooting. She cringed as dry skin scraped between her legs, shoving himself where he was not welcome.

The thrusting created waves of nausea as he drove against her.

The moon came into view from the tiny corner basement window. A blur of a silvery glob, only visible if she craned her neck backward. A smidgeon of light the universe offered while Michael kept moaning, squirming, taking. As blood drained from her body, she grew weak. Too weak to fight back. Too weak to care. Reese had given up on reaching for the wooden stake. He was too strong for her to get out from under him. She gave up on pushing him away. She gave up on squeezing him out. She gave up on saying *no*.

Maybe he'd take so much she would pass out for a while, black out and forget it happened. Or maybe this would be the end and she'd never wake up. Perhaps that would be okay. Her fingers went cold and her strength weakened beyond the ability to keep the moon in her view. Reese's vision narrowed, blackening around the edges.

Michael's body tensed and he exploded inside of her. When they'd done it before, he either wore a condom or pulled out, but now he hovered over her, teeth pulled out of her neck, the long spindles dripped claret onto her breasts.

No matter how hard she pushed on him, it went unregistered. Michael was locked in place. She shoved at his belly to push him away and Michael's eyes returned from their shroud of blackness to meet hers. His teeth receded, and he relaxed enough to allow her to scrabble out from under him.

"What did you do?" She scooted into the corner against cement walls, cold against her bare back.

"It's okay. I can't get you pregnant."

Fluid spilled from her. She reached between her legs and fingers squished into a pool of Michael's ejaculate. Reese brought her shaking fingers into the blue light of the fish tank, revealing a viscous, black substance coating them. Her gag reflex brought vomit the back of her mouth, but she swallowed it.

"It's just a little blood," Michael said.

Reese kicked blankets away and crawled out of her bed as fast as she could move. Legs rubber, her feet found a way to stagger backward across her room. The loss of blood made her head dizzy, but she clutched her bedsheet to her chest and hurried toward the door.

"I mean, you should be used to blood down there, right?" he laughed.

Stunned by his comment, she couldn't manage to reply. She opened the door.

Michael had a hand on her before she could step out of the room. "I'm sorry! It just kind of happened."

"I have to go to the bathroom." Her words were strangled by hyperventilation.

"I said, I'm sorry." Michael released her, and she hurried up the steps as fast as she could, blood clots rolling down her thigh, sheet trailing behind like the train of some tragic princess's gown.

In the shower, she sat in the tub, hot water pouring down, scalding her between her open legs, as she tried to burn it all away. She'd set herself on fire if it would rid of the gore leaking from her.

Michael stood outside the door, knocking every few minutes, asking if she was okay. She'd muster an, "I'm fine," or "Just a minute."

Blood diluted in the steamy water, but some came out in clots and clumps. Her mother had kept a stash of Summer's Eve in the cabinet under the sink, and she fumbled through the instructions on use as her vision blurred.

The worst part was she didn't know whose blood it was since Michael's was no longer his own. It could've been the nameless donors in the IV he'd received at the hospital or the blood of the Belinskis. She wanted to scour every last cell out of her vagina, out of her uterus, rip her reproductive organs clean out of her body if it would take away the contaminated feeling within. She scrubbed herself until she was raw and painful, until the water finally ran clear. She would've stayed in the shower until her skin scoured off her body if the hot water hadn't run out. The icy stream of water exacerbated her trembling, and she fought to breathe. Unstoppable violent tremors rattled her body while her eyelids grew heavy. She'd lost too much blood.

No help was coming, no opportunity was going to present itself, and she may not have lived to see another moment if she didn't leave right now. Reese left the shower running, and cranked open the window. The screen popped out of its frame with little effort and fell to the snowy earth below.

She wrapped a towel around her body and put her foot on the shampoo ledge to climb up to the should-height window. Her depleted strength was now her enemy as she struggled to pull herself up. Her eyesight tunneled, darkening at the edges and blurring in the center. A clot of blood dribbled from between her legs and her foot slipped out from under her. Reese crashed to the bottom of the tub as the blood clot circled the drain. Cold water rained onto her body and she slipped into darkness.

Chapter Forty-Six

Trevor

Red incandescent lamp light bathed the dark walls. An IV bag of blood hung to Trevor's right. A catheter in his forearm delivered a steady drip of sustenance. Trevor grabbed his chest where Michael had stabbed him with the tree branch. A set of stitches ran down the center, but there was no longer a wound beneath.

"You've been nothing but a pain in my ass." The harsh, baritone voice came from the corner, where Jensen sat with his arms crossed. He leaned forward, round, polarized glasses sat on top of his head. He wore ripped denim jeans and high-top sneakers, and slicked his hair back with his hands.

Trevor eased to a sitting position and slid the IV from his vein, applying pressure.

"You were reckless," Jensen said.

"So were you."

Jensen lunged out of his chair with a snarl. "You think you're tough now because you turned someone? Don't fuck with me, Trevor."

"You screwed this up as much as I did, man."

"Yeah, but you …" Jensen paced with clenched fists. "I mean look at you. How the hell did you let some fledgling shit get the best of you?"

"He was stronger than me."

"The only way that's possible is if he changed someone."

"I tried to tell you—"

Jensen held up a hand, signaling for Trevor to keep his mouth shut.

Trevor spoke anyway. "Did you find him?"

"We tracked his footprints through the snow but lost them in the woods. If you gave us an address, we could've caught up to him."

"I wasn't about to let you get anywhere near his family."

"His family is a liability!"

Trevor dropped his feet to the floor and sat upright, refreshed like he'd just taken a power nap.

"What the hell happened to me?" He reached for the tray of tools beside him and lifted a pair of suture scissors.

"It took a while before the surgeon could see you, so it's been a couple days."

"I thought I was a goner." Trevor worked his way down the row of stitches, clipping and letting the pieces fall to the floor. He wiped away the dried blood at the suture holes and they healed instantly.

"Yeah, you were shredded. That kid did a number on you. Looked like you got attacked by a rabid bear." Jensen laughed. "You have the Blessing of the Immortal now. You created life when you turned Michael. That makes you untouchable. Dude, if you ever fucking listened to me, you'd know that!"

Trevor picked at the last stitch on his chest.

"Stake to the heart is like an off-switch, but with the Blessing, we can flip it back on so long as we can fix the heart. The surgeon had to remove a shit ton of splinters, but she got them all, and voila! You're back in business, baby."

"Would've been good to know. You didn't tell me all that."

Jensen leaned closer, speaking through clenched teeth. "If you stuck around, maybe I woulda had the chance."

Trevor hung his head. "So now what? Michael could've killed a dozen more people by now."

"Hoo boy! He did a number on that family. Wow! I almost wish I coulda seen it happen, you know?" Jensen clapped his hands together.

"No," Trevor said. "I don't know."

"All right, you big prude." He rolled his eyes. "They cleaned up the Belinski place real good. They made it look like they moved all of a sudden or something. I don't know, I don't work in that department."

"And there've been no other random murders in Byron on the news?"

"Nothing we seen. He got a good fill-up so he won't need to for a while. He's laying low, I bet. Or running away like you did."

"I'm done running away." Trevor stood.

"Good! Now let's go fetch this psychopath. I gotta meet this kid."

***

It was only a few hours before dawn when they arrived at the Braxton trailer. The Chevette was parked in the driveway beneath a layer of snow, even though Eleanor was supposed to have escaped to a safehouse. Curtains were drawn over the trailer's windows, backlit by the faint glow of flickering candlelight.

Jensen turned the ignition and the black Buick silenced.

"Shall we?" Jensen said, gesturing for Trevor to lead the way. He stepped out of the car to silence; there was no barking dog tonight to announce his arrival. Trevor hesitated on the steps, and lifted his fist to knock on the door.

"No need for formalities." Jensen pushed past and kicked the flimsy door in, knocking it off its hinges.

They stepped inside, and Dan jumped to his feet. A Bible dropped to the floor as he held up his hands. Eleanor was slumped over the arm of the couch behind him. She lifted her head with a gasp and scrambled upright out of a deep sleep. She reached for a wooden crucifix on the coffee table, clutched it to her chest and whispered a prayer.

Jensen turned to Trevor. "Who the fuck are these people?"

Eleanor's head struggled to stay upright. Her fingers lost their grip on the crucifix and it dropped to the floor. She sank into the couch and her arm went limp, punctures and bruises marking her skin.

Dan held his praying hands together. "She said it was okay, but I couldn't stop. I wanted to stop, but ..."

Jensen approached Eleanor and squatted beside her. "Bro, she's good as dead now."

Dan collapsed to his knees and his face contorted in grief. "Eleanor?" He groveled, taking her hand in his, then turned to Trevor. "She told me it was okay. She said it was okay."

"Why is she here? I told you to let her go!"

"She came back." Dan knelt before her, sobbing, then twisted to face Trevor. "You said you'd come back! Where were you?"

"I'll explain later," Trevor said. "We have to find Michael. He's dangerous."

Jensen laughed and looked toward Dan. "Looks like this dude is too."

"It was an accident!" Dan jumped to face Jensen.

"It always is," Jensen hissed through clenched teeth.

"If we can find him," Trevor said, "we can keep him from hurting more people."

Eleanor's eyes opened, and her dry, cracked lips parted. She lifted a hand as if it weighed a hundred pounds and let it fall to her chest. "Is Reese okay?"

Jensen whipped his head around. "Who the fuck is Reese?"

"His girlfriend," Trevor said. "But she's out of town. She doesn't know anything."

Jensen tensed, clenching his fists. "You didn't tell me there was a girlfriend."

Dan spoke up, eager to help. "They're inseparable, and when Michael left, that's where he was going. To find Reese."

"Okay, then, where do we find this girlfriend?" Jensen asked.

"She's not home," Trevor said.

"How the hell do you know?"

"I asked her."

"Now you're making friends with these people?"

"She doesn't know anything, and she's out of town, so this trail is dead," Trevor said.

"Well, if she's out of town, she won't mind if we swing by and snoop around for Michael," Jensen said. "Let's go."

Trevor turned toward the door and the whoosh of Jensen speeding across the living room rattled the knick-knacks on the shelf. Jensen lunged at Eleanor and grabbed her by the throat before she could scream. In a swift squeeze and jerk, her head twisted to the side, snapping. Her body went limp and she collapsed.

Trevor winced, as the memory of Rebecca tumbling down the stairs and Jensen standing over her body came flooding in. He froze in a pool of his trauma and regret, and he wanted nothing more than to rip Jensen apart.

Dan howled, arms raised to the ceiling as if his god might change the course of history. He fell to his knees, fawning over her lifeless body.

"This is on *you*!" Jensen's eyes blackened. His chest heaved. "You fed on her. Anyone who knows we exists dies. Those are the rules!"

"We could've taken her with us," Trevor said.

Jensen threw his head back, laughing. "I'm not babysitting for the rest of this road trip. We came to get Michael and this asshole. That's all."

"She was a good person. She was kind." Dan folded in half like a knife had been driven into him.

"Then you should've left her out of it," Jensen said.

Dan took one threatening step toward Jensen, but Jensen grabbed him by his face and squeezed.

"What the hell are you doing?" Trevor leapt between the two men and shoved Jensen away.

Jensen heaved, hackles raised. "The bitch was gonna die anyway. I did her a favor. Dan, is it? You took too much." Jensen pushed Trevor to the side and flung open the trailer door. "Clean up your own fucking mess. I'll be waiting in the car."

CHAPTER FORTY-SEVEN

MICHAEL

If there were a heaven, Michael wanted nothing to do with it anymore, because he had arrived in his own personal version of it. Here, in the cool dark of Reese's basement bedroom, with the soft glow of a tropical tank highlighting the curves of her flesh. Her softness. The fine hairs of her arms stood erect as he kissed along the bruises he'd created.

Reese's skin was pale and sickly when he'd found her in the bathtub basin passed out. He'd heard her fall, so he busted open the door, lifted her from the cold water, and brought her to bed where she could warm up. She'd been in and out of consciousness all night, and there were moments he worried he'd taken so much she might have changed. But the scab on the top of her head was still there, and there was no swelling in her gums.

"How do you feel?" he asked.

She sat up in bed and put her hands on her body; he'd dressed her in pajama pants and a sweatshirt while she was out. She swayed and held a hand over her mouth like she might throw up.

"Lemme get you some food." He swung his feet over the side of the bed.

"I think you took too much."

"No," Michael said, staying by her side. "I would never take too much. Just enough to get me through."

Reese's eyes drifted to the window, as if she were thinking of leaving again. Thinking about opening it up like she'd done in the bathroom earlier. When she was feeling better, he'd ask her what the hell she was doing. If she was trying to leave him. If she was ever going to love him as much as he loved her.

***

"Who do you want to die first?" he'd asked her before. Michael had posed the hypothetical question while sitting in the field behind her house. Dry autumn weeds reached for the sky.

"Neither." She'd locked her eyes on the stars. Gaze latched to their beauty. Sometimes he wasn't sure if she loved the sky more than she loved her own boyfriend, but he tried not to get upset about that.

"Like, say, when we're old," he'd said, "and you have to pick which one of us dies first. Who's it going to be?"

"Fine." She stood up, dusted off her bottom and told him, "Me. *I'll* die first."

"That's selfish," he'd said.

"Well, I'm not going to say I want *you* to die first." Reese stopped looking at the stars, baffled by his statement.

"Think about it," he'd explained. "I'd want *you* to die first, so you wouldn't have to live in grief for the rest of your life. If *you* die first, *I'd* be the one to suffer, so you wouldn't have to."

***

And now, as he sat beside her, he understood with full clarity that neither of them had to die at all.

"I don't ever want to spend a day without you by my side."

Her eyes lowered and she returned her head to her pillow, body curling into itself like a dying spider. He covered her with a blanket. "What do you want? I'll give you anything you want. I'll go get it for you right now."

Her breaths turned shallow, and he could hear her sluggish heartbeat within her chest.

"Maybe some crackers and juice? Like after a blood donation?" he asked. He didn't wait for an answer before running upstairs to the kitchen. He grabbed a bottle of orange juice from the fridge and some Ritz crackers from the cabinet.

Reese was at the edge of her bed when he returned to her room, slipping her feet into a pair of house slippers. "I want to leave."

"It's not safe." He handed her a sleeve of crackers.

She struggled, but Reese picked at the wrapper to peel it open. "You say you want me to be happy."

"Yes!"

"Then you have to let me go." Her hand ran along the bruising on her arms.

"I'm working on a plan, I promise."

She took a sip from the bottle of orange juice and whispered, "I don't want to die."

"That's just it!" Michael said. "You don't have to … ever. Neither of us have to worry about outliving the other."

Reese's hand froze on its way to delivering a cracker to her mouth.

"Reese." He knelt on the floor beside her, taking her hand into his. "Will you be with me forever?"

She didn't say anything. She just sat there frozen, with a cracker paused by her lips, like time had stopped. For every second without a word, his anxiety grew. He couldn't handle rejection now. Not after everything that had happened to him.

"I want you to be like me," he said. "If you're like this, we can be together, literally forever." Michael moved in for a kiss and she turned her head away.

He grabbed her chin, forced her back to him, and he was met by dry, soft lips. Her heart picked up its pace, beating with intensity, and his pulse matched hers, thrumming in his ears, his lips, his cock. If she'd let him, he could carefully take the rest of her, binding her to him infinitely.

He lay Reese down while she shook her head, eyes locked on the window above her.

"It will be quick. And then I'll get you blood from someone else, and we can get out of here. You and me."

Reese's body tensed, pushing against him. Her arm was stretched over the edge of the bed, bent and fishing between the mattresses.

"What are you doing?" Michael asked.

A white, glaring light flashed through the window as a car pulled into the driveway.

"Damn it." Michael glanced at the clock on Reese's dresser. It was already five in the morning. "Your mom said she was staying longer." He bounded up the basement stairs, ready to meet Reese's mother in the driveway, while Reese staggered up the steps behind him.

Michael peeked between the curtains to see a black vehicle he didn't recognize. "What's your mom's boyfriend drive?"

Reese held one fist to her mouth, looking like she might throw up.

"Hey," Michael ran to her side as she wobbled. "Okay. I don't have to take anymore today. It can wait. I can wait as long as you need. We'll wait for you to feel better first. I'd wait forever for you."

Reese hobbled across the kitchen, trying to find her balance by holding the countertop.

A crash, then a whoosh of cold air rushed into the house as the front door was busted in. Michael grabbed Reese by the arm and shoved her into the kitchen nook, out of view from the front door.

"Well, well, well ..." a stocky man said, storming into the house wearing a hypercolor windbreaker. "You must be the infamous Michael Braxton." Behind him, to his surprise, Trevor stood alive and strong, then Dan Delgado stepped into view.

"What the hell is going on?" Michael said. In his periphery, Reese had crouched under the table.

"This is Jensen," Trevor said. "We're here to talk."

Jensen closed in, "I'm beyond talking. I'm here to tell you flat out that you are coming with us."

"I'm not going anywhere."

"You're leaving a pile of bodies in your wake, bro," Jensen said. "You need to learn some manners and start cleaning up after yourself."

Michael cringed at the accusation. "You've got the wrong guy. I've been here the whole time."

"Michael, please. Just listen." Dan stood several steps back on the threshold.

"You here with your girlfriend?" Jensen asked, extending his neck to snoop into the living room.

"I told you," Trevor interrupted. "The girlfriend is out of town."

"Yeah," Michael said. "Florida. To meet her dad." He eyed Trevor, wondering what the guy's deal was. Wondering if he could trust him, or Dan, or anyone.

Jensen inspected the room. "And what about the girl's mother?"

"Her mom is in the Poconos on vacation," Michael said.

"So, you're here alone?" Jensen asked.

"Unless you count the fucking fish. Yeah. I'm here alone. These traitors didn't tell you my mom kicked me out of the house?" Michael nodded to Dan. "So where is she, Dan?"

"Well." Jensen stepped past Michael into the kitchen. "You don't gotta worry about her no more."

Michael kept himself placed between Jensen and the table at every step. "What's that supposed to mean?"

Trevor and Dan eased into the kitchen from the foyer. Dan's eyes shot straight to Reese, giving away her position without a word.

Jensen grinned and sprinted lightning fast toward her. The table flipped upside down with one swipe of his arm, and Reese guarded her head with her hands.

The moment played out as if he had all the time in the world to calculate each move. Time paused for him to make things right, to protect her. She was all that mattered. The table legs spun upward while Reese's trembling legs brought her to her feet. Her eyes clenched shut with tears dripping down her cheeks. Tears he wished he could take from her and cry himself. Tears for every punch his father delivered. Tears for each bruise and mosquito welt left on his skin. Tears for never earning his love, nor his mother's. None of it mattered anymore because he'd never have to cry real tears again, and he was so close to having the life he deserved. But that life included Reese. Without her in it, he may as well die.

Jensen closed in on Reese, but Michael thrust himself between the two of them faster than he'd ever moved before.

CHAPTER FORTY-EIGHT

REESE

Reese had grabbed the wooden stake from under the mattress and charged up behind Michael, sliding it behind her out of view when he'd asked about who was in the driveway.

Lightheadedness overwhelmed her and she had been staggering to the bathroom when the front door busted in.

Despite her languid state, when Jensen made eye contact and flipped the table, it sent a jolt of electricity through her muscles. She was on her feet in a fraction of a second. Moments ago, she'd lost the will and strength to push Michael away, but some instinct to stay alive was still within her.

Michael intersected Jensen's attack, but she was trapped between the upturned table and the counter. Jensen threw Michael to the floor and Trevor motioned to her to come to him, but they were fighting in the only pathway out of the breakfast nook.

Michael struggled beneath, but Jensen held him by his biceps and kept him down, ramming him against the floor.

Michael locked furious eyes with her and clenched his teeth. "Run!"

"Don't worry about her. We're not interested," Jensen said.

Reese scrabbled over the tipped table and onto the opposite peninsula counter, rolling and falling on the other side. The point of the stake tucked in the back of her pajama pants scraped her back.

Beyond the counter, there was commotion, Jensen yelled *grab her*, there was shouting, furniture knocked over. Background noises were blurred by her focus to get away. She righted herself and was about to sprint for the garage door, but it opened. Dan Delgado stood blocking her path.

"Don't you touch her!" Michael said.

Jensen kept Michael pressed into the floor and turned to look at Reese. His eyes traveled her body from top to bottom.

Michael headbutted Jensen, while Trevor stood with his arms to his sides near the front entrance on the opposite side of the kitchen, doing nothing. Watching. Waiting for something, but Reese didn't have the time to consider what his motives were. While Michael and Jensen thrashed, Dan closed in on Reese.

"Are you okay, dear?"

Bodies tumbled behind her. Michael threw a fist that connected with Jensen's jaw. Jensen yelled something about going willingly, getting *all the blood he wanted*. But it was muffled sounds in the background to Dan's blackening eyes.

She reached behind and lifted her shirt, wrapping her fingers around the stake, calculating in her mind how she'd swing it at him so that it could plunge into his chest. Perhaps she'd aim for the thigh, just to slow him down so she could get away.

Before she could do anything, Trevor was between them. "Get out!" he said to Dan, but Dan held his gaze.

Michael raised his hands in abdication, eyes locked on the other men. "Okay, okay, okay! I give up."

Jensen pulled a short stake from under his coat and held it over Michael. It was polished and stained dark cherry with an embellished handle. "I don't want to have to use this, because it hurts like a bitch. So quit fucking around, kid. Come willingly and nobody gets hurt."

Michael scooched back and stood slowly, palms raised. "Okay. I will."

Through the gap in the curtain over the kitchen sink, daylight beamed through and reflected off a glass on the counter. Reese kept her hand clenched around the stake and steadied herself.

"Dan." Michael calmed his tone, but his chest still heaved, veins bulging in his neck. "You killed my mom and you're gonna kill the only person I have left?"

Dan shook his head, eye color returning to normal. "I didn't kill her!"

"Then where is she?" Michael asked.

Dan's eyes darted to Jensen. "I'm sorry, son."

Michael's face dropped. His arms fell to his sides, and he stood silently, chest swelling, and she imagined him getting bigger and bigger with each breath. He was like a dying red supergiant, burning up all its fuel and collapsing in on itself. Too much mass to contain, it would explode in a supernova, sending an explosive shockwave across the universe. Reese backed all the way to the kitchen sink.

She slunk to the floor crouching and eased closer to the peninsula counter.

"Is she really dead?" Michael asked. "Didn't you at least turn her?"

Jensen stood directly behind Michael with a smirk on his face. "We can't just run around turning everyone."

Another foot forward and Reese could round the edge of the corner and slip away toward the front door, but Trevor spotted her. He made eye contact for a second, then turned his back to her, situating himself as a shield. Reese kept low and made her way across the kitchen.

"It was him, Michael." Dan pointed to Jensen. "He killed her."

"She was good as dead anyway," Jensen said. "You practically drained her!"

Reese's queasiness rushed back to her. Her head was dizzy but she continued forward quietly.

"We could've saved her!" Dan said.

Jensen pinned Dan against the wall and Reese made a break for it. She sprinted toward the foyer but, before she could get to the door, a hand fell onto her shoulder and flung her across the living room. She landed on the couch and it tilted, banging into the wall behind it. Her arms smacked against the coffee table and her fingers lost their grip on the wooden stake. It fell to the floor.

Michael and Trevor were both between her and Jensen before he could get to her.

"Ooooh!" Jensen picked up the stake from the floor. "Clever girl!" He tucked it into his jacket and held tight to his own cherry stained weapon.

Trevor said. "Just let her go."

"You know the rules," Jensen said. "She's a liability."

"I know," Trevor said. "But she's just a kid. Nobody's gonna believe her."

Without a word, Michael charged at Jensen, and the two tumbled to the floor.

Dan's eyes had darkened again, stalking toward Reese. She ran for the door, but he blocked her. "I'm sorry Reese."

Trevor grabbed Dan's arm while Jensen and Michael tumbled, fists flying and ribs breaking.

Reese was again backed into the breakfast nook. She reached for the knife block and pulled out the largest Ginsu blade. The chef's knife that Handsy Hank had used to unsuccessfully cut through watermelons in one strike. She clutched it in her palm and dove over the counter at another attempt to escape. Trevor kept Dan in the foyer, and Jensen had Michael pinned against the wall.

Cuts and gashes had broken open on their faces and arms, and Michael fell to the floor. A wound on his forehead stitched shut on its own, but grief took him. Reese could see it on his face. The loss of his mother weighed him down and he curled into a fetal ball. She could see the aimlessness he'd shown her the night he'd called claiming to be suicidal. The hopelessness of despair over how his life had turned out. Michael caved under Jensen's power and gave up.

Michael's met eyes with Reese from across the room. He nodded to her, blood tears seeping.

Jensen's back was to Reese now and she could slip away unseen. He straddled Michael and elevated his fancy wooden stake over his head. "Just gonna turn off the lights for a bit, dude."

Michael sobbed. A guttural, primal thing that rose from his core and filled the room. An animalistic scream like the one she'd heard from the side of the road a week earlier. The desperate, agonizing cry for help that had called her to take action. To traverse the icy embankment and go to the victim's side.

Her feet froze in place. If she ran now, there'd be no time to get away. Jensen would be behind her in seconds. No matter how fast she drove, they'd find her.

She hurried across the kitchen faster than she could think.

Trevor's back was to her, keeping Dan from going after her.

She gripped the knife in a sweaty palm and raised her arm, then swung it out away from her body so she could use what was left of her dwindling strength to bring it down.

Michael's eyes were shut, blood squeezing between his lids.

Jensen turned his head, but it was too late.

The knife came down with all the force she could congregate. It sliced through flesh, meeting resistance instead of cutting clear through.

She shrieked as the metal reverberated through her palm. Jensen buckled, but she yanked the knife from the back of his neck and swung again. Every nerve in her body sparked alive, screaming, weeping, swinging … swinging … swinging. The spine snapped and the knife sank through the meaty thickness of Jensen's neck. Reese released her grip, the knife dropped, and she staggered backward. Jensen twitched on his knees as Michael climbed out from under, backing himself against the adjacent wall.

Jensen's head teetered from side to side and fell forward. His neck severed, head dangling from sinew upside down, eyes still blinking for several seconds before finally losing life. His body crumpled to the floor.

Trevor and Dan stood in stunned silence.

Reese's lungs struggled to pull in enough air as hyperventilation took over. Her body quaked.

Michael staggered to his feet and approached her side.

His wounds closed in front of her eyes, blood smeared over his face and body. He stepped over Jensen and scooped an arm around Reese. "Let's get out of here."

CHAPTER FORTY-NINE

REESE

Reese held her stiffened hands to her sides with the steel of the Ginsu knife handle a memory in her hands. Michael stood in front of her, squared up to Trevor and Dan.

"Nobody touches her," Michael said.

Trevor groaned. "She can go."

"Get your coat!" Michael said.

Reese's vision pulsed with her heart as she fumbled into the closet. She traded out her slippers for a pair of sneakers by the door. The backs of the sneakers folded over when she jammed her feet into them, but she didn't bother to fix them. Michael grabbed her arm and looked in her eyes. A darkness was there. Not the pitch black orbs she'd seen when he wanted to feed, but something else behind the eyes.

"Get me a coat too," he said.

Trevor stepped closer and said, "Dude, just come with us for the day. Let her go."

"I'm not going anywhere without her."

"Son," Dan said. "She's not safe here. She's not safe with us."

Michael stormed closer to Dan. "Us? Or she's not safe with *you*?"

Dan held up his hands in prayer. "Forgive me. I couldn't protect your mom."

Michael's voice lowered, his shoulders tensed. He kept his back to Reese and said, "Go start the car."

Without a moment's hesitation, her trembling hands found the keys on the hook, and she swung open the garage door. She hurried across the cement floor as Dan Delgado screamed from inside. Trevor began shouting and the raucous sounds of a fight followed.

Michael would end both of their lives today, and if he didn't, one of them would kill Michael. Light poured through the garage door window, and she flung open the outside door.

Sunshine hit her face, and she stood in the sweet liminal space between Michael and freedom. Her feet wouldn't move forward. Thrashing continued within the house. Screaming melded with growling and clamor.

Reese couldn't move another step out the door without knowing for certain they wouldn't be following her. But the part that scared her most was the fact that her hesitation was because she still loved him. Not a romantic love—not anymore. But a familiar one. Michael was her best friend. He was her family. He was just a broken kid—much like herself—who could've had a better lot in life if it weren't for all the things that had happened to him. He could've grown up to be a better man had he had an ounce of helpful guidance during his upbringing.

Reese, against all sensibility, against all reason and rationale, closed the door to the outside and headed back to Michael.

∗∗∗

Blood streaks painted the kitchen floor and walls. Chairs were upturned and broken. Dan Delgado lay lifeless on the floor, neck ripped open and a dark crimson puddle beneath him. His palm was open at his chest, holding the gold cross pendant he wore around his neck. Jensen's body was a few feet away, head detached from his body.

Reese's ears pulsed and her vision narrowed. Nausea and dizziness battled with her senses as she headed toward the living room, navigating between the dead bodies. Michael pinned Trevor to the floor. Muscles tensed and his back was like a beast, hunched and rippling with every swing.

Trevor flipped him over and they tumbled while Reese drew closer. She knelt near Jensen's body and wrapped numb fingers around the wooden stake. Blood splattered onto her clothes as she shuffled closer to Michael and Trevor. If she stepped between the two now, would she feel the blows of their fists? Or would they'd go right through her and shut her down like a computer switch.

"Reese! Help me!" Michael straddled Trevor against the base of the couch, hands clutched around his neck.

With trepidation, she eased closer, remembering why she once loved Michael. She remembered the late night talks under the stars. She remembered solidarity through their broken lives. Every good memory she thought had been drowned by the bad washed over her mind in a shockwave of emotions. A nebulous hint of light still glowed in the vast expanse of hopelessness.

"Reese?" Michael held Trevor down and leaned to the side. He nodded to the stake in her hand. "Hurry!"

Trevor didn't look away from Michael as he struggled beneath him.

"Babe, it's okay," Michael said. "You're doing great. Just one more of these assholes and we get out of here."

She saw the light of the moon on his face the night he held her hand when she read a letter from her estranged father. She saw the stars twinkling overhead as they laughed about neglectful parents. She felt his lips against hers and tasted his tears when he cried about his football career coming to an end. She felt his sweaty palm in her hand as they walked to school, just the two of them against the world.

And she hated that he took it all away from her. She hated he made the choice, over and over again, to be just like his father.

Reese charged in while Michael leaned to the side with his hands still locked on Trevor, opening up a space so she could impale him. She dove in, dropping her keys so she could clutch the stake securely with both hands.

Reese thrust with all her body weight behind the stake as it plunged into Michael's back. Her mouth opened wide with a scream that wouldn't release, and if she didn't see the tip of the stake pierce his back, she'd think her own heart had been impaled.

Trevor's eyes went wide.

Michael's back arched but the stake stopped short. He howled, releasing Trevor, reaching for the stake that had only sank an inch deep. Reese staggered backward, and without a moment's hesitation, she used every emotion unleashing within her as fuel to raise a foot, and kicked the end of the stake, lodging it deeper.

Michael's arms shot out to his sides and he froze, choking on his breath as Trevor crawled out from under him.

A look of betrayal cast over Michael's eyes as he turned to face her. Heartache like she'd never seen him experience before. Michael struggled to a stance, clutching the pointed tip of the stake that had exited through his chest. He ran his fingers along the apex, never allowing her to leave his gaze. His eyes filled with blood and it spilled over his lower lids.

"Get out." Trevor coughed from his slumped position on the floor. Blood sprayed from his mouth.

She backed away from Michael, mouth agape, and a high-pitched whisper of a scream escaped. Drool dribbled over her lower lip and tears poured into her mouth.

"I'm sorry!" She backed against the dividing wall at the foyer and folded in half.

Michael took another step closer, arm stretched toward her. He was inches away when she turned and ran out the front door.

She'd dropped her keys inside, but didn't consider for second going inside to retrieve them. She'd have to get away somewhere on foot.

Michael stumbled out behind her. Blood dripped from his chest into the packed snow. He flinched, raising his arms over his head to protect himself from the rising sun.

The street was still engulfed in shadow from the tall trees, so she headed behind her house and up the slope to her stargazing field, flooded with the morning sunlight. Her sneakers slipped on the climb.

She'd expended all her energy. Every step through the deep snow was an epic struggle but she had to keep moving.

Her stomach wretched and Reese forced herself to keep walking though debilitating dry heaves, while Michael continued to limp behind her.

"Reese!" He shouted her name between sputtering coughs.

He stood against the backdrop of the sun. The shadow figure whom she couldn't escape no matter how hard she fought to move her legs. But finally, Michael stopped his pursuit, turning to face the sun, and his scream echoed across the empty field. A war cry of fury and defeat. To Reese, it was his desperate call to the universe for salvation, which would go unanswered. His silhouetted body emitted snaking trails of steam, evaporating in the icy morning air.

Reese, drawn by gravity or curiosity—or perhaps love or pity—no longer walked away from him, but toward him.

Michael dropped to his knees facing the sun. The stake in his back sizzled at the point of impact. Blood soaked through his shirt, turning the fabric the color of wine. She kept a couple meters between them, moving around to the front of him.

Michael's roar diminished to a pulsating whimper. Skin blistered and popped, and flesh blackened on his knuckles. Flames engulfed his eye sockets like two small campfires eating away at his lids. Burnt flesh turned to black smoke that swirled into small clouds, disappearing against the blue sky.

He reached out his hands. "I know you're there." A stream of blood seeped from his lower lip, drooling to the snow around his knees. "I know you didn't mean to do it." Michael coughed, cupping his hands around the pointed end of the stake. Blinded in the vast emptiness of the wintery field, he may as well have been floating through the abyss of space. Cold, dark, and alone.

Careful not to alert him to her location, Reese covered her breath with her hand.

Skin on his forehead rippled like water about to boil. His arm hair singed, and his skin crusted and charred to a black crisp. Michael coughed, spraying blood across the snow and onto her face.

"Stay with me, Reese?" He sat in the snow with his legs extended before him, like he had on the curb the night he called her to save him from killing himself. Shoulders slumped, arms limp in his lap. Defeated. "This is the last thing I'll ever ask of you. Just stay with me until I die?"

She didn't understand why, but her heart broke for Michael. For the soul-crushing agony he'd felt over the loss of his mother. For her betrayal as his best friend. Blistering and burnt, his bottom lip quivered. Blood tears soaked his scorched face, filling the blackened gouges and grooves with a scarlet glaze.

He picked up handfuls of snow, pressing them against his skin, but no relief came to his expression. He clutched his chest, losing the strength to speak. "Don't leave me"—he gagged on blood, spewing it out in a mist—"to die alone."

Part of her wanted to open her window and let him in, give him a warm and comforting place to heal. She wanted to place a hand against his heart, to at least soothe his anguish for this moment. A blister popped on his face, blood oozed out, and she considered kissing him.

The open field had plenty of room for her to take a seat beside her old best friend and let him feel loved while he died in excruciating pain. But if she did, she feared she'd be sitting with him forever. She'd never have the strength to pick herself up out of the snow. She'd forever be trapped in his gravity, in his atmosphere, and choking on the fumes of his ashes.

The snow crunched underfoot as she stepped away.

"Just tell me one thing before you go," he said.

She paused, ready for him to ask her if she loved him. The answer was *yes*. A resounding, pitiful, hate-filled, disgusting *yes*.

Michael collapsed to his side in the fetal position, hugging his knees to his chest. "Will you tell me *why?*"

She offered no explanation.

Tears and mucus dripped from her eyes and nose, freezing in the icy air. But she held her breath so as not to make a sound. He didn't get to hear her cry.

She turned her back to Michael and walked away.

"Reese?"

She continued forward, eyes locked on the opposite side of the field about a hundred yards away.

Don't look back. But as she neared the tree line, she glanced over her shoulder to be sure he hadn't followed her. He lay motionless against the morning sun as another man walked toward him.

It was Trevor, she assumed. Draped in a blanket to protect himself from the sun, he looked like a cloaked harbinger of death. He stood facing her and Reese crouched low, hoping to remain out of sight.

From the distance, it was difficult to tell, but it looked as if Trevor raised a hand to her. A goodbye, perhaps. The forest beyond the field was still in shadow and she wondered if anyone lurked in the darkness, waiting for her to exit the safety of the rising sun.

Uncertain if she could make it out the other side, Reese buckled, body finally succumbing to her lack of energy. Adrenaline wore off and she fell backward into the snow. The icy cold on her head was a welcomed discomfort. She lay in the field, close to the woods, at the edge of light and dark. It was her terminator line between her past and future, the beginning and end.

An electric blue sky hung overhead. The kind of sky that typically came before a crystal clear night of stargazing. Her vision faded again. She needed to rest for a moment before moving on. The edges of the sky blackened, creating a blue tunnel of light. Her mind raced up the tunnel, beyond the atmosphere, where she could float among the stars. She would've liked to stay there for a while, but shouting from across the field brought her back to reality.

She'd have to keep moving, or everything she'd done would be for nothing. Reese excavated the last of her strength and pushed herself from the ground. There was no time to raise her eyes to the sky for now. There was no object up there that could offer comfort. She had to keep going.

CHAPTER FIFTY

TREVOR

Six months had passed since he'd called for a clean-up at the place in Byron. Extensive cover-ups were necessary, but the organization in Syracuse was quick and efficient. Forged documents and planted travel vouchers led missing persons investigators to dead ends with no foul play suspected. Fortunately, the girl was smart enough she didn't try to go public with her story, and there was enough evidence in the Perkins' house to prove to the organization she had traveled to Florida, and the mother was out of town during the incident. There was no reason to pursue either of them.

He wanted to reach out to Reese after everything had happened and let her know she'd be okay. That nobody would be after again. He had watched her house for a month after things settled down, but he never saw her coming or going. The mother returned home and her boyfriend Quentin moved in, but Reese was gone. For all Trevor knew, the kid could've been driven to suicide. He tried to not to think about that though. He also tried not to think about the moment he stood over Michael's burnt body in the field and considered lobbing his head off with a Ginsu knife and burying the parts so nobody could ever bring him, or Jensen, back. But he called for the clean-up crew instead. He let them gather the two most vile men he'd ever known and take them in for surgery.

Who was Trevor to judge what they'd become? They were a version of himself in some ways, and despite the things they'd done, maybe they deserved a chance to do better.

When Michael woke after having the stake removed from his heart, after the burns healed, Trevor was by his side, warning him not to say a word about Reese to anyone. If he really loved the girl, he had to let her go, or the organization would silence her. Michael came at him, furious fists swinging, eyes black, but was quickly sedated by staff. The kid would need a lot of help. He checked in with Michael periodically over the months, but the kid spiraled into depression, with fewer outbursts of rage, but more attempts at taking his own life. Trevor had failed him.

All Trevor could do now was to think forward. He'd fed from bags and willing donors in the city. He'd trained himself to be sated by the blood from animals. There were times, as he sat alone in pa's hunting cabin, hunched over the carcass of a fresh doe, that he realized how traumatizing it must appear to see him feed. How haunted Reese must be by her experience.

Now, he stood outside a bar in Oswego, NY at closing time. Concealed in the shadow of a dumpster, he'd be unseen by patrons stumbling out all evening. It was spring in New York, but there was still a crisp chill in the air coming off Lake Ontario.

The bar door jingled, and a group of college students stumbled out laughing. Among them, Trevor spotted his oldest—now his *only*—son, Ryan. He wanted to run to his boy. Scoop him into his arms and squeeze him. He needed Ryan to know that he was loved. That his dad still cared about him, and would always be watching out for him. That Ryan's mother and brother did not die in some random attack, and that his father didn't abandon him.

Trevor dreamed of leaving a note for him. An apology. An explanation, perhaps. What he'd give to stop him on the street, offer to buy him a coffee and chat about how he was doing in school and whether he had someone special in his life.

But the only person who would benefit from making contact would be Trevor. The only person who'd feel any better would be himself. Trevor needed to leave Ryan alone. Even if that meant Ryan believed his father to be a villain. It was the truth, after all. He would accept this curse. Accept his fate for what he'd done, and that he would forever long to hold his son in his arms.

However, he would follow Ryan for as long as he could, unseen. He'd be waiting around the corner as he entered adulthood. He'd lurk in shadow for every important moment. Graduation, marriage, promotions … and Trevor would even keep his distance the day he became a grandfather. Nothing in the world could keep him from keeping his son; his only light in the ever-growing expanse of darkness.

Chapter Fifty-One

Reese

It'd been nearly a year since she'd driven a stake through the heart of Michael Braxton. A year since the man, Trevor, chased her down in the woods after her escape and warned her never to say a word to the authorities, or else they'd be after her and her family. A year of nightmares and medications. She'd missed the remaining school year, and graduation.

Several days after that bloody day in Byron, Reese's mother returned to find the house spotless. Exactly the way it was when she'd left. Someone had snuck inside, fixed the cracked doors, scrubbed the bloodstains from existence, and removed any sign that there had been two brutal murders in the kitchen. Despite the lack of evidence, Reese had told her everything as calmly as possible. As *not-crazy* as a person could tell such a story, but Mom didn't believe her. Her face twisted and she yelled at Reese for making up lies about *a good boy like Michael.*

Several days had passed, and Reese was adamant in convincing her mother she had been telling the truth. She'd refused to walk out the door, and she'd wake screaming in the middle of the night. Within a week, Mom sent her daughter away for someone else to deal with her. She'd spent her nineteenth birthday alone in a state-prescribed, drug-induced numbness that blocked any sense of anxiety, along with most other emotions as well.

According to her psychiatrist, who had connections with police, there was no proof that anyone had died or gone missing. Plenty of evidence existed to support that Michael maintained the residence in Byron, but worked out of the area. His mother and Dan Delgado had eloped to Mexico, and the Belinskis had started new lives in the Virgin Islands. None of the missing persons or deaths could be corroborated. After a few months, Reese began questioning whether any of it happened at all.

Reese's brain—according to her psychiatrist—created the story to justify her abandonment issues. Everyone left her, and she broke. After showing substantial progress in recognizing that her delusions of trauma were simply fabrications of her fractured mind, the doctors at the Psychiatric Center of CNY released her.

Mom agreed to give her a lift home. Mom hadn't visited much since Reese had been institutionalized, and Reese didn't care to speak to her anyway, considering how her mother responded to her traumatic experience. She hugged her mother for less than a second and followed her into the parking lot, scanning for danger.

Reese slid in the passenger side.

"I'm glad you're coming home," Mom said. "I've got all the paperwork for getting your GED. Fat Joe's said they'd be happy to have you back, so long as you don't scare the customers."

Reese crossed her arms over her body and eyed the lot. Thick clouds hung low, like they were about to spill.

Mom continued, "So, you're all better now?"

She looked to her mother but didn't know how to answer, so she gave a subtle shrug of her shoulder.

Mom started the engine and put the vehicle in drive. They pulled out of the parking lot and she said, "I love you, honey, but you can't say the things you were saying. Especially if you want to get a job."

"Even if some of it was true?" she asked.

"Jesus Christ, Reese." Mom sighed, gripping the wheel. "You want to know what part was real? The part where you were found miles from home with track marks up and down your arms."

Reese picked at the edge of her fingernail. "No. The part where Michael was abusive."

Mom went silent and made the turn onto the highway ramp. She didn't say anything for several miles as they headed home.

Reese stared out the window as snow-covered trees whizzed by. She'd like it if time would do the same. Fast forward to her future when this was all behind her. When she was better, healthier, stronger in spite of it all.

They pulled into the driveway and Mom cut the engine, finally breaking the silence.

"What does it matter now what he did? Let it go."

Reese went to her basement room and closed herself inside. She hit the switch on her aquarium hood and the tank lit up with a green glow. Algae covered the glass walls, it clung to plastic plants and gravel, and there were no neon tetras swimming within.

She lay on her floor because her bed held memories she didn't care to revisit. She flipped through the pages of an old Astronomy magazine from the previous year. Comet Hale-Bopp was a spectacle she never had a chance to observe. She'd seen pictures in the newspaper, and on TV, but she never ventured out at dark to view it. Maybe when she was feeling brave enough, sometime in the years coming, there'd be another chance to see a comet. Another chance to go outside under the stars and witness the beauty of the universe once again.

A scratch at her window startled her to her feet. Every nerve ending in her body sparked to attention. A chipmunk skittered along the base of her window outside. She pictured it nuzzling up close to the window for warmth, then she tapped against the glass to scare it away.

Mom came down the stairs and opened the door but didn't enter. "Sorry about the fish. I fed them, but they started floating to the surface after a couple months."

Reese stared into the algae-ridden water without a word to say.

"Maybe you weren't ready to come home after all," Mom said.

"I'm fine."

"Good. I've been thinking about what you said. About how Michael … abused you." The last two words fought to exit her lips.

Reese faced her mother and waited for some sort of advice. Something that would help her through this nightmare of a phase in her life.

"I don't know what *really* happened," Mom said. "Drugs? Abuse? I don't know. And I don't know if I ever will."

"I told you—"

Mom held up a hand and closed her eyes, impatience and annoyance painted all over her face. "Maybe I screwed up as a parent. I'm not so proud that I can't admit that. But you're a grown-up now. And it's time to do just that. *Grow up*."

The words pierced her heart, but maybe it was exactly what she needed to hear.

Mom went on. "That means—especially for us women—that we have to be tough. We have to take all the bad things that happen and bury it six feet under, or we will not survive in this world. It's a man's world. I can't tell you how many times I've seen woman after woman speak out against some guy and nobody ever believes them. Guess who loses their career? It ain't the guy." Mom sighed and turned her back. "You're welcome to stay here with me for a while until you're feeling better. I'm not a monster. I'm not going to kick you out unless you do something that forces me to. So, get your GED. Get a job. And get on with your life. That's the best advice I can give you."

Chapter Fifty-Two

Reese

Reese Perkins sat in the manager's office of Fat Joe's while a couple walked in up front. From the back, she had a view into the lobby, partially obstructed by the sandwich chute. The couple stood eerily still, wearing black cloths draped around their faces and necks. Dark goggles concealed their identities.

She stood to approach the counter and more wrapped figures came into view. Her staff was out back on a smoke break as the lobby filled with more of them. They all dressed in black, fully cloaked head to toe without a sliver of skin exposed. They stood shoulder to shoulder, facing her. Their presence exhausted the air from the room. Shadows elongated from beneath them, stretching toward her.

Reese had been waiting, hiding for so many years; it was only a matter of time before they'd find her. None of them said a word, nor moved a muscle, until she turned to run. Her feet caught in the black sludge of the restaurant floors. She sank, ankle-deep, as if trudging through snow. She couldn't move. She couldn't scream …

Reese woke with a startle in her bed, safe in her Florida apartment. The nightmares didn't come as often as they used to, but they still came. It'd been twenty-five years, and nobody had come for her yet. There were days, early on after everything had happened, that she could've sworn she'd seen someone lurking outside her house, but those incidents grew further apart. Or perhaps she noticed them less. Or maybe they never happened at all.

Over two decades should have been enough time to heal from the trauma, but there wasn't a day that passed when she wasn't watching over her shoulder. While she was still living in Byron with her mother, she'd changed her name to Sara Smith. Something simple and common to make it more difficult to be found. She got her GED, cleaned out her bank account, and caught a bus to Florida, but she never went to visit her biological father. A few years after she'd moved there, George passed away from liver failure.

Reese couldn't find it in her heart to care. Abandonment was the norm. People fled from her with rocket speed, like she was a dying planet. There was not a single human in her life whom she could trust. Even the friends she'd made at work were kept at a distance, never allowed close enough to know her. Never allowing them the opportunity to do any damage. She'd tried dating, but nothing stuck. Eventually, she would have to explain to the person why she hadn't been outside between sunset and sunrise since 1997, and she couldn't risk that. In the rare cases when the relationship turned physical, she shuddered at intimacy. The new guy's embrace would become Michael's controlling grip. Her body remembered every touch. Every unwelcome grope and kiss and thrust and *bite*. The new guy's kiss became the cold, toxic lips tainting her skin. The desert wasteland of her heart and soul had eaten away through her flesh, making her untouchable. So, she gave up on dating a long time ago.

She'd taken some courses on computers while working days at random fast food joints across the panhandle, making just enough to pay for a small studio apartment. Eventually, when internet moved to cable rather than dial-up, and working remotely became more common, she took a job in website design that allowed her to stay home. This wasn't the life she thought she'd be living. She never attended Berkeley, never took a course on astrobiology, never upgraded her telescope or viewed anything through it again. The only stargazing she'd done was in the glossy pages of *Sky and Telescope* magazine. But it was safe.

Her German Shepherd rested his head on her bed as her heartrate slowed from her nightmare. It was nearly dawn, and after a dream like that she didn't predict she'd fall back to sleep.

"Good boy, Orion." Reese scratched between his ears.

He let out a low growl, ears perking up at something inaudible to her. Reese moved to the window to steal a glimpse between the curtains. The well-lit street was quiet and still. When she craned her neck, pressing her face to the window, she could spot a few stars fading in the pre-dawn sky. She longed for cool summer grass beneath bare feet, lounge chair reclined, her skin caressed by a soft breeze, and her eyes absorbing photons from lightyears away. But each time she dreamed of a starry sky, she remembered the long, creeping shadows surrounding her, and the figures who lurked there. Those shadow people, draped in cloths, black-orb eyes hidden behind glasses. They were out there, everywhere, taking what they had no right to take. Every time Reese watched the news, she couldn't help but wonder if it was one of them. A violent murder? A missing girl? It was always one of them in her mind. And among them was Michael, waiting for his opportunity to take her back. Waiting for her to let her guard down so he could swoop in and take everything away from her.

In her periphery, a shadow moved in the street below. Reese sank away from the window, careful not to make any sudden movements that could draw attention to herself.

She sat on the floor beside Orion with her back pressed against the couch. Her pulse hammered in her ears. Knees squeezed into her chest, she rocked, waiting … waiting … waiting for the sun to rise. Orion growled again and lay his head against her.

"Everything's fine," she said, petting him along his back, even though she was smart enough to know nothing was fine. It was a lie, a mechanism to keep her going, to keep her alive and functioning. She pressed her forehead against Orion's, knowing that everything was not okay. Nothing in her life was okay, and it never would be.

Reese was a nebula. The remnant of what used to be a star, her matter far too scattered and disorganized to regroup. She'd be forever adrift in the vast emptiness of space. A ghost of a star with no future to coalesce and shine bright again.

Acknowledgements

I've been needing to tell this story for a long time, but I couldn't find the voice to do it. Then, in 2021, I attended a Scares That Care event that was so inspiring, I knew I had to write this book, no matter how difficult it was to dig into those past traumas, and no matter how much I thought people wouldn't want to hear Reese's story. Thank you to Joe Ripple, Brian Keene, and the Scares That Care team for an inspiring event. There were four stand-out authors at that event who truly inspired me to 'write the thing!'

Gabino Iglesias' public reading taught me to be unapologetically brutal when the story called for it. Jonathan Janz encouraged me to be vulnerable and to pour that old trauma into my writing. V. Castro showed me what it was to be fearless and strong in a male-dominated industry. And Cynthia Pelayo read an excerpt that taught me all stories should be told, especially the ones people turn their heads away from.

A huge thank you to Steve and Heather Ventura at Brigids Gate Press for giving this book a home and allowing it to be the story it is: a tragedy.

Thank you to Elle Turpitt for a keen editing eye.

To my pancake-therapy friends, Gemma Amor, Laurel Hightower, Sonora Taylor, and Todd & Erica Keisling: thank you for your kindness and being there for all the little bumps in the road, all the wins and losses. I value your friendship, your industry expertise, your confidentiality, and all the jokes.

My very first beta-readers on this book were invaluable. Thank you to Matt Brandenburg and Elford Alley for your feedback when the book was in its earliest and most vulnerable stages.

To Jason Lagoe, thank you for showing me what a healthy relationship looks like and for supporting my creative journey every step of the way.

ABOUT THE AUTHOR

Red Lagoe grew up on 80's and 90's horror and carried her fear of slashers, sewer creatures, Hitchcockian birds, and psychos into adulthood where she now purges her horror-ridden mind onto the page. She is the author of *In Excess of Dark* and three horror collections including *Impulses of a Necrotic Heart*. Red has stories published in various anthologies and magazines, and she enjoyed her role as curator and editor of *Nightmare Sky: Stories of Astronomical Horror*. In addition to writing, Red loves creating art using traditional fine art mediums like paint, ink, and charcoal, as well as some dabbling in the digital art world.

About the Cover Art

I had the honor of creating my own cover art for *Bloodstains by Gaslight*. It began as concept art that I had planned to pass along to a cover artist, but as it built in digital layers on my screen, it became evident I was creating more than just a concept sketch. Being in a violent relationship is to be perpetually battle-ready within the inescapable shadow of a threat, as all signs of identity fade away leaving a silhouette of one's former self. To convey these themes (and also vampires!) in one image was challenging, but satisfying when I finally pulled it off.

More from Brigids Gate Press

FOOD FOR THOUGHT

Ariana Ferrante

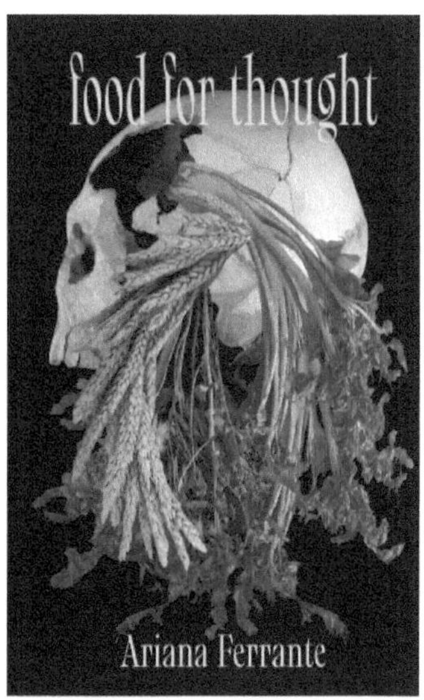

Limos is the goddess of starvation. Whatever she touch withers and wastes, crumbling to dust. She aids those seeking destruction, plaguing fields with famine and waters with drought. When mortals see her, they yearn.

Her opposite, harvest goddess Demeter, makes life flourish wherever she goes. She supplies mortals with fruits and vegetables, piling their tables with sustenance and satisfaction. When mortals see her, they are contented.

Given their opposing natures, The Fates themselves have decreed Limos and Demeter are never to meet, promising only ruin and mutual destruction should they ever unite.

But when Demeter arrives at her doorstep, begging for her assistance, Limos can't help but fall victim to the same yearning her mortal worshippers feel …

IN THE GRIMDARK STRANDS OF THE SPINNERET

Keith Anthony Baird

Betrayal brings grave ending to a noble bloodline. Forced to flee, its sole surviving heir is spared this fate by the timely intervention of a haunter of the wilds. In his charge, the maiden embraces the lore of the dark arts and rises to become the watch-keep of the woods. As decades pass, with her legend growing, the 'witch of root and earth' weaves subtle deceits in a tangled web of vengeance.

But will there be a fairy tale ending, or will poisoned legacies and pacts with dark forces see ambition unravel in her relentless pursuit of power?

Bloody, and brilliantly realised, Baird's dark fantasy nightmare spins a lavish tale of dread, desire, and fantastical fury.

THE FIVE TURNS OF THE WHEEL

Stephanie Ellis

Welcome to the Weald. The Five Turns of the Wheel has begun. With each Turn, blood will be spilled, and sacrifices will be made. Pacts will be made…and broken. Will you join the Dance?

In the Weald, the time has come for the Five Turns of the Wheel. Tommy, Betty and Fiddler, the sons of Hweol, Lord of Umbra, have arrived to oversee the sacred rituals… rituals brimming with sacrifice and dripping with blood.

Megan Wheelborn, daughter of Tommy, hatches a desperate plan to free the people of the Weald from the bloody and cruel grip of Umbra, and put an end to its murderous rituals. But success will require sacrifice and blood as well. Will Megan be able to pay the price?

MARIONETTE

Antonia Rachel Ward

On the run from a life of prostitution and poverty, exotic dancer Cece Dulac agrees to become the main attraction at an erotic séance hosted by an enigmatic mesmerist, Monsieur Rossignol. As the séance descends into depravity, Cece falls prey to Rossignol's hypnotic power and becomes possessed by a malevolent spirit.

George Dashwood, an aspiring artist, witnesses the séance and fears for Cece. He seeks her out and she seduces him, but she is no longer herself. The spirit controlling her forces her to commit increasingly depraved acts. When the spirit's desire for revenge escalates to murder, George and Cece must find a way to break Rossignol's spell before Cece's soul is condemned forever.

Marionette is an erotic horror novella inspired by traditional folk tales and set in fin de siècle Paris.

Visit our website at: www.brigidsgatepress.com